MW01129283

Edited by Alicia Shields, Jessica Dalusma, and Cynthia Dotson.

Series Order:

Secrets of a Side Bitch 1

Secrets of a Side Bitch 2

Secrets of a Side Bitch 3

The Simone Campbell Story

Secrets of a Side Bitch 4

Previously on Secrets of a Side Bitch...

Simone

As I lay on that bed, naked and cold, watching Jimmy approach me, with thoughts of my mother in my mind, I refused to go down without a fight. Like my mother, I had made mistakes. Hell, the mistakes that I made were way worse, but I refused to go down like this.

My heart began to beat out of my chest as his hand came closer and closer to my face. However, I was relieved when he ripped the duct tape off my mouth. It burned, and I knew that he had also ripped skin off as well.

But I began to plead through the pain. "Jimmy, please don't..."

His smile was so evil that I stopped mid-sentence, but he began to taunt me. He stood back and looked at me. "Don't what? Kill you? Like you did Tammy?"

"She was fucking somebody else anyway! More than one person! Fuck that bitch."

He just shook his head and came towards me. Again, anxiety filled my body. He was over me, so close that I could smell his stench. I could feel him untying me.

"Jimmy, please don't kill me. We can go on the run together. Didn't you like this pussy, baby? You felt so good inside of me. I can love you better than Tammy ever did. She didn't love you like a man like you needs to be loved. She deserved to die. I can make it up to you, baby. Just let me."

My hands were now untied as he stood straight up and looked at me. Jimmy's head tilted as he stared at me. There was so much disgust in his eyes. "I think you're more of a monster than I am."

Now, he was untying my feet. "Where are you taking me?" I asked.

He chuckled. "I can't kill you in my apartment. Get dressed."

When he bent down, I could see that my clothes were on the floor beside the bed. He was picking them up to give to me. Now that his attention was on something else, it was like a light bulb went off in my head. I took my chance. I attacked him with all of the strength in my body. I hadn't eaten. I was dehydrated. I was battered and bruised from both his and Omari's beatings. But the adrenaline rush had given me strength that I didn't think that I had.

I kicked, screamed, and bit, all while trying to get the knife out of his hand. If I could only get that knife, I was prepared to cut him from the top of his head to the soles of his feet.

As we wrestled, I finally saw the knife fall to the ground. He was so busy trying to get ahold of me that the knife was no longer his focus. But it was mine. So as he wrapped his arms around my waist, I reached for it, grabbed it, and began to swing, hoping that the flesh that I was slicing would subdue him.

"Arrrgh!" He let me go in order to use his hands to protect himself from the blade, but it was of no use. I was on top of him, attempting to force the knife through every vital organ that I could. "Arrrgh!"

"Die, motherfucka!" I wanted him to die so that I could live. Yes, I had done some pretty fucked up things. I had taken three lives. But I'd be damned if I was going to go out like this.

Not like this, is all I kept thinking until finally Jimmy stopped moving. Blood was everywhere—on me, flowing from him, and even in my eyes. But I could see my clothes that had gotten scattered everywhere during our fight. I scooped them up as fast as I could, while standing over Jimmy as he clutched his chest while it bled out. Then I ran into the living room frantically with the knife still in my hand. I was looking for his car keys, which were thankfully on the couch. I was shaking as I threw my clothes on and frantically looked down the hall towards the room where I left Jimmy. His moans were now faint and became more and more in the distance as I darted out of the house.

The sun felt incredible as it hit my skin. I thought I would never feel the sun ever again. But as I jumped into Jimmy's car and turned the engine, I began to feel the sweet feeling of relief. I quickly drove away from the building. Once I approached a street sign, I realized that I was in Calumet City. I also realized that it was not over. I was out on bail for murder, and I had nowhere to go. I couldn't go to the hospital. I couldn't go back to Omari. I didn't have any money. I had nothing. As I drove, I used a towel that I spotted in the back seat to wipe my face free of blood. It stunk and smelled like gas.

I wished that I could just go somewhere and start over; I wanted a chance to do it all over again. But what was fucked up was that, even as I envisioned starting over, I doubted that if in the same position that I would do anything differently.

I ain't shit; I know.

I was an evil and vindictive bitch, and the evilness blossomed as I approached a light on 159th and Torrence.

"Spare any change, ma'am?"

The voice caught me off guard. I was initially in a complete daze as I sat at the light trying to think of what the fuck to do now.

The young lady looked at me as strangely as I looked at her. I was expecting to see some crack head standing at the driver's side window, and I am sure that she wasn't expecting to see a battered woman.

I chuckled. "My boyfriend. Long story," I said to explain my black eye and busted lip. "What do you need change for?"

"I'm trying to get on the bus. I lost my transfer."

"How far are you going?"

"Chicago. Southside."

"I'm headed that way. You want a ride?"

She looked skeptical at first but then shrugged her shoulders. I guess I appeared weak to her, with a beat up face and all. Cars began to honk as the red light changed to green. The young girl jogged around to the passenger side and hopped in.

****

I sat inside of Jimmy's car across from the forest preserve trying to figure out my next move. I really had nowhere to go now. Without any money, and now without an ID, I was stranded in this city.

However, I had a lot more options now that I had, hopefully, fixed everything.

There was mayhem all around me. Cops were everywhere. There was an ambulance pulling away. There was nothing that they could do for that girl. She was toast... literally.

As I watched cops put up the yellow tape, my heart kind of went out to that girl. I really didn't want to kill her. There was enough blood on my hands that would never wash away. But as she sat in the passenger side telling me that I should leave the nigga that beat me, it hit me; if everyone thought I was dead, I could easily get away and start all over.

When I banged her head against the passenger window, knocking her out, all I was thinking about was survival. When I tied her to that tree and set her on fire, it was purely to make sure that any DNA was burned away and that the body would be found sooner than later. I cringed when I heard her screams. I never expected her to regain consciousness. Apparently, I hadn't been successful when I choked her, after dragging her inside of the woods.

The tap on the window nearly made me piss my pants. I looked up reluctantly to see an officer. Yet, he merely waved his baton, signaling for me to move along as he shouted to the car in front of me that this area needed to be clear. He never even made eye contact with me.

I started the car with a heavy heart. This was one life that I didn't want to take, but I had no other choice. I had done so much wrong, but it wasn't in me to give up without a fight.

You didn't think that I was just going to go away that easy, did you?

Detective Howard

"Jimmy! We've been looking all over for you."

I smiled at him as I walked into the room in the ICU unit at Ingalls Hospital. I was so happy to finally catch this son of a bitch. He had been on the run for a little over a year for the murder and attempted murder of his ex-girlfriend, Tammy Douglas.

I chuckled as I scoped out his injuries. "Damn, who fucked you up?"

Luckily, this crazy motherfucker was handcuffed to the bed. When the paramedics got the call from 9-1-1, reporting a man stabbed in his apartment, it was just my luck that it was Jimmy Straton. I guess he would have rather been apprehended than allowing himself to bleed to death.

When he spat, "Simone Campbell," I nearly lost my cool.

"Who?" Unbeknownst to him, Simone was a suspect on another murder case that I had been investigating.

"Simone Campbell. That bitch stabbed me."

He went on to tell me some fucked up ass story about him and Simone fucking with each other and getting into some kind of lover's quarrel, but I wasn't buying that shit. It all sounded and looked suspect. I knew that Simone had recently been on the run in Atlanta for months. This nigga was lying. Since Simone was out on bail, I planned to put a warrant out for her arrest to get to the bottom of this. That bitch should have never gotten bail in the first place.

"Look, I know that I'm going to jail for a long time, but I didn't kill Tammy. I know I tried to, but I didn't do it. It was Simone."

This bitch was one crazy broad, but Jimmy wasn't too sane his damn self. So, I just looked at him, assuring myself to get to the bottom of all of this when I got back to the station.

"Okay, Jimmy..."

"Seriously!"

"Even if she did, you still attempted to murder Tammy, and you've been on the run. You're going down for this Jimmy. You're going to do time. Lots of it. There is nothing you can do about it," I said with a pleased chuckle.

"What if I have information about a murder?"

I waved my hand dismissively. "I wouldn't believe any information you gave me. Of course, you would blame Tammy's murder on someone else."

He looked at me and proved me wrong. "No, not Tammy's murder... A baby's."

Chance

I couldn't believe it as I stepped outside of the County Building. I was wearing the Levis and white tee that I was arrested in. Unlike that day, my locs were fuzzy. I had mad new growth. I needed a fresh lining and shave bad as hell.

But I didn't give a fuck about any of that. No matter how rough I looked, I felt like a million bucks on the inside. It was almost three in the afternoon, so there was very little traffic going in and out of the building. I spotted Gia's white 300 sitting a few feet up the street with the hazards blinking.

Thomas was standing beside me. He'd stayed with me during processing to make sure that everything ran smoothly.

"Thanks," I told him as I shook his hand.

"It was our pleasure, Chance," he assured me.

However, he was hesitant. I knew that there was a lot he wanted to say. As my attorneys, they never asked me had I done it. They only asked me certain questions, because they said that they didn't want to commit perjury. But I knew what his look meant. The State could turn around and offer Simone the deal that they'd offered me. Knowing her, she would take it without thinking twice. And then I would be back in jail fighting for my life.

"I hope I never have to see you again," is what I told him.

He laughed, saying, "I hope so too."

He walked away, looking like Agent K from the Men in Black. I wish he had one of those neutralizers to flash in my face to make me forget everything that happened in my past. As I walked towards Gia's 300, listening to the "Too Much" lyrics that spilled from her speakers, all I wanted to do was remember my future from that day forward. I was so sorry for killing Aeysha. I was so sorry for the pain that I saw Omari live with every day. But I was dead too. My soul would never live freely because I would always remember that day that I killed her. I would live every day in pain because I punished myself every day. I lived in fear every day. I hadn't grown up in church, but I knew that God promised that I would reap what I sowed. I had sowed death. I lived every day waiting to reap that.

♪ *Don't think about it too much, too much, too much, too much*
There's no need for us to rush this through
Don't think about it too much, too much, too much, too much
This is more than just a new lust for you ♪

Still, Drake's voice was like a breath of fresh air to me. I opened the door and the music hit me like the sweet breeze of freedom. Gia's face itself was like a breath of fresh air as she sat literally smiling like Chester Cheetah as I climbed into the passenger side.

She squealed before wrapping her petite brown arms around me.

"Thank you, baby," was all that I could say.

She began to kiss me all over my face; my cheeks, my lips, my forehead, and, hell, even my eyes.

"What's all that?" I looked at Gia curiously after spotting a backseat full of luggage and bags.

"That's our stuff," she said nonchalantly. Then she smiled at me. "Where do you want to go?"

"Go?"

"We're out of here, baby. I have money saved up and a tank full of gas. Let's go and start over. Anywhere you want to go. If they want to charge you with anything, they'll have to come find you."

Just the thought of that made me relax in the seat even more. "Where are we going?"

"Where do you want to go?"

I sat back feeling the happiest I'd ever felt. The windows were down, so the warm air blew on my face. I couldn't believe how much I missed that simple feeling.

"Somewhere where it feels like this every day," I answered.

"California?"

"We can't drive to California. It will take us days and a ton of gas."

"Boy, I told you I got a pocket full of money!"

Just then, my heart felt like it had skipped a beat. I didn't realize how much I missed that wittiness and smile until that very moment. "Then let's go. California it is."

She smiled, and I caught her letting out a sigh of relief. She started the car and pulled off as I sat back, relaxed, and slid my hand onto her exposed thigh.

I didn't grow up with a family that loved me. I didn't grow up being shown what love was. But I did know that sitting in that driver's seat was love in its purest form.

Omari

I had been held up in Eboni's bedroom since the night before. For the life of me, I couldn't bring myself to get out of the bed. Eboni had been trying to feed me since I got there, but I didn't even have an appetite.

I couldn't wrap my head around all of this. I felt so bad for being so blind that I brought this crazy bitch into my life. I had been chasing Aeysha's murderer for a year, ready to kill him, when ultimately I was sleeping with the enemy and the person at fault was me.

I couldn't live life knowing that I had done this to my family. I didn't know how to live with this amount of guilt on my chest every day.

"Omari, you awake?"

Eboni's voice came over a round of light knocks on the door. I didn't say anything as I lay in the dark. I knew that it had to be the late afternoon. I was sure that the sun was still shining. But the shades were drawn.

Despite the darkness, I could see Jamari in her arms, along with someone coming in behind her. It was Capone, so I sat up.

He fussed at me as he flipped the lights on. "Man, I been calling you."

I squinted and groaned.

"Omari, get up. You gotta see this shit," Eboni told me. She put Jamari in my arms. She had been doing that a lot since I got there– as if she was trying to show me what I had to live for. Capone had called her during the night to check on me and told her that he found me with a gun pointed to my head. She talked to me all night about what I had to live for, but I didn't talk back.

There were no chairs in her bedroom, so Capone sat on the bed next to me. "You good, bro?"

"I ... I don't..."

As I stumbled over my words, I noticed Eboni frantically fumbling with the remote.

Capone sternly put his arm around me. "Its all good, fam. We gon' get through this."

I looked at him like he had a third eye when he said "we".

He answered my curiosity. "Yea, nigga! *We!*"

When he laughed, I actually laughed too.

Then Capone told me, "And if you put yo' hands on me again, I'mma kill you myself." He was wearing a faint grin as he talked to me. He knew that I would never do it again.

I apologized, even though I knew that sorry wasn't enough. "I'm sorry about that, bro"

"It's good. You been goin' through a lot. You get a pass. *This time.*"

Having him by my side again actually relieved some of the pressure that I was feeling. My niggas was there with me, Jamari and Capone. They were my family. If my mother wasn't enough to live for, these two men were my reason to shake this shit off and continue to live. I had mouths to feed and people to take care of. I may have fucked up with one family, but I had a chance at another family to get it right. I just wished, with every fiber of my being, that I could have that second chance with Aeysha and Dahlia.

They say that everything happens for a reason. Maybe one day, I will know what that reason is. Until then, I would live everyday correcting my wrongs.

I could only pray that Aeysha was looking down on me, forgiving my stupidity but still proud for the man that I had become.

"Here it go! Here it go!"

I looked curiously at Eboni. She sat at the foot of the bed with her eyes glued to the television.

The television was on the channel–nine news. Alicia Ramon was standing near what looked like a forest preserve.

She spoke unbelievably, as if what she was about to say had even shocked her. "We're coming to you live from the Calumet City Forest Preserve. Just a few hours ago, authorities were called to this location. A group of people celebrating a family reunion could hear the screams of a woman over the music that they were playing. They followed the screams inside the forest. Just a few feet into the forest, they made the gruesome discovery of a woman hanging from a tree by her wrists. Her body was on fire, the majority of her body completely engulfed in flames as she screamed for her life. Within seconds, the woman was dead.

However, witnesses still attempted to put out the blaze as they called 9-1-1. Witnesses describe the scene as one from a horror movie, the smell of the burning flesh and the sounds of her gruesome screams as she burned alive, indescribable. An ID was located on the body. Though damaged by the fire, authorities were able to identify the victim as Simone Campbell."

DAVID WEAVER PRESENTS

SECRETS OF A SIDE BITCH 4

by JESSICA N. WATKINS

CHAPTER 1

Omari

It had been three months since Simone was killed. Knowing that that bitch was gone allowed the burden to lift slowly but surely as the days passed by.

"Hello?"

"Hey, Omari."

"What's up, Eboni?"

"Nothing. Just wondering if you can pick the kids up from daycare for me. I have to work overtime."

"No problem. Bet."

I helped Eboni out a lot with Jamari and her kids. It helped keep us both grounded. She was taking classes at Malcolm X. She wanted to try to get into their X–ray tech program once enrollment opened up. For right now, she was taking prerequisites while working at a beauty shop as the receptionist and shampoo girl. As far as I was concerned, she didn't have to work. I was willing to take care of her. Though Eboni and I maintained a platonic friendship over the last few months, she and her kids were my family. But she insisted on working; trying to be an independent woman and what not.

Once I hung up the phone, I hopped out of my ride and walked through the parking lot towards Chicago Ridge Mall. It was mid–October. The weather was changing, and it was time to do some fall shopping. Now that I was back feeling like myself, I was ready to get some new gear and start living the life that I fought so hard to obtain for myself and Aeysha. I had done so many things for her and my daughter. They weren't here, but, instead of grieving, I wanted to live life to the fullest for them.

Just as I entered the mall, the sweetest smell came over me. I looked down and saw a woman texting on her phone, clearly not paying attention to what she was doing until she collided with me.

"Ooo, I'm sorry! I am *so* sorry."

Man, she was beautiful. Her smile was like a light, as she laughed at her own clumsiness. She made a nigga feel like somebody when she finally stared into my eyes and literally lost herself.

"It's okay," I told her. She was stuck a little bit, and so was I. Man, this girl was beautiful, and she was built like a racehorse. And it was something about her presence. Just standing there with her was different. I felt comfortable and right.

It was weird…in a good way.

I was actually nervous. She obviously was hesitant to walk away. She was waiting for me to say something, and I was waiting for something smooth to come out of my mouth.

"What's your name?" she asked, taking the lead with a smile that was full of confidence.

"Omari Sutton." She laughed at the fact that I had given her my first and last name. But fuck that. This girl was something else. I wanted her to know me! "Where are you from?" Her accent caught me off guard. She spoke much more proper than chicks from the Chi.

"I'm from Chicago, but I just moved back home a few weeks ago."

Man, I couldn't believe that I was gazing at this woman like this. Mind you, yes, she had an ass the size of Texas and she was a pretty brown–skinned girl. But it was something about her smile. It was so genuine and real, much like Aeysha's.

I finally figured out how to make a complete sentence. "I'm sorry for staring, but you are so beautiful." She blushed as I asked, "Can I have your number?"

Just asking that question was so weird to me. I hadn't done that in, what felt like, years. I hadn't courted a new woman since Simone. And just the thought of that bitch made me want to avoid every woman in the world, including my own mother.

We moved to the side to exchange numbers. As I followed her, I admired the maxi dress that she was wearing. She was only about 5'4," so the long dress swept the floor as she walked. Her ass jiggled below hair that hung down her back. It definitely wasn't real. It looked like that banana boat shit that Simone always wore and that Aeysha wished I could afford back then. But it looked good.

I was happy to save *this* number into my phone. "What's your name?"

Again, she was smiling into my eyes. I did everything that I could to squint and make these gray eyes work magic on her. "Jasmine. Jasmine Mays."

Chance

"Damn, baby. What's your name?"

Honestly, I was drunk as fuck. I had drowned my irritations in a bottle of the cheapest fifth of tequila that I could afford and stumbled into a bar on the furthest part of the North Side of Chicago that I could find. It was the one part of the city that I figured I wouldn't run into Omari, Capone or anybody in their crew, while getting some space from Gia at the same time.

"I'm Georgia, baby." Figures; her smile was bright and warm, like the southern sun. Plus, she was thick like gumbo, like I heard most of the women were down south.

"Georgia?" I was immediately taken back a bit.

She giggled. "I know. Weird name, right?"

"I've never met a woman named Georgia."

"And you probably never will."

I had never met a girl that looked like her either. My eyes rode low from the heavy amount of liquor that I'd inhaled in the parking lot of the bar before coming in. They also squinted at the abundance of ass that was sitting on the back of this chick's long legs that had her standing at about 5'7." Gia was nicely shaped, but she didn't have a big round, ghetto booty like this chick. She was casually dressed in jeans and a long sleeve fitted tee. Since it was early October, the weather had dropped from the unusual sixty-five degree weather that Chicago had been having earlier that day. Her skin was dark, and her natural hair was long and in a simple ponytail. Her simplicity was a major fucking turn on. My dick got hard when I noticed how gorgeous she was without an ounce of makeup or a strip of lashes.

I invited her to have a seat, and she had no problem sitting closely next to me at the bar.

"It's rude to ask someone their name but not offer your own."

Drunk or not, I knew better. "My name is Reginald."

She gave me that pretty ass smile again as she extended her hand to shake mine.

As my hand met hers, I asked, "Who you here with?"

"Myself," she answered with a sigh. I looked at her sadness questionably, and she answered my curiosity with, "I came in town to handle some business. I decided to get liquored up first before I get on this roller coaster tomorrow."

"I feel that." I felt that more than words could say. Gia and I had been going through one hell of an emotional roller coaster since we returned from Cali.

Gia's mother died suddenly about a week ago. Since Gia was the eldest of two sisters, she had to come home to handle the funeral arrangements. Of course, I was irritated with the fact that we had to come back. Last thing I needed in my life was to be back in the Chi, living with the possibilities of running into Omari every day. But she had to come back to bury her mother, and I couldn't let my girl deal with that alone, even if death was a possibility waiting for me when I stepped foot off of the plane.

"I just got back in town myself," I told her as I smiled and licked my lips. "We got something in common already."

She smiled and flirted back. On the inside though, I was frowning. I hated being back in the Chi, while I honestly felt like Gia was ecstatic to be back. Though the circumstances were unfortunate, I could see it in her eyes that she was relieved being back in Chicago. During the three months that we had been in Cali, she hated it. She wasn't making the same money at the strip clubs out there that she had been making at Sunset. To a true hustler and go-getter like Gia, that shit was fucking with her heavy. Even I had been having issues establishing myself financially. I had a high school diploma and no job experience, and I was accustomed to the fast money that working under Omari and Capone had given me. A minimum wage gig wasn't cutting it for me, and it was taking time for me to break into the streets of Cali, especially since I didn't know anyone out there.

Anyway, Georgia and I kicked it for hours while techno and rock music played over our drunken conversation. Since we were on the North side, white people were everywhere. For whatever reason, when white people see Black people in a bar, they think we are cool as shit and get us drunk. This time was no different. White people thought that Georgia and I were a couple and treated us to shot after shot. I was relieved too. She was so fucking pretty and a breath of fresh air. Even though I had a girl back at the crib, and would most likely never see Georgia again, I really wanted to show her a good time. I couldn't afford it, though. But the white folks did a hell of a job of taking care of that for me.

By three in the morning, we were so fucking wasted.

"Can you drive?" Before she answered, I could look at her and tell that the answer was "no." Her eyes were riding so low as she leaned back against the brick of the building.

"I don't have to drive. I'm walking."

"Walking?"

"Yea. I'm staying right across the street." Then she pointed at the Sheraton hotel.

I felt relief ... and my dick get hard. I had never cheated on Gia. As a matter of fact, I couldn't remember the last pussy that I was in before Gia's; had to be one of those random bitches at Lexington House before I moved out. So, I ignored my dick getting hard at the sight of Georgia's nipples hardening against her t–shirt as the cold wind blew. Clearly, she didn't have on a bra. Clearly, her nipples were big as shit.

Nigga, you need to go home, I thought to myself as Georgia smiled at me. She saw me staring at her. She probably saw how hard my dick was inside of my jeans too.

"Can you walk me inside?" she asked.

Fuck, I thought to myself, but I told her, "Sure."

Needless to say, after I helped her across the street and into the building, she was on me as soon as we got into the empty elevator.

"Shorty, stop. You're drunk." I had to laugh as she continuously attempted to cuff my dick. "You don't even know me." I was pushing her away ... but barely. I wanted her more than I was willing to admit. I loved Gia, but shit was so fucked up at the crib. My dick inside of this bitch would have made me feel a hell of a lot better than how I had been feeling for the past few months. I wasn't chasing pussy.

I was chasing happiness.

Even if it was temporary.

"You know you want this pussy." She was breathing heavy as she spoke into my ear. She was leaning against me as I finally gave up and let her caress my dick through my jeans. "Gawd damn, this dick is so big, Daddy."

Fuck. I rolled my eyes into the back of my head and bit my bottom lip. *Did she just call me Daddy?*

It was a wrap after that. My tongue found hers. As soon as our lips connected, we attacked one another. Swear, I wanted to take shorty's clothes off right there in that elevator. My life had been one of poverty for ninety-nine percent of it. Even as I sold dope out of Omari's trap house for those few months, I trapped so hard that I didn't live much. Gia was the only life in my life. So never would I have ever dreamed that I would be in some hotel elevator about to

9

bang a beautiful woman. But that's exactly what was about to go down as the elevator doors opened and she pulled me out by the hand. My dick was so hard that I could hardly see straight.

Luckily, her room was only a few feet away from the elevator. Within seconds, she had unlocked the door and we were stumbling inside. She'd left the television on, so we were able to see one another. Again, my tongue found hers. We sucked each other's mouths as we tore clothes off of one another's backs.

With my dick exposed, she salivated at the sight of it. "Gawd damn," she moaned in amazement. She immediately dropped down to her knees, but I was so ready that I didn't even want head. "Uh uh, ma. Bend over. Let me see that pretty ass, baby."

She grinned seductively as she stood upright and sashayed over to the table in the suite. I followed her, waddling since my jeans were still around my ankles. Georgia lifted one leg onto the table, giving me the most beautiful view of that pussy and ass and allowing it to spread perfectly for me. It fell open like a heart, and I fought the urge to put my face right in it.

"Condoms are in my purse, baby," she said, pointing to it on the floor near the door.

I nearly tripped trying to get to it. Luckily, it was a Magnum that was inside.

When I heard her moan and say, "Fuck. Hurry up," I glanced over to see her leg still on the table, that ass still arched as she played with her pussy. It was so wet that the light of the television illuminated the juices.

I put that condom on fast as hell.

Simone

"Gawd damn, it's cold."

I don't know why I was surprised. It was almost winter. Though we were managing to stay in the sixties during the day, it was a good thirty at night, with a wind chill that made it feel like twenty. We were all reluctantly waiting for the moment that it got artic around this motherfucker, though. Then, it would be especially cold for the girls and me as we stood outside on Cicero Avenue in Garfield Park.

Standing out there in booty shorts and fishnets was sure to give me the worst cold ever. I could only hope that the leather jacket that I was wearing would keep me warm. But it was so thin that it wasn't much help. I would have preferred to have on a full-length mink, but Slim would have been super pissed that I was covering up my body. I was highly anticipating the moment that a guy drove by in his warm car and invited me in.

"Fuck. My feet hurt," I heard Tanisha complain. I glanced back and had to giggle at the six and half inch stilettos that she was wearing.

Hell yea, your feet hurt, bitch. Duh.

I was grumpy, as always. I was out there by no desire of my own. It was what I had to do to eat.

For three days after escaping from Jimmy and killing that girl, I was able to sleep in Jimmy's car. I knew that I would eventually have to ditch it, but I held on to it for as long as I could. On the fourth day, I heard on the radio that Jimmy had been arrested and plead guilty to the attempted murder of Tammy. The fact that he had yet to be charged with her murder let me know that the son of a bitch was in jail singing like a motherfucka. I knew that he would though. Therefore, I was forced to ditch the car right then. But with no money and no identification, I had nowhere else to go but a homeless shelter. I stayed in that stinky, nasty, horrid place amongst the homeless, drug addicts and even some unfortunate single mothers for about a month. One day, I was walking down this very street, in a daze and wearing a blond wig that I'd stolen from the Beauty Supply to hide my identity. I was ready to give up on life. I was hungry. The food at the homeless shelter was nothing to crave. My back hurt. The beds at the shelter were cheap and hard as boards. The bed in the county jail felt like luxury in comparison. I knew that I had brought this all on myself. The Bible says that you reap what you sow. I had killed with little thought or guilt. Now, I was begging for death, because living like this was unbearable.

Just when I was wondering what would be the easiest, less painful way to kill myself, a guy blew his horn. He was in a tricked out Tahoe. It wasn't new, but the fact that a man was propositioning me made my heart skip a beat as he called me over to his ride.

"Damn, sweetheart. You look way too sexy to be walking out here."

As I stood at his driver side window, I slightly rolled my eyes into the back of my head. I was far from sexy. I was wearing clothes that had been donated to the shelter. They were worn and faded. I had lost so much weight from stress and the unavailability of the delicate foods that I preferred, like a cheeseburger. Yes, at that point, a double cheeseburger on the dollar menu at McDonald's had become a delicacy to me.

Yet, I knew what he meant by sexy. With so much weight shedding from me, the fake ass that I'd spent thousands on looked huge on my small frame.

I managed to smile and say, "Thank you, baby."

He wasn't all that fine. I could look at him and tell that he was older than me too, but only by a few years. His facial hair was thick and his lips were full. His hair was lined to perfection, but it was nearly growing into a small fro. He didn't look like he'd ever seen a gym. He wasn't fat, but his thick frame was lacking any muscle whatsoever. What got my attention was his jewelry. It was minimal but dripped of expensive taste and quality. It was obvious that he wasn't rich, but did have some money.

He peeped me checking him out and with a smile told me, "This is like my fourth time seeing you walk up and down this street. Where are you going?"

"Nowhere," I answered with a sigh as I wondered how in the hell I missed this truck drive by. "I'm just getting some air."

"Getting some air?" he asked curiously. "You live around here?"

"Yea. Right over there," I said pointing towards the shelter.

Right then, it was like a light bulb went off for him and me.

At that point, I was ready to use my pussy to get into a soft bed and that cheeseburger. I was ready to slut myself out for a room at the Quality Inn and a combo meal. And for two weeks, that's what happened. He treated me nicely; took me out to dinner and let me ride with him while he ran errands. But he never fucked me. He made me feel human and like a woman again. He gave me life with his encouraging and strengthening words. The more I threw pussy at him, the more he acted like it was far from what he wanted.

I was confused. I didn't understand why this man had been rocking my world for two weeks without penetrating me. I didn't understand it until one day we were at dinner at a Mexican restaurant and I told him, "I really like you."

He smiled bashfully, asking, "Is that so?"

"It is so. I can show you better than I can tell you."

Slim grabbed his drink and took a gulp as he stared at me for a few seconds. "You aren't ready for this, mama."

I felt defeated, but I was never a woman to back down from a challenge. "I believe I am. If you let me show you, I know you'll believe me." Then I licked my lips for emphasis on what I wanted to show him.

15

"I'm sure you could fuck the shit out of me, but it's not about that." He was so blunt that it was almost offensive.

But of course, I am not one to give up when a man tells me "no." "What is it about? Tell me."

"The women in my life don't just fuck me. They work."

"Work?" I asked with curled eyebrows.

He chuckled. "Yes, they work. I'm a pimp."

I am sure that he thought that would scare me away. My daddy was a pimp, so I wasn't new to the game whatsoever. However, I didn't think that in this decade pimps still existed. Women knew how to sell their pussy on their own, so I thought.

As I sat listening to my stomach growl in the homeless shelter for weeks, I had thought about that very notion. Stripping was out of the question. I wasn't much of a dancer. Plus, being in that scene would increase my chances of running into Omari or any of his crew. I couldn't stomach fucking every dirty Tom, Dick, and Harry that drove by a street corner either. Therefore, I was stuck in that shelter until I figured out another way.

Slim saw it in my face that I wasn't down. I didn't have to say a word, but I was taken aback when he quickly wrapped up dinner. I didn't see him for a week. He would usually come by the shelter or drive by the street that I walked on to get some fresh air, as I did the day that we met. But I hadn't seen him. I missed him: his conversation, the affection, the security... *the food*. Therefore, I was so happy when he showed up on a Monday night.

"You think you ready for this now?" he asked through the opened window of his truck.

I was so happy to see him that I said, "Yes," without even thinking about it.

That was two months ago. I had been hooking ever since. Despite giving my pussy up for a hundred dollars five or six times a day, I was full, I had decent clothes and I finally had that room at the Quality Inn.

Detective Howard

"What is taking so long on those dental records, Sam?"

Sam blew his breath as he pulled away from the microscope. "It's coming. You know how long it takes, Keisha."

He was calling me by my first name to fuck with me.

He ignored the stern look on my face. "They're coming. Give it time."

I huffed and stormed out of the lab. I probably had way too much attitude but I couldn't take this shit anymore. I just had to know.

I wasn't convinced that that body found in the Calumet City Forest Preserve was Simone Campbell. That bitch was way too sneaky. Plus, after listening to Jimmy's story, it was way too coincidental that a body was found near her ID moments after she fled from Jimmy's house.

Jimmy told me everything in exchange for a plea deal for the attempted murder of Tammy. I listened in horror and disgust as he told me the things that he saw as he stalked Simone. That motherfucker was one crazy bastard, but I was appreciative for the lengths he'd gone to get that bitch. Because of his obsession, he saw Simone creep back into her own home through the patio door the night that Dahlia died. He also saw Simone at Tammy's mother's house the night that Tammy was killed.

Though I had kept the conspiracy to myself and out of the media, for the past three months, I had dedicated most of my time into proving that Simone Campbell was indeed dead. I needed proof before I breathed a sigh of relief. The body was burned beyond recognition, but the teeth were intact. My captain was quick to call this an open and shut case. It would take money from the department to prove that that body wasn't Simone Campbell; money that he claimed we had little of and therefore needed to spend wisely. He would have rather spent it on cases that involved innocent victims. To me, this was that case. Simone wasn't innocent, but all of her victims were.

It took me a month to convince my captain to give the go ahead to further investigate this murder. After weeks of arguments and damn near getting fired, I was given permission. I had turned to a team of dentists and technicians from around the state to positively identify the victim. Like a fingerprint, no two sets of teeth are identical. Unlike fingerprints, almost everyone who has visited a dentist has a record of their teeth.

I was on pins and needles, waiting for proof that Simone Campbell wasn't dead so that I had the full support of my boss to lodge a full–fledged investigation into getting this bitch.

CHAPTER 2

Chance

The next day, I was lying in bed with Georgia's pussy on my mind.

I had my hand on my dick as visions of her bouncing up and down on it, reverse cowgirl, played in my mind like a nasty-ass porn. That girl's sex game was amazing. I'm not sure whether it was so good because I hadn't fucked another woman in so long or what, but I couldn't take my mind off of it.

I didn't call her though. She wanted me to call her to let her know that I had made it home that night, but I never did. I had never cheated on Gia, and after watching the shit that Simone went through just to get a nigga that was never hers, I didn't want to even initiate no shit like that. It was what it was, and what it *was* ... was a booty call: nothing more, nothing less.

A man can always dream and reminisce though.

And that's exactly what I did. I thought about that ass bouncing as she stroked my ego. "Fuck!" she would femininely growl. "Gawd damn. This dick is *so* good." Her voice in my head had my dick rock hard in my hands underneath the blanket.

I stroked it and pretended that it was the tight, dripping wet pussy that I was in the night before. Just as I was about to bust a nut inside of Georgia in my imagination, I heard Gia's voice.

"Babe?! Come here!"

Instantly, the nut that was about to spill from my dick ran away and my dick went limp. Gia had gotten back from picking up her sister way faster than I'd expected.

I hopped out of bed before she could make it inside of the bedroom. All I needed was for Gia to catch me jagging off. She would swear that I was doing it because I wasn't into her anymore. I didn't need another argument on top of all the present bullshit.

I reluctantly threw on a pair of pants and a shirt, and got myself mentally ready to meet yet another family member that would most likely get on a nigga's nerves. Their mother's funeral was the next day. Family was in and out of her mother's house, which we were staying in while we were in Chicago. Gia was arguing with her aunts and uncles because certain ones were already staking claim on some of her mother's assets. She died without a will, so everyone was trying to put their claim on her car, properties and everything else. Fortunately, she had an insurance policy, but it was just enough to pay for the funeral and pay off the debts that she left.

Going through this shit with Gia made me happy that I didn't have any family for the first time in my life.

As I left the bedroom, all I could think about was boarding the next plane back to Cali.

I strolled into the living room and that thought became even more intense. Suddenly, I needed to get back to Cali way sooner than later.

More like immediately.

"Hey, babe. Come say hi to my sister."

I tried hard to hide the fact that it felt like I had just swallowed my own shit. Georgia, who stood behind Gia, wore a smile that Gia couldn't see through. "Hi, *Chance*. I'm Georgia."

Since she was obviously pretending, I played along. I walked towards them and extended my hand to Georgia, but she lightly smacked my hand away. "Nigga, you've been with my sister for damn near a year. You ain't no stranger. Give me a hug."

I don't know whether she was trying to be funny or real, but I hugged her nonetheless, as I heard Gia giggle at her sister.

"Nice to meet you," I managed to say. On the outside, I looked cool, *I hoped.* But on the inside, I was freaking the fuck out. The sex was good and Georgia seemed cool, but I had full intentions of leaving her at the Sheraton and never seeing her again. I had chosen to cheat on my girl, but I wanted to leave it in yesterday and only have it come back to haunt me in my dreams; not in my face as my girl's fucking sister!

This shit was crazy!

I tried not to stare at Georgia, but I couldn't help it. I was wondering if she was freaking out as much as I was. I was also waiting on her to pop off at any moment.

Hearing Gia's sigh brought me out of my thoughts. "Georgia, you can stay in mama's other guest bedroom, I guess."

The mention of their mother had brought depression into the living room just that quick.

"That's cool," Georgia said.

"Let me go make sure that there's sheets on the bed. Mama wasn't using that room much."

As Gia left the living room, Georgia stared into my eyes with a slight smirk. I wanted to follow Gia, but it would have looked too suspicious. I wasn't comfortable being alone with Georgia. I didn't know what the fuck she was going to do or say.

But I couldn't help but notice how cute that smirk was.

"So," she said as Gia could be heard on the second floor of the house. "I guess that's why you didn't call me to let me know that you made it home."

I was stuck. I didn't know what the fuck to say. I was caught and my dick was still hard from the memories of how her pussy wrapped around my dick.

"Reginald, huh?" she asked me with a smirk.

"Don't look at me like that," I told her. "You didn't know I was your sister's man?"

I knew better than that. Because of my situation, I never took pictures. Facebook, Instagram and spiteful bitches will get a nigga in trouble before a snitch. Even though my murder case had been dropped, I didn't need Omari and Capone knowing where the fuck I was.

"I'm sure you know that me and Gia aren't that close... Besides, maybe if you told me that you had a woman ... or your real name, I would have never fucked you in the first place."

She got me there. Shit. "I'm sorry," I managed to say.

"And I'm sure that heffa never showed you a picture of me. She don't fuck with me."

As I thought about, it dawned on me. I *had* saw pictures of Georgia, but she was much younger and didn't look like the beautiful girl with mature, womanly curves that was standing in front of me.

Crazy as this situation was, my dick was still responding to this chick. In my mind, I was ready to recommit to Gia and never fuck up like this again, but my dick was trying to bust through my pants and get back in that pussy.

I even caught her staring at my dick. I mean, it wasn't hard to see my erection in the jogging pants that I was wearing.

She didn't hide the fact that she was staring. It took her a few seconds to look up and into my eyes before saying, "Don't be sorry. I fucked a nigga that I met at a bar. What else can I expect?"

"Not for the nigga to be your sister's man."

24

Georgia slightly shrugged. "Shit happens." She noticed my confusion in her nonchalant demeanor, winked and said, "Don't worry. I won't tell."

Jasmine

"RIP Simone."

I shot daggers at Tasha as she actually poured a little Vodka down the drain of her kitchen sink.

I had to laugh. "Girl, you stupid. Don't even waste no liquor on that   bitch."

"Don't talk about your cousin like that."

I rolled my eyes into the back of my head. "That bitch was never my family."

It's crazy, but the stunt that Simone pulled with Kendrick and me still affected me twelve years later. I hated that bitch for taking away who was possibly the only man that I was meant to marry. After twelve years, I had never met a man that had the same connection to me that Kendrick had. I never had the same friendship with a man. I never vibed again with another man. I had dated and even been in relationships, but nothing was the same and I hadn't been in love again since.

After the day that I walked off of his mother's porch, I couldn't get in touch with him. I would go by his mother's house, clearly hear that someone was inside, but no one would even come to the door. He had even changed his cell phone number and soon the number at his mother's house was no longer in service. I was sick. I was heartbroken without him but it killed me that it was all my fault. When I got accepted to North Carolina A&T State University six months later, I was on the first thing smoking out of this city. I had been in North Carolina for the next twelve years, heartbroken over Kendrick and hating Simone. What she had done had caused such a rift in our family that even our mother's relationship had become estranged, even until Cecily died. I didn't even go to her funeral. That's how much I loathed Simone. I wanted absolutely nothing to do with that bitch. She was crazy as shit. Many of my family members thought I was taking my hate to the extreme. That is, until they heard on the news that the bitch had killed that girl. I don't know too many details of the case. A lot of what I heard was hearsay that I got from my mother while in North Carolina. When I heard what she had done, I wasn't surprised at all. That bitch was a desperate psychopath in need of a lot of therapy.

Luckily for us all, she got killed. No one knows who killed her, but I assumed that she had finally fucked over the wrong person.

"How you feel being back in the Chi?" Tasha asked me as she handed me a mix of Vodka and cranberry juice.

"It's okay."

"Is Ant okay with it?"

I sucked my teeth. "Hell nah."

Just the thought of Ant made me take a big gulp of my drink. It burned like hell too. "Damn, is it any cranberry in this?"

"Stop being a punk. You need it."

I didn't argue with her. She was right. I hoped that the Vodka was burning away the pain in my heart like it was burning my chest. Hopefully, it burned away any memory of Ant.

Ant was my ex. We had been fucking around for about four years. It was off and on for the first two and became official after that. I met him through one of the dope boys that Tasha was dating. He had family in North Carolina and was often there. He met Ant through a friend down there and they had become good friends over the years. Ant was also a dope boy. He was also chauvinistic, had an ego the size of Texas and was extremely bipolar. Though we had been living together for the past year and half, it was like I didn't exist until he wanted to bust a nut. He made no effort to be a father to my son, Marcus. Everything was about him. Between his ego, his five kids and three baby mamas that couldn't let go of his ass, I'd had enough. When my mama told me about the teaching position at her friend's school that was open, which she could hook me up with, I was so game.

For years, I stayed away from Chicago because of Kendrick. I got a gig straight out of college that was only bringing in forty-five thousand after years on the job. It didn't matter though. Ant paid all of my bills. I hustled here and there with Ant because hustling was always in my blood. At the end of the day, the position that I eventually got hired for sounded like a much sweeter deal than what I was dealing with in North Carolina, so I brought my ass on back to the Chi, despite the very air of this city when I got off of the plane heartbreakingly reminding me of the love that I lost and never got back all because of Simone.

"Is he still blowing up your phone?"

Again, I sucked my teeth, as I answered, "Every hour."

"I told you that he didn't think you were leaving for real."

I marinated in my bitterness. "If he would have paid attention to me long enough, he would have."

Ant waited until the day that I was leaving for the airport to express his undying love for me. I knew that he loved me. We had been fucking around for years; we loved each other. But, unfortunately, the way that he loved me wasn't good enough for me. For a nigga that never even committed to one woman or claimed her, he believed that I should have known how he felt because I lived with him and I was tagged in a relationship with him on Facebook. The fact that he kicked me down with bread was an added bonus and a reason for me to keep the complaints to a minimum, so he thought.

That wasn't good enough for me. There was no chemistry and no connection. It wasn't what Kendrick and I had, so when Ant begged for me to stay, I kept lugging me and Marcus' luggage outside. I knew that it was a shock to Ant. He had been completely oblivious to the fact that I was unhappy dealing with his baby mama drama, cheating, and degrading me with his narcissism. He didn't listen when I told him over and over again that I needed something more and different.

He was listening now though.

My cellphone began to vibrate against Tasha's glass table. I peeked at it as the memories of the hard emotional years that I'd been wrapped in were running rampant in my mind. Despite the somber thoughts, a small smile crept across my face when I saw the text message that was on the screen.

"Who is that?" Tasha asked, watching my smile.

"That fine ass nigga that I met at the mall yesterday." I sighed as I deleted the text message. Omari was fine …. *as hell*… but I had way too much going on in my heart at the moment. I was tired of niggas and tired of drama, so, despite his sexiness and those amazing gray eyes, I had to pass.

Omari

"You gotta be fuckin' kidding me."

I couldn't even believe that this bitch knew where I lived. After I found out that Simone and Chance killed Aeysha, I moved out of the trap house. I was now living in Orland Park, twenty miles outside of the city. The brick home was twenty-five hundred square feet with four bedrooms and three baths. It was the perfect size for me, and Eboni and the kids when they were over. Of course, Jamari had his own room that was decked out with Cookie Monster everything. When I closed on it two months ago, I wished to God that Aeysha could have been alive to see me make such a nice purchase for my fam.

Nowadays, I tried to think of Aeysha and Dahlia in the most positive ways that I could. No longer did I mourn for them. I celebrated them by living my life in the way that I wanted to live it with them.

That's the exact reason why I didn't feel like talking to Detective Howard, who stood standing on the other side of my door. I hadn't seen her since she accused me of killing Aeysha. So it behooved the fuck outta me why the hell she was at my door.

That era of my life was over.

When I opened the door, I could instantly tell by the look on her face that this visit was far from a pleasant one.

"Detective Howard," I huffed. I didn't hide the fact that I didn't want to see her. I had shit to do that day. Though I had escaped to Orland Park, I still had a large presence in the hood back in the city and suburbs. My trap houses were still booming. Capone and I were flipping bricks like crazy. We were pulling in over damn near fifty thousand a week. My residual income had me living real fucking comfortable. I didn't want anything that Detective Howard had to say to fuck that up.

"Hey, Omari. Can I come in?" She chuckled when she saw the reluctance on my face. "I know. You hate me, but I need to talk to you."

A deep, heavy, irritated- than -a -motherfucka sigh came out of my throat before I even knew it. But I gave her space to walk into the house and tried my best not to slam the door shut.

She took it upon herself to get comfortable on the sofa. The highlights of this week's football games caught her attention as I leaned against the wall with my arms folded. Even though she was a detective, she was feminine, so I didn't take her to be into sports. She didn't look to be over forty and she was in good shape. She was dressed down in jeans, so I could see the definition of her legs and the curve of her ass. But that big ass blue CPD jacket turned me all the way off.

"This is a nice house," she told me as she looked away from Eric Allen and glanced around the house.

"Thanks," I spat as I sighed again. "So what's up?"

Her sigh was as heavy as mine had been as she said, "I need to talk to you... We arrested Jimmy Straton a few months ago."

"Okay...?"

"He confessed to the attempted murder of Tammy, but was adamant about his innocence in her death."

"And what does that have to do with me?"

Again, she sighed and ran her hands over her pants nervously. Seeing her nervous made me nervous.

"He was stalking Simone. He was the person that attacked her in her condo, so he said."

Though I didn't give a flying fuck about Simone, that shocked the hell out of me, but it made sense. I always wondered how the crackhead she claimed that did it would have even gotten into her building past the security door.

"Why would he be stalking Simone?"

"He saw her go into Tammy's mother's house the night that Tammy was killed. His obsession turned to Simone, after figuring out that she killed Tammy–"

"The fuck?!" That caught me off guard. I had learned long ago that Simone was a sneaky, evil bitch, so it shouldn't have surprised me at all. But the depths of this bitch's insanity was mind boggling, to say the least.

Detective Howard bit her lip and nodded her head. She looked like she didn't even blame me for being so shocked. "He started stalking Simone as well. Saw her creep back into the condo the night that Dahlia died–"

"Wait. What?" I couldn't believe what I was hearing, what she was insinuating.

"He saw you leave, saw her leave, and then watched her come back through the patio doors. She left back out the same way a few minutes later."

I could only stand there silent. I was waiting to feel some sadness or anger, but I felt nothing. Simone had caused such havoc in my life that I no longer felt emotion; pain, happiness, *nothing*.

I already knew that someone smothered Dahlia. Three months ago, the autopsy reports had come back. Usually, it took thirty days to get back results, but since she was so tiny, the autopsy was complicated and took a little over ninety days for the results to be analyzed. I was pissed at Tiana about the alleged abuse, but I knew that she didn't have the heart or reason to smother my baby. Now, her nigga was a different story. My little Dahlia Rose had been buried for quite some time. I had buried my last little bit of heart with her. When Simone was killed, I vowed to move on from all of the hurt. I couldn't keep walking through life pissed and ready to pop a motherfucka because I was angry at the world. So, I told the police to do whatever investigations they had to, but really didn't give a fuck about who did what: Tiana or her boyfriend. I had cut Tiana off a long time ago. If I wanted to stay out of jail, she had to remain cut off, and I had to let the police do their thing. But the case went pretty cold because of lack of evidence.

I guess this was why.

Instantly, I felt remorse for the way that I had been treating Tiana. Since she was Fred's sister, before Dahlia passed, she was part of the crew. She had helped me so much with Dahlia. I was now realizing that Tiana was yet another victim of Simone's games. I felt terrible for accusing her of such a thing and planned to do whatever I could to make it right ASAP.

Detective Howard took my silence as disbelief, so she thought she had to further convince me. "I read over Dahlia's case files and talked to the detectives. Tiana has always been adamant that she never went in that room until she checked on Dahlia, and at that point she was already dead. The last person to see Dahlia alive was Simone. I know that any story coming from Jimmy is questionable, but his details are pretty specific. How would he even know the day that your daughter died?"

I felt the sudden rush of sickness, but fought it. I felt the room trying to spin, but I fought it. There was a large lump in my throat that I managed to swallow. Simone had yet again destroyed me. It was crazy how a lustful decision had caused my world to end. I was a dead man emotionally, trying real hard to keep on living. If it weren't for Eboni, the kids and Capone, I wasn't sure where I would be.

"Thanks for letting me know," was all I said, and she looked disappointed at my lack of emotions. But she also looked like she understood.

"Can I ask you a question, Omari?"

"You're probably going to ask me anyway."

She chuckled, but it was a dark laughter. It was heavy, as if telling me this was affecting her like it should affect me. "When was the last time that you saw Simone before she died?"

"The day before her body was found. The day she was granted bail. We got into it because I found Eboni's number in her phone. She ran out my crib. Left her purse and everything."

Detective Howard's eyes widened. "Left her purse?"

"Yea. Purse, cell phone, even her credit cards and shit. I thought she would come back to get them..." My eyes turned deadly, and I didn't bother to hide it. "...I was hoping she would. I waited on her. But she never came back. I bounced. The next day, she was burning in the woods... Why did you ask?" "Jimmy claimed that he picked her up that day, so I was just curious," she quickly said as she stood.

"Was he the person that killed her?"

"No. They got into an altercation and she stabbed Jimmy multiple times. That's how we were able to take him into custody."

Damn. That fucking Simone was a beast.

"Then who in the hell killed her?" My heart started to beat like crazy. Memories of Detective Howard accusing me of killing Aeysha came rushing to mind. "You don't think that–"

"No," she quickly told me.

"Real talk, I wanted to, but–"

"Omari," she insisted. "I know you're innocent. I'm not here for that."

"Then who did it?"

I was just curious. I wanted to go find the motherfucker and congratulate him or her.

"We're investigating that," she quickly said as she stood. "Sorry to bother you with all of this, Omari. Just thought you would like to know about Dahlia so that you can put the matter to rest."

"I would say thank you, Detective Howard, but –"

"Call me Keisha."

Her compassion let me know that she felt sorry for me. She now knew that Simone had not only killed my girl, but my daughter as well. She had taken everything from me. She had taken my woman, my daughter, and, hell, my dreams too. Detective Howard looked how I felt on the inside; she was looking at me like a dumbass nigga that fell for the wrong, crazy bitch. This was like one fucked up episode of Snapped or Fatal Attraction that I did not want to be in anymore, so I started walking towards the door before Detective Howard did.

"You have a good day, Keisha," I told her as I opened it.

"You try to as well, Omari." She comfortingly squeezed my shoulder as she left.

I immediately went into my pocket for my phone. I had to get the fuck out of the house. If I sat still, this shit would hit me, and I would be no fucking good. I remember putting that gun to my head three months ago. Though it hurt like hell to live without Aeysha, I didn't want to join her on the other side just yet. I had to live for the people that I took care of like I would have liked to take care of her and Dahlia.

I went to text Capone to let him know that I was on the way to the city. As I opened my inbox, I caught a glimpse of the unanswered text message that I sent that fine ass chick that I met the day before at the mall. Beautiful she was, but at the moment, I was happy as hell that she hadn't responded to my text. Just thinking of Simone, and the trouble that followed after I stuck my dick in her, made me straight on any female.

I hadn't fucked with another chick since Simone and that slip up between Eboni and me a few months ago after she had Jamari. Something in me had really wanted to get to know shorty from the mall, but at the moment, it reminded me of that same feeling that I felt when I hooked up with Simone.

I deleted the message and Jasmine's number.

Beautiful or not, phat ass or not, I was straight on the bullshit.

CHAPTER 3

Simone

"Urgh.... *Fuck*. That's it, baby."

My eyes rolled into the back of my head as it bumped into the steering wheel. My stomach was pressed against the center console. It was the most uncomfortable way to suck a dick, but I had gotten used to it.

On a good day, Slim hooked us up with John's that found us on Craigslist and Backpage. But on slow nights like tonight, me and the girls were outside in the cold, fucking and sucking in cars.

This wasn't escorting in a luxurious hotel. This was bottom of the barrel hoeing.

Luckily for me, this guy, Hose, who was a regular, finally bussed into the condom after *twenty gawd damn minutes.*

I was holding my hand out, waiting for the fifty dollar bill as I adjusted my blonde wig in his vanity.

"Always a pleasure." His heavy Latino accent was so annoying only because he had to be damn near sixty.

I took the money without even looking him in the eyes and I opened the door.

As I hopped out, I heard him say, "See you next week, Brandie."

"Lucky me," I grunted under my breath as I slammed the door of the Altima.

Brandie; that was the name that I had been going by. Slim, his hoes, the homeless shelter; everyone knew me as Brandie.

Since the sun was rising and most of the hoes had disappeared off of the Ave, I decided to take my ass in as well. The motel that we stayed in was only a block away, so the walk was short.

As I walked up to our room, I could hear Katie's voice clear as day. I rolled my eyes into the back of my head and prepared for her attitude. Katie was Slim's bottom bitch. Out of the six girls that worked for Slim, she had been hoeing for him the longest. She was obviously in love with him. Though Slim fucked all of us every now and then, she was his regular. She tried her best to ignore the fact that he fucked other women, but she knew that, as his bottom, she came first. But when I started hooking for him, she felt some kinda way instantly. The other girls embraced me and treated me like family. Katie, whose street name was Sunshine, had a distaste for me that got annoying at times.

"Brandie, baby," Slim greeted me as I strolled into the double queen room. This was his and Katie's room, but he only stayed overnight sometimes. He had a townhouse somewhere that we never saw. It was always a toss-up who slept where for the night in the other room, which also had a double bed with a let-out couch.

Slim watched me with a lustful grin. "Bring that phat ol' ass up in here, girl."

See? That's why Katie hated me. Out of all of the girls, I was the finest. I wasn't just being cocky either. His other girls were either drug addicts, meth heads, or the streets had gotten to them so bad that they were now alcoholics. They looked older than their age and it showed in their skin. I was fresh, so my skin was still clear and my body was still tight.

I sat in a chair at the table near the window and immediately kicked off my stilettos. My toes seemed to scream out in relief. What's worse than walking in stilettos all night is walking in cheap ones. My feet screamed relief as my legs warmed against the radiator next to me that was blazing.

After reaching in my purse, I handed Slim a wad of cash.

"How much you make tonight?"

"Five hundred."

Immediately, Katie sucked her teeth. "That bitch lyin'."

Francesca, a Mexican chick that also hoed for Slim, was lying on the bed nearest the bathroom. She sucked her teeth as soon as Katie started in. I had actually gotten cool with Francesca, so she knew that Katie fucked with me for no reason.

I rolled my eyes at Katie. "What the fuck are you talking about?"

Immediately, she started popping off. "Bitch! I saw you gettin' in and out of cars all night. You a motherfuckin' lie all you made is five hunit!"

I looked at her like she was crazy. "Are you high?"

She was way too amped up for it to be six in the morning. But I knew that she wasn't high. She was showing off for Slim. We all went out of our way to show our loyalty to Slim. The more he knew that we were loyal, the more he took care of us. But, since I kinda knew the game, my mind wasn't as warped as the other girls. Katie always took it overboard. She had Slim's name tattooed across her stomach like Tupac's "Thuglife" tattoo.

She was all in.

"What, bitch?! Who the fuck you think you are talkin' to me like that?! That's your problem! You think you're the shit."

Before I knew it, I had rose to my feet. "No, I don't think I'm the shit, but you do."

I knew there would come a day that I had to fight this bitch, and I be damned if after sucking and fucking all night, today was the day. Katie came towards me like a raging bull. I was all kinds of bitches, hoes, cunts – you name it. Slim and Francesca was looking back and forth between us like a Ping–Pong game. By the time that she was in arm's reach, Katie swung. Immediately, she pulled on my wig, which I had been smart enough to sew down. It was a short bob, but she had her fingers intertwined tightly in it while her other hand hit me over and over again in the face.

I could hear Slim yelling for her to stop while Katie pulled me all over the room. I was swinging with all of my might, but no matter what, she would not let go of my hair.

I could smell Slim's cologne nearby. I could also see the black Timbs that he was wearing. He had grabbed a hold of Katie, which had only pissed her off even more. Her hits became harder and her grip on my hair was tighter.

"Bitch, didn't I say stop?!" Slim's deep voice echoed all over the room. "Chill before you get us kicked out!"

Finally, the blows stopped. I stood up straight and glared at Katie. If I weren't dodging a few murder convictions, I would have told her my record of what I did to a bitch that got in my way.

"Stupid ass bitch!" Katie fussed as Slim blocked her in a corner. "I told you–"

Whack! Slim had slapped the living taste out of her mouth. "I said shut the fuck up!"

Katie stood in the corner holding her face. I could see that her pale skin was already turning red from the blow. I only snickered to piss her off. When Slim didn't chastise me, it pissed her off even more.

Gia

Georgia joined me at the kitchen table. She picked up the cup of cappuccino that I'd made her with my mother's Keurig and sniffed it.

"The hell is this?"

I giggled. "It's a cappuccino. Drink it. You'll like it."

"When did you start drinking this boojie shit?"

I shrugged. "It's a habit that I picked up in Cali."

Georgia's eyes rolled into the back of her head as she mumbled, "Figures."

I closed my eyes and sighed as the cappuccino rolled down my throat. Finally, I had a little peace. It was a week after my mother's funeral, and finally some of the drama had died down. I told my family to kiss my ass. They were going to have to fight me if they thought they were getting any of my mother's things.

"Sooooo..." Georgia practically sang with a sneaky grin.

"Oh shit," I interrupted. "What do you want?"

I knew she wanted something. All of her life, she had that specific smile and sparkle in her eyes when she looked into the eyes of whoever it was that she wanted something from.

"What happened when you went to Sunset last night?"

Luckily, Georgia knew that this was a secret, so she kept her voice low. When she got here last night, I lay in bed with her and told her how much I wanted to stay in Chicago. I figured if I started back dancing at Sunset and Chance saw the money that I was making, he would agree to stay.

It was a gamble, I knew. He wouldn't be able to move around the city too easily without bumping into Omari and Chance, but we needed the money.

I didn't know how fast two people could run through money. Three months after being in Cali, all the money that Chance and I had was pretty much gone. I was stripping in Cali, but men in Cali liked a different look or had their favorites. I wasn't making the same cash and neither was Chance. I needed to be in Chicago, stacking my paper. We would be able to stay rent–free in my mother's house since it was paid off. It was perfect, until we came up with a better plan.

"Of course they hired me back. I was the best bitch on the pole at Sunset."

Georgia giggled along with me and then asked, "What would they think about your sister dancing too?"

I nearly choked as I sipped from the coffee cup. "What?!"

Georgia laughed at the way that my eyes bulged out of my sockets. "I know, sissy. But I don't want to go back to Idaho." She frowned and poked her lip out.

I should have known this was coming. My sister and I weren't that tight. She had always been a problem child that kept my mother with a headache. She had chased some nigga to Idaho, of all fucking places, three years ago, when she was only sixteen. She had dropped out of high school and followed this grown ass, nothing ass nigga to God only knows where, which gave my mother so much grief. My mother was older, damn near sixty. She had us very late in life. I didn't like that my sister had been so disrespectful with her cutting class, drinking, fucking and fighting. Once she ran away with that nigga, I washed my hands.

However, when she hadn't gone back to Idaho after my mother's funeral, I knew something was up.

"So, you're done with Rodney?"

Her eyes rolled into the back of her head at the sound of her boyfriend's name. "Fuck him."

"You sure?"

She reached up to the collar of the long sleeved t–shirt that she was wearing. When she tugged on the collar, she revealed bruises along her neck and chest. "I'm done," she assured me.

My insides winced and cringed, as she told me, "I'm fine, but I'm done."

She didn't look like she wanted to talk about it, so I left it alone. "Okay. I'll talk to the manager at Sunset tonight. Can you dance?"

She cheesed and started to twerk in her chair. "Girl, bye. Hell yea, I can twerk."

"Its way more than just twerking, Georgia."

"I'm sure it is, but you'll show me, right?"

For the first time in years, I saw drive in my sister's eyes. She looked determined, so I was willing to help. "Sure. I'll show you."

Chance

"When in the fuck were you going to tell me that you didn't plan on going back to Cali?"

I went in on Gia's ass as soon as she stepped foot into the bedroom. Her eyes bucked, and she immediately closed the door. "Wh .... What are you talking about?"

Then my eyes bucked. I had never known Gia to lie so fucking easily. "I heard you!" I told her before she even tried to lie. "I was on the stairs."

She just stood there, in the middle of the floor, stuck and biting her bottom lip nervously.

"So you just gon' do what the fuck you wanna do?! So fuck me?! Fuck my life?!"

"We need the money, Chance!"

"We can figure that out in *California...*" I lowered my voice to keep Georgia from hearing me. "... where a nigga ain't tryin' to kill me because I murdered his girl."

I guess Gia had forgot about that. Her shoulders hunched down and she came towards me. She reached out to touch me, but I lightly pushed her hand away. She looked surprised, but I didn't give a fuck. She was trippin' if she thought I was staying in the Chi.

She told me, "It will only be for a few weeks," but I knew she was lying. I saw the light in her eyes as soon as we got back. She was happy to be back home.

But there wasn't anything that I could do. Now that I wasn't hustling, Gia was my means to an end. I couldn't eat, have a roof over my head, or even wipe my ass without her help. When we first moved to Cali, I appreciated it. She was a down ass bitch. I wanted nothing but to do what I had to do to be able to take care of her more than she was taking care of me. But, as my life had always been, I had no luck.

She saw the wheels in my head turning. She took advantage of my mind wandering and came closer to me. This time, I didn't push her away. She wrapped her arms around my waist and tried to convince me that this shit made sense. "We'll be able to save money here, baby. We don't have to pay rent. My customers at Sunset have been asking about me; I'll be making bread in no time. We can take it, go back to Cali, get you some product and we'll be back on. Then the money that I make in the clubs down there won't matter. Just let me make this money, baby, please."

I could only roll my eyes in the back of my head. I had nothing to say; I had no choice. I couldn't go back to Cali without her, even if I wanted to.

I had never seen Gia be so selfish. Since I met her, she had been all about me. She did everything for me. She made sacrifices for me. She hustled just to save my life. Now, she was thinking about herself and it hurt.

I wasn't used to Gia hurting me. Since living in Lexington House

I was taught to be hard, not to have emotions, and not to let other people hurt me. Otherwise, I would never survive. Now, no matter how hard I tried not to, I was feeling pain on the inside, and I didn't like that shit at all. Gia was actually hurting me. She was being money hungry. Her hustle mentality had overshadowed her love for me.

They say money is the root of all evil; it was definitely about to be the root of mine.

CHAPTER 4

Eboni

"The fuck?" I swung my front door open and glared at Terrance, who was standing on the other side of the door. "Are you serious? It's three in the morning. What the fuck are you doing here?"

I was fronting. It didn't matter what time of the morning it was. I was awake anyway. I had been reading *When A Bitch Is Fed Up*. The girls at school were raving about it. Omari heard me bitching about not having a Kindle, so he got me one the other day. That Kevina Hopkins sure knew how to write a book. I felt like she was telling my story. I was engrossed in the book and could not put it down. So I was more so irritated with Terrance for interrupting my juicy read, than him knocking on my door at the crack of dawn.

I wasn't that surprised to see him. He had been acting strange for the past two months; calling the kids, spending time with them, asking if they needed anything... You know, *being a father*; shit he hadn't done since he left me. He had even invited me out to dinner when he was taking the kids three weeks ago and apologized to me for leaving me, especially for leaving me for my best friend.

"Can I come in?"

"For?"

He blew a deep breath. "Please, Eboni?"

I scratched my head through my bonnet cap nervously. I couldn't figure him out. I assumed he was drunk, but taking a closer look, I could see that he was sober. He did look sick though; emotionally sick. He wore a Pele, but I could see that underneath it all he had on was a wife beater. Taking into account his jogging pants and unlaced Timbs, it appeared as if he'd just stumbled out of the house.

"Please?" he reiterated as I looked him up and down in confusion.

Reluctantly, I stepped back to let him in. As he walked inside, I caught him looking at my ass. All I had on was a sports bra and some boy shorts that could barely hold half of my ass. But hell I was in the bed; what the fuck did he expect? Since he was somebody else's man, I probably should have put on some clothes before joining him on the couch. But since he was in a relationship with my ex best friend, whom he'd left me for, I didn't give that much of a fuck.

"What's going on?" I asked with all the attitude in the world.

Terrance didn't even bother to complain about my attitude either. Like I said, he'd left me for my ex best friend. She and Terrance were living like the fucking Cosby's in the suburbs while I was struggling to take care of all these gawd damn kids; that is, before Omari came into the picture. Terrance did not only leave me, he left his kids. I had to beg him to see them, and getting any child support from him was a miracle from God. We stayed at each other's throats. We beefed like niggas on the street. Though he had gotten better recently, his presence on my couch was confusing, to say the least.

"I'm sorry. I had to get the fuck out of there. I had nowhere else to go."

I looked at him like he was crazy. "Huh? What do you mean? What happened?"

He sighed as he took off his jacket. His smell escaped and washed over me. After all of these years, he still wore the same hypnotizing cologne.

Get it together, bitch. I had to check myself super-fast.

As a single mother –a single mother that is truly single; no booty calls because I have four kids that I always have that prevent me from going out and meeting anyone to... *shiiid*, just fuck! Damn a relationship – having a man in my home is a turn on in itself. The fact that I knew how the dick swung and how he immaculately ate pussy was a plus.

"Felicia and I been gettin' into it for a minute...."

The moment he said her name, the effects of his smell were stomped all over, and I was reminded why I hated this motherfucker.

"Tonight was the last straw. I had to get the fuck up out of there. It's over."

"Umph," was all I said, as if I barely cared. But I can't lie; on the inside, I was jumping for joy. I felt validated. I had been waiting for karma to come around and get them back for deceiving me, for how they treated me and my kids. By the look on Terrance's face, indeed karma had showed her face and kicked their ass. Even if he went back to Felicia the next day, I felt better.

"Well," I sighed as I stood. "I guess you can stay here tonight." I didn't want to have some long ass conversation with him about what happened. I didn't care. Knowing that they were no longer together was good enough for me. Long as I knew that Felicia was at home wondering where he was, was good enough for me.

She deserved it.

"I don't want the kids to see you, though…"

"Why not?" he asked.

"I don't want them to see you sleeping here. I don't want them under the impression that you're back. They just stopped asking why you don't live here anymore. I don't want them confused, so you'll have to sleep in my bed. Sorry."

"It's okay."

Even though my back was to him as he stood and followed me inside my bedroom, I could feel his shadow after me. He was a beast of a man, standing at 6'3" and weighing almost three hundred pounds. He was thick from head to toe. His solid build gave him so much presence, and I could totally feel it as we walked inside of my bedroom.

I closed the door behind myself as I told him, "You can sleep on the inside. I like the outside now."

He used to always sleep on the outside of the bed. He said that he needed to in case of emergencies, if he ever needed to get out of the bed quickly.

"That's cool."

I could feel him staring at me. He wanted to say something. He wanted to talk. But I kept my shoulder cold and my eyes away from his. I was battling myself. I hated him, but I couldn't deny how good it felt to have him in "our" home again, even if only for a moment.

I sat on the bed and powered off my Kindle. I would have to get back to Mia and Seantrel later. I couldn't focus if I wanted to.

I caught Terrance staring down at Jamari as he took off his pants. Even though we weren't comfortable with one another like that, he knew that I didn't like anybody sleeping in my bed with their street clothes on.

"He's gotten big," he said in a whisper.

Lil' T had a birthday party two months ago. Omari funded the whole thing. That was right around the time that Terrance started to act strange. He actually showed up to Lil T's party with an abundance of gifts. I don't think he could stand that Omari was starting to upstage him. That was one of the few times that he'd seen Jamari.

"Yea, he has." I got comfortable under the covers and immediately turned my back to where Terrance would be sleeping.

As soon as I felt him climbing into the bed, I reached over and turned off the lamp.

Awkwarrrrd.

I closed my eyes and tried to sleep, but my heart was beating so fast that I couldn't. I was scared that he could hear it. I was upset with myself for even being nice enough to let him stay. I was biting the hell out of my lip, trying not to go off on him for all the hurt that he'd caused me.

"I'm so sorry for how I left."

The sudden sound of his voice made me jump a bit in fright. Then it took me a few seconds to digest what he said.

"Eboni? Do you hear you me?" As if he was trying to get my attention, he put his hand on the curve of my waist.

Gawd damn it, I thought as I pressed my lips together tightly. Though my back was to him, we were close. I could only fit a full–sized bed in my room. When we were together, we always joked about him barely being able to fit. I could feel his breath on the back of my neck. I fought the chills that ran down my spine. He didn't have to touch me to cause this excitement though. Just having a penis in this bed that wasn't Jamari's or Lil' T's was like the second coming of Jesus. My pussy was tripping; like she completely forgot how this nigga had played us.

"I... I hear you."

Am I stuttering? I couldn't believe my–motherfuckin'–self. *Damn my hormones. Damn! Damn! Damn!*

That quick, gone was the "fuck him" attitude that I had had for two and half years.

I couldn't believe *myself*. The man wasn't even trying to have sex with me. He was only lying behind me. He had only slightly touched me and my body was reacting. It had nothing to do with him. Sure, he was nice looking. But it was purely because I hadn't had any action since me and Omari's slip up at his trap house a few months ago. Even before that, the only dick that I had was sparingly from Omari. After Terrance left, I was too depressed to date to anyone else. Terrance was the only dick that my pussy knew. He broke my virginity when we met in high school eleven years ago. I had never cheated on him. Even when I slept with Omari, it wasn't the same. There was no love or affection in those strokes. My body missed everything that Terrance used to be before he left, and there he was, in the bed with us.

"It was bogus, I know. I know it doesn't make it right, right now, but I'm sorry, Eboni."

In the darkness, my eyes rolled into the back of my head. "You've said you were sorry already. And, nah, it doesn't make it right at this very moment."

"How long are you going to hate me?"

Fuck if his voice in this room wasn't overpowering! I just wanted him to shut the fuck up!

When I didn't answer, he grabbed my waist and turned me over. Even in the darkness, I could see him staring down at me.

"I'm sorry," he reiterated in a more convincing tone; a sweet, caring, and seductive tone that I hadn't heard him use in a long time.

"Now that the relationship that you left me for is over, you're sorry?"

"I've been sorry."

"Not this sorry. Why now?"

"I'm sorry because it should have been said. Because you never let me close enough to you to say it like this. You cussed me out every chance you got-"

"Because you...!" I had to stop myself because I was getting loud. "Because you fucking left me for my best friend. You-"

Now I stopped because Terrance's hand went beneath the comforter and started to rub my stomach. *"I'm sorry."*

I lay there thinking about how if I had done better with my life, if I had been a little smarter, if my credit was better, Felicia wouldn't have had an advantage. He wanted to buy that shop with me. He wanted to buy a home for us. He couldn't do it alone, and I wasn't in the position to help my family either.

There it was; that sickening feeling of low self-esteem that was with me for years after Terrance left. Every time he rubbed my stomach, it was as if he was rubbing it away. It made me feel good to know that, yes, he did still want me in some way, and, no, I wasn't repulsive to him.

It was cliché for him to try to kiss me right then. Even more cliché, and even more stupid, was that I let him. Fuck that. I was horny! He had called me every name in the book, as I had him. He had made me feel like a bum bitch. He had left me for my best friend. But right then, with his hand on my stomach, with the smell of his Gucci Guilty in my sheets, I felt better.

His hand roamed from my stomach to the lake presently between my legs. I was embarrassed of how wet I was when his hand found its way inside of my shorts, but it turned him on. His breathing got heavy and his kisses got more aggressive.

Yes, I felt stupid. I felt like he was just using me. I was sure of it. He had left me for someone smarter, more responsible and more established. I was sure that he was going to wake up in the morning and go right back to her as soon as she batted those full, long lashes that I always envied.

But did I care? No. All I cared about was that he was with me at that moment. For that moment, for hours, things were back like they were; back two and a half years ago before my world turned upside down. It was like nothing had changed. As he kissed the stomach that he always praised for staying small kid after kid, I felt like my heart had never been broken, crushed and run over by that truck that he pulled up in, packed his shit in, and drove off in with her in the passenger seat.

Before I knew it, he slid on top of me and quickly into me.

We were like kids on a playground, except we had to keep our screams and giggles quiet in order not to wake Jamari.

I got every nut off that had been lying dormant inside of me.

"I didn't realize how much I missed her," he breathed as he rode me missionary. My legs were up and my knees were on the mattress. Usually, I wouldn't be able to take this much dick, but my body was still accustomed to his length and width.

Damn, it felt so good to have him on top of me. The dick was good, but what made my body cry juices was the feeling of his body on top of mine.

There was no magic in it. I was fully aware of the stupidity that was swimming in the atmosphere of my bedroom. But it felt so damn good. Until 6am, I kept my eyes closed and basked in the feeling. As soon as he pulled out and bussed on the sheet, I opened my eyes and looked at him. The incredible feeling of him delivering countless orgasms, the best ones when he was hitting it from the back, was still all over me. I could even see the pleasure and excitement in those dark eyes that naturally rode so low. He looked a lot more at ease than he did when he got there.

But he had to go. "You gotta go, Terrance."

Now that the thrill was gone, reality was back, and I had to look out for my kids. Just because Terrance was there that morning, reality was that he probably would not be the next.

He looked down on me; at my breasts that still dripped with sweat and wild hair that had become disheveled once my bonnet fell off.

"Huh?" He was still breathing hard, but the shock was still

evident in his voice.

"You have to go," I reiterated as I sat up. "The kids will be up in a minute. I told you that I don't want them to see you here."

I could feel his eyes following me as I busied myself by getting out of bed and putting some clothes on.

"I can put my clothes back on and act like I came to get them ready for school."

"Don't play with their feelings like that. You haven't been doing it before."

"But–"

"Terrance, you needed to stay, I let you stay, and now it's time to go."

Silence. I didn't hear the bed moving, signaling his movement, so I glanced over at him as I stepped into a pair of pajama pants. The way that he was looking at me was damn near humorous. He was actually hurt. I had hurt him.

Imagine that.

"Terrance, you've been broke up with Felicia for how long? A day? Has it even been twenty–four hours? Last night was good, but let's not fake the funk. You left me for her before, and I'm not about to allow you to play house until the moment comes that you leave when she calls again… It is what it is. I'll give you ten minutes to get dressed before I wake up the kids. I'm going to wash off. Be gone when I get back."

And with that, I was out.

Omari

"What's up, fam?"

Obviously Capone was concerned when I called him in the morning and told him that I needed to holler at him. He was even more concerned that I wasn't ready to talk until Eboni got to my house.

"Yea, what's going on?" Eboni asked as she sat on the couch holding Jamari. He was wide-awake. Those big gray eyes looked like moons. "And hurry up because I have to go to work."

I chuckled. "I have to go to work." "I have to go to class." She was always quick to say that shit; she was so proud of herself. She reminded me of when Aeysha finally got her job: "I gotta go to work." She was so proud to say that and was quick to throw it in my face.

My heart warmed with the thought of that as I sat across from Eboni and Capone in the loveseat in the corner clutching a glass of Hennessy X.O. No matter how much I wanted to just forget about Simone, what Detective Howard had laid on me was heavy as hell.

Capone stared at me as I stared at them. "Speak, nigga," he urged.

I nervously rubbed my hand over my mouth. I hated to fuck up their day, but I had to. They were the closest people to me. They were family. I had to tell them.

"Detective Howard came by here yesterday."

Eboni's eyes immediately frowned up as she asked, "For what?"

Again, I took a deep breath and prepared myself. "They finally caught Jimmy."

"Who?" Capone asked.

"Tammy's ex. Remember Simone's friend that we ran into at the club that night? I told you about how her ex had went crazy and shot her best friend that she was living with. He was stalking her and ended up killing her."

"Riiiight," Capone recalled with a nod.

"Okay. What's that got to do with you?" Eboni asked. I could see the nervousness rising on her skin.

"He confessed to trying to kill Tammy, but he said he didn't actually kill her. Since he was stalking her, he saw who did..." I was so scared to say it. I'm a grown ass man. I fear nothing or no one but God... and Simone Campbell. Saying her name was like saying "Candyman" three times in the bathroom with the lights off when you were ten-years-old.

Fuck it, I thought before forcing myself to blurt out, "Simone did it."

Their faces were pretty much like mine when Detective Howard told me the same thing; stuck. But I went on and took advantage of their silence to further fuck up their day. "Since he saw her do it, he started stalking her. He stalked her for a minute.

That's who attacked her in her condo that day, Capone." The realization caused a telling smirk on his face as I continued. "The day that Dahlia died, he saw her leave out of the house, creep back through the patio, and then leave back out a little while later."

The air in the room was eerie and still. I took a sip of the Hennessy in attempts to prevent the oncoming headache.

"So... Wait a minute... Did she...?" Eboni was trying to wrap this all around her brain while fighting tears. We were both tired of crying at this point. "She's who smothered Dahlia?"

With a heavy heart, I answered, "Yea. She killed Dahlia."

I could hear the heavy breath that Capone let out. This shit was heavy. She was my daughter, but she also meant so much to the two people sitting on that couch. Capone loved Dahlia because he loved me. Eboni loved Dahlia because, no matter her mistakes, she loved Aeysha.

"Well, good thing the bitch is dead. Saves me a murder wrap," Capone said coolly as he stood. I knew my nigga. He was being hard. He didn't want me to see him down because he didn't want me to fall apart after it took me so long to get myself back together. "I'm out, bruh. Let me go handle this business on the block. You good?"

He stood in front of me with his hand stretched. I shook up with him and told him, "Yea, I'm good. You?"

He nodded, but I knew better. When it came to me, he was a bad liar. He could never lie to me with a straight face.

My eyes fixed on Eboni's as Capone walked towards the front

door. She was always fighting tears. Neither one of them wanted to be weak in front of me. Ever since a nigga had a weak moment and kinda put a gun to his head, these motherfuckers treated me like a patient.

I chuckled after I heard the front door close. "That nigga gon' cry in the car."

Eboni's eyes found mine, but there wasn't an ounce of laughter in them.

"You okay?"

"No," she spat. "That crazy ass bitch. I'm glad she's dead. Did Jimmy kill her?"

"He was in the hospital when she was killed. He says he and Simone got into it. Simone stabbed him a few times and got away."

"So who in the hell killed her?"

"I don't know, and I don't care. I'm just glad they did."

Eboni just stared off into space. She was cradling Jamari a lot closer to her chest now.

"You okay?" I asked her again.

"I told you, no."

"No, I mean, before I told you all this. You looked like something was bothering you when you walked in."

Even though she said, "I'm fine," I could tell something was off about her. It was obvious that she played nervously with Jamari's hair to avoid my questioning eyes.

I didn't force it though. I had enough on my mind. I just hoped she hadn't done something stupid, like get pregnant again or something. She was on the right path for once in her life, and I sat there hoping that she stayed on it.

CHAPTER 5

Detective Howard

"Hey, Michelle. Is everything okay with the kids?" When I heard the crying, I knew that it wasn't. "What's wrong?"

"Everything is okay," Michelle, my night sitter, told me. "Khryssa just had a bad dream and wants to talk to her mommy."

I was relieved but still felt sick to my stomach. As my five-year-old daughter got on the phone, her tears pulled at my heartstrings. Even though her bully of a big sister, Krislyn, had made her watch a scary Halloween movie and she was only scared of Chucky, I felt horrible. My job had taken me away from my only two kids for years. Late nights and early mornings had left a sitter to raise my kids for me; take them to school, pick them up, cook them dinner and help them with homework.

After a few promises to Khryssa that her cop of a mom would be home soon to shoot any boogie man, her tears slowed and she gave Michelle back the phone. "Sorry about that, Michelle."

"It's no problem, Miss Keisha."

She was twenty-three. I was only old enough to be her auntie, but she insisted on calling me Miss Keisha.

"As soon as I am done with this paperwork, I will be home."

I hung up with desires to be a mother more than anything. But I couldn't. I was a homicide detective, what I had fought long and hard to become for most of my life. I fought against all odds, including my ex-husband, Will, who hated the long nights and early mornings. He wanted me at home; barefoot, with a spatula in one hand and his dick in the other. But that wasn't my life. I wanted to be a detective, just like my dad. But Will wanted a stay-at-home mom, just like his mom had been to him and his brothers, so he found that stay-at-home mom in the pussy of one of the many babysitters that I had hired over the years.

I think that's why I was so adamant to get Simone Campbell. I hated every willing side bitch that walked this earth. Sure, some women fell victim to a lying man. But a bitch like Simone Campbell was a deceitful hoe that deserved her day in court.

"Keisha! So glad you're here!"

I looked up to see Sam walking towards my desk through the pretty empty Homicide Division. It was two in the morning. Most detectives were outside investigating murders. In Chicago, every murder was usually a gunshot victim. I was sitting at my desk finishing up paperwork on a fifteen-year-old victim that had died from a gunshot wound to the head in a park three days ago. Luckily, the doer had been running his mouth in school and someone defied the street code and snitched. This was one case that was luckily open and shut.

"You better have some good news for me, Sam," I said not even looking up at him. I continued filling out the paperwork so that I could get to my baby as fast as I could in order to shoot that boogie man. That is; until Sam slapped a manila folder in front of me.

I reached for it cautiously, as I eyed him through my Chinese bangs. "What's this?"

"That, *Keisha*, is twenty–two–year–old, Brianna Daniels."

I stared at his content grin. Shit, I had so many cases on my desk that I couldn't recall who the hell he was talking about.

"That, *Keisha–*"

"Say my name one more time and I am going to shoot your ass."

He chuckled. "Damn, I like it when you act like a cop." I rolled my eyes as he went on. "Anyway, those are your dental records on that burn victim in the park..."

As the words left his lips, my eyes brightened and my heart started to beat fast with excitement. "Yes! I knew it!" I jumped to my feet. "Thank you!" I even hugged him.

"Mmmm. How thankful are you, baby?"

I immediately let him go and smacked the shit out of his arm.

"Ow!"

That was it. That was all I needed to hear. Sam watched me as I began to shut my computer down. I was going home to have a celebratory drink and pop the shit out of that boogie man. "Keep this out of the media, Sam. I don't want Simone Campbell tipped off."

"You got it."

I caught his eyes on my ass. "Get shot, Sam. Keep it up."

He held his hands up in defense as he walked away. "It's cool. Drinks on you then."

I agreed with a smile and grabbed my purse out of the drawer. This was the best news that I had gotten in a long time. However, now the real detective work began. I had to find Simone Campbell. She hadn't touched her accounts since the day she went missing. Without any money or identification, I knew that she couldn't have gone far.

Jasmine

"C'mon, Jasmine. Let's go kick it."

I rolled my eyes in the back of my head as I turned the engine off of my 2015 Jeep Compass. I would have rather been riding around in the Audi that Ant had given me for Valentine's Day that year, but, hey, this is the type of shit that happens when you leave a dope boy; you have to downgrade...severely.

"I don't feel like going out, Tasha." I really didn't. I had spent the last few weeks settling into my new apartment and my new job, an eighth grade English teacher at Beasley Academic Center. I was super excited because I had graduated from Beasley, so it was pretty cool to now be working there as well. I had a hell of a time getting the kids to respect me though. The girls thought I was young enough to be their friend, and I couldn't get the little boys to stop looking at my ass.

I rolled my eyes in the back of my head, listening to Tasha fuss at me for being a lame. Then, my other line rang. I pulled my ear away from Tasha's nagging to see who it was. It was Ant, so I ignored him.

Ain't nobody got time for that.

All he wanted to do was threaten me if I didn't come back and remind me how I was living like common folk without him. His voicemails and text messages were full of the same egotistical words; not a word about how much he loved, needed, or missed me.

Fuuuuck him, I thought as I grabbed the Subway that I bought for lunch and climbed out of the car.

"So, are you coming or nah?"

"Nah."

Tasha sucked her teeth and started back ranting as I tuned her out and fought wind.

It was so damn cold. One thing I did not miss more than the drama that I left in this city was the bitter cold. It was taking some getting used to. In late October, I was used to being in eighty-degree weather, not thirty. I adjusted my earpiece in my ear, dropped my lunch in my purse before securing the tote bag on my wrist and shoved my hands in the pockets of my leather blazer. Suddenly, I was regretting choosing to wear a pencil skirt that day.

"Jasmine, we haven't been out since you got back. Damn."

I groaned, "Not tonight, Tasha–"

"But today is Fridaaay," she whined. "There is a Halloween party at Sawtooth..."

The vision before me rendered me speechless. I stopped dead in my tracks. I could no longer hear what Tasha was saying. I damn near lost my balance when I laid eyes on him. My heart started to beat at least a hundred miles per hour. The earth was literally spinning under my Louboutin pumps. I could *not* fall in these shoes. They were probably the last pair of high–end shoes that I owned since I left Ant. But I was sure that I would fall the closer he got to me. He wasn't paying me any attention. He was holding the hand of a little girl, who couldn't have been more than six and looked just like him.

I hung up on Tasha mid-rant. Just as he walked by me, I reached for him, grabbing him gently by the elbow. "Kendrick." His name felt so foreign to me as it left my lips.

It didn't take him long to recognize me at all. Sure, it had been twelve years, but when a man spent nearly every day of three years inside of you, he will never forget your face.

"Jasmine... H... Hey."

"Hi," I breathed. I didn't know quite what the fuck I was feeling right then. It was a mixture of happiness, pisstivity and jealously. I was so happy to lay eyes on him again after so long. I was just as happy to see that he was alive and well. The same anger that I felt when he cut me out of his life because of that bitch Simone rose to the surface of my brown skin. And I was jealous of whoever this child's mother was because I was supposed to be her mother.

By the look on his face, he didn't know what to feel about seeing me either. He didn't look happy; that's for damn sure.

"Hi." Luckily, the little girl was the only one with sense enough to break the awkward silence.

"Hi, baby," I greeted her. "What's your name?"

"Sierra."

"Wow, that's a pretty name for a pretty girl. You look just like your dad." I tore my eyes away from her. I had to. I couldn't look into those eyes any longer without breaking down. But as I looked at Kendrick, it was a large feat to keep my composure. "She's beautiful."

"Thank you," he simply told me.

He was so casual, so dry, so not like we had been madly in love before.

"How have you been?" I was literally forcefully pulling conversation from him.

"Good."

"I see. You look great." That he did. He still had the thug appeal about him. His Moncler jacket, jeans, and Timbs gave him that local, Chi, hood boy feel. As always, he was perfectly lined with waves so deep and luscious that you would want to swim in them. The only difference now was the full facial hair that lined his face and gave him a grown man look.

"Look at you," I smiled. "You look so grown up."

"Hey, married life and kids will do that to a nigga."

Whoa... Ouch... Don't trip, bitch.

I tried so hard to keep it together. I really did. "Married?" I tried to smile to hide my heartbreak. "And kids? Wow."

"Yea. I got three of them. Sierra is the youngest."

"When did you get married?"

"It's been about eleven years."

Ouch!

He watched me, waiting for my response. Eleven years meant that he had married the bitch within a year of leaving me.

"Wo... Wow! That's... that's great, Kendrick. Congratulations."

Breathe, Jasmine. Breathe. Don't cry.

He totally ignored my shock, asking, "How is Marcus?"

That made me feel like a complete ass.

"He's good. Grown man now. He'll be eighteen next year."

His eyes bucked. That was the first time that he smiled or showed any excitement whatsoever.

He started to say something else but a strong gust of wind blew by. "Whew!" I said. "Let me let you get your baby out of this cold. It was good seeing you." And I scurried away as I heard him say, "You too."

I had just talked to the love of my life like we were complete strangers. I can't lie; I had so many daydreams of seeing him again and us picking right back up where we left off. This was a hard dose of reality. Obviously, what I had been struggling to let go of for years, he had so easily let go of within a year. Did I even mean as much to him as he did to me? Apparently not.

I called Tasha back as I entered the school.

"Bitch, you wrong for hanging up on me–"

"I'll see you tonight." I needed a fucking drink. Lots of 'em. "Do I need a costume?"

Omari

"Sawtooth? Really, nigga?" I looked at Capone like he was crazy.

"C'mon, man. Do you know all the ass that's gon' be there in some sexy ass costumes? You know the hoes gon' be naked!"

No homo, but I wasn't even really trying to look at no hoes. It had been a week since the visit from Detective Howard, but the reality was still fresh on my brain. I was still in the positive spirit that I was trying to adopt before she came by, but I had a real sour taste in my mouth for women.

"You already know I ain't interested in no hoes."

"That's your problem, man. You need to get back in the game. Take your frustrations out on some pussy." Then Capone bit his bottom lip and moved his hips like he was deep in some pussy.

Again, I looked at him like he was crazy. "Stop, nigga."

He was so young and full of life. I envied that. He was a club junky too. He was still too young to get in them, but he went where he either knew the bouncers or knew that he could slide them a few bills to let him in.

"For real though," he said with a chuckle. "C'mon, man. You my nigga, and we ain't kicked it in a while. 'It's Friday. You ain't got no job. And you ain't got shit to do!'"

Now this nigga wants to be Chris Tucker.

I sighed heavily. "Ah ight man. Anything to shut you up."

****

"Bruh, this party is whack as fuck. I knew I should have stayed at the crib."

Capone shook his head as he bobbed his head to the sounds of Lil' Boosie. "Nigga, when did you turn fifty? I missed it."

I chuckled at his little joke but decided to stop complaining and try to enjoy myself as best I could. Luckily, we were in VIP, sectioned off from everyone else by a velvet rope, so I could just chill and not be bothered. The two bottles of Hennessy XO on our table was attracting the attention of a few girls on the other side of the ropes in nurse, Cat Woman, and other costumes that left little to the imagination.

Never knew a nurse to have her ass out.

Anyway, if you clubbed enough, you knew that bottle service for that brand of Hennessy was six hundred a piece. These chicks obviously knew that. They figured that we had bread and was shaking their ass to get our attention. The view was nice, but I wasn't impressed.

As I stared down on the first level of the club, I instantly got very impressed, however. In my eyesight was a chocolate drop dressed in an Air Force jumpsuit. I recognized the hair that fell from underneath the hat. I definitely recognized the ass that the hair fell on top of.

"Aye! Aye!" I was smacking Capone's arm to get his attention. He was lit by now and was rapping along to Lil' Boosie's every word. "Bruh!"

"What, man?!"

"Look! That's shorty." I sat back on the couch to give him a good view of the bottom floor. I pointed towards the bar, at the beautiful woman in the jumpsuit next to the pretty, high–yellow chick dressed as, yet another, Cat Woman.

"Shorty from the mall?"

I stared at her as I nodded.

"You haven't called shorty yet?"

I didn't want to tell him that I had talked myself out of it and deleted her number. I didn't need to hear his shit. So I just shook my head and told him, "Nah, not yet."

I couldn't even hear what he was saying. Shorty mesmerized me. More than being bad on the outside, it was something about that smile that told me she was just as nice on the inside. I had seen a lot of women in my day. Capone and I had so much cash that women of all races, ages and body types flocked to us wherever we went. They were all the same, but something told me that this one was different.

Jasmine

"I'm so sorry, Jasmine. I can't believe that shit."

I had opted to wait to tell Tasha about seeing Kendrick until we had a drink in us. I could only handle allowing the horrific details to leave my lips if I was tipsy. Two drinks in, I had managed to give her every grizzly detail.

"I felt so stupid, Tasha." I stood closely next to her at the bar. Clutching a double shot of Coconut 1800 with anger. I couldn't believe that I had spent twelve whole years holding on to someone who had so easily let me go after just one. "He said it with such ease. Like he didn't even care about hurting me. He looked like he was just as disgusted with me as he was the last time I saw him." My lips pressed together tightly. I knew that it was wrong to speak ill of the dead, so, in my mind, I cursed Simone. I would have cursed her existence if she was alive. I hated that I allowed that bitch to manipulate me out of my happily ever after. But, just as I should have known better, if Kendrick loved me as much as our connection told me that he did, he should have forgiven me.

"You think he married somebody that he was fucking around on me with? I mean, he married her a year later. He had to know her already."

"Don't even worry about that," Tasha told me. "Fuck him, friend. Don't trip. You'll find the right guy one day."

That sounded good but it didn't feel like it. "Umph," I grunted. "Maybe so. But..." I frowned as I looked around. "... I definitely won't find him in here."

Clearly, we hadn't gotten the invite to the party were the *men* were at. This party was full of *boys*; niggas with their pants around their knees drunkenly swaying into people and spilling their drinks on unsuspecting women.

"You really shouldn't frown like that. You're a lot prettier when you smile."

My eyes rolled into the back of my head so hard that I thought they would get stuck.

Here we go, I thought as I didn't give the brotha any eye contact that found it necessary to be *allll* up in my ear.

"Jasmine, right?"

Okay, that got my attention. My eyes darted up to look into those gray eyes that had me feeling all kinds of ways a few weeks ago in the mall. His presence was so dominating. I was barely able to maintain eye contact with him. His intense stare was so damn intimidating.

"H–hi." *Wow, I'm stuttering.* But it was warranted. This guy– this adorable, sexy, man – made me nervous with the way that his eyes looked at me. He looked at *me*. Usually, guys looked at my body with eyes full of lust and hunger. But he looked at me in pure interest, like I was a piece of art; the same way that he watched me when we first met. There was a bit of intimidation in his eyes, like he couldn't believe it as much as I.

It took my breath away.

"What's your name again?"

He pretended to clutch his chest. "Ouch, ma. It's that easy to forget about me?"

Damn, even his voice went straight through to my soul. I'm sure he was putting some extra sexy and bass in it to further blow my mind.

It was working.

"Omari," he told me.

Right.

"You would have remembered that if you would have responded to my text." His eyes were full of sarcasm as he sipped from the glass in his hand.

I tried to sound as feminine and charming as I could, "Touché."

"Me and my boy have a VIP table upstairs. Come join us."

"We sure will." Tasha's voice had completely caught me off guard. I had actually forgot that she was even standing there. "I'm Tasha."

Omari shook her extended hand as he said, "C'mon."

I followed him and Tasha with shaky legs. Guys didn't usually faze me, but, like I said, it was something about this one that excited me and put fear in my heart. The fact that he was actually making my heart feel anything scared me even more.

Up in VIP, Omari and his friend, who he introduced as Capone, kicked it with Tasha and me like they had been knowing us for years. Thankfully, they were cool as shit, especially Omari. There wasn't any tension. We laughed and joked, even danced.

"'If it ain't about the money, don't be blowin' me up. Nigga, I ain't gettin' up. If it ain't about the money, ain't no use in you ringin' my line. Stop wastin' my time!'" I was throwing my ass back against Omari as I rapped along to T.I. with my finger in the air.

Above the music, I could hear his chuckle in my ear. "Girl, you betta stop that."

I just giggled and kept dancing and rapping, "*I pack an 11, I pack an 11, ooh!*" Then Omari joined in. "*I ride in a gator, my shoes are Giuseppe, ooh!*"

I giggled even more and leaned back against him, pressing my back against the simple black tee that he was rocking. I could feel his muscular build against my skin, and was highly impressed.

I caught Capone glancing at him as he and Tasha danced as well. He had a smirk on his face that looked tickled to see Omari dancing with me. I knew something was up with that, but it wasn't my business. I wasn't trying to pry in the man's life. I was just trying to drink and dance the hurt away.

By the time the DJ made the last call for alcohol, I was sweating underneath my tightly-fitted jumpsuit. I had even removed my Air Force hat and pulled my weave back into a ponytail.

"Thanks for inviting us up. I had a good time."

Omari smiled at me as we walked down the street towards

Tasha's car. She and Capone were a few feet ahead of us. Capone was trying hard to get her number, but Tasha was deep in a hood love relationship with a few dope boys, and she wasn't trying to add any more to her list.

"Hopefully, we can do it again," Omari told me.

It sounded good, but as the nighttime air hit my face and sobered me up, my heartbreak came back.

Married life and kids will do that to a nigga.

I could hear Kendrick's voice clear as day. It caused a sickness in my stomach every time it rang in my head.

"Can I ask you a question?" As Omari waited for an answer, his look was so intense. It was so happy and full of lust.

I smiled as I looked up in his eyes. "Sure."

"Can I kiss you?"

I figured he was tipsy. So was I though. So as he pulled me back and stopped my strides, I didn't fight it. Even if I never saw him again, who could resist that face and that mouth?

Fuck it, I thought as he leaned down. I didn't budge. Those big pretty lips damn near swallowed mine. Without any tongue – with just a slow, intimate kiss on the lips – I had been completely woo'd.

Sometimes a nigga can kiss you and it goes straight to your pussy. The kiss is full of lust; emotions nonexistent. But it's those rare moments when a man kisses you and your world shifts. You feel it in your heart and chills run rampant all over your body. Your head is so full of excitement that it feels like it's going to burst and you feel faint. As my nipples hardened against his chest, I realized that that was what was happening to me.

It scared the fuck outta me and made me pull away. "I... I should go."

He actually whined. "Don't, ma." When I stood firm, he sighed and seemed to check himself. "Ok. Cool. But we gotta do this again.... kick it, that is.'

I giggled nervously. "Right.'"

"And since you don't like it when I hit you up, I'll leave it up to you."

"Will do," I lied.

"Promise?"

His eagerness was so adorable, but I couldn't help but question it. Men did a good job of acting like they were at your beck and call until you were at their beck and call.

But I put on a fake smile and said, "Promise." Tasha had already got in the car and started it, so I reached out to Omari and hugged him, saying, "Thanks again."

"You're welcome, ma. More than welcome."

I inhaled deeply, basking in the intoxicating, masculine smell of his cologne as I let go. He opened the door for me and allowed me to climb in. I waved goodbye as he shut it.

"Damn, he's fine!" Tasha spat as I watched him walk away. "Shat! Capone is a cutie too, but he's too young for me. But that Omari? Whew, girl! Thank you, Jesus!"

I chuckled as we pulled off. He *was* fine. He was too good to be true and too much like right. Any man that fine had to come with a shitload of baggage that I was not willing to carry.

"I can't wait 'til you get a piece of him, girl."

I let Tasha gloat. I was too much a friend to break her heart. But I didn't plan on getting any piece of Omari. I wasn't in the mood to have yet another man filling me with false hopes of happily ever after.

But it was damn sure fun while it lasted.

Simone

I couldn't complain about life. I was eating, had a roof over my head and I wasn't in jail for murder. However, as I stood out in the frigid temps on toes that were screaming out in agonizing pain, I figured that there had to be another way.

I had fell off. I had allowed the fear of being caught scare me into submission. I was submitting to the hand that I had been dealt. But that wasn't me. Usually, if I wasn't given what I wanted, I took it. And that's what I needed to do now.

Obviously I wasn't above my current situation, but I didn't need a pimp taking my money in the process. If I had my own money, I could skip town and get by in the same way and in an even safer place.

As I stood on the Ave all night, I wracked my brain, trying to figure out how to get my own cash, when it was in my face all along. These hoes were walking gold mines. They had hundreds of dollars on them at a time.

That's too risky, I thought to myself as I eyeballed the rest of the girls on the stroll with me. I couldn't just rob these chicks. Slim would whoop my ass before I made it to the Greyhound station. *There has to be another way.*

The complexity of the situation had my mind gone all night. I was mentally absent as I turned every trick. I walked back to the hotel in a daze. Francesca was walking along with me. She was telling me about some John that she actually had feelings for, like an asshole, but all I could think of was how to get the hell out of there.

"Big Booty Judy." I giggled as Slim greeted me when Francesca and I walked through the room at the motel. Just like Little Miss Old Faithful, Katie was inside with him, sitting closely next to him on the bed.

Francesca was tired, so she quickly kissed Slim on the cheek, handed him her earnings for the night, and made a quick exit to the room next door that she and I shared, with Priscilla, Renee, Tanisha and Peaches.

I attempted to do the same as Francesca. Despite Katie's sneers behind Slim's back, I kissed him on the cheek and gave him the six–seventy–five that I'd earned that night and turned to leave. I was obsessed with the hot bath that was waiting on me next door, if Peaches wasn't hogging the shower with her constant and obsessive hair washing. The best thing that I had going for me was my ass, and the best thing that Peaches had going for her was that long Indian mane that she managed to maintain, despite a meth habit that kept the rest of her looking like shit.

"Hold on, Brandie," I heard Slim say as soon as I reached for the doorknob.

I turned to see him watching my ass lustfully as Katie's eyes were cutting daggers in the side of his head.

He didn't even make eye contact with her when he told her, "Let me holla at Brandie for a minute. Get out."

Katie was all but crushed. She knew that the girls would make slick comments all night about getting kicked out of her own bed while they argued over which of them would have to sleep on that busted ass let–out couch.

Katie glared at me as she got out of bed and threw on a pair of jeans. She didn't even bother to put shoes on her bare feet as she stomped by me, still glaring. With Slim watching me, I smiled at her, and he laughed.

As she swung the door open, Slim barked at her. "Don't slam that motherfuckin' door either!"

She knew better than to do that. As she inched the door closed to make sure that it made no sound at all as the metal met, I inched towards the bed. I knew what he wanted, so I kicked off my shoes and began to undress without him asking or even attempting to get me wet first. Even though I had been fucking all day and I was tired, I knew better than to say one word in discontent. If I wanted to keep eating, if I wanted to continue to have a warm bed, I had to comply.

It wasn't that hard to comply. Compared to the slimy men that I fucked all day, Slim was a Greek God. He never kissed me in the mouth. Never gave me oral. He didn't even bother to suck a tittie to arouse me. Yet, he smelled good, he wasn't a stranger and the dick was halfway decent.

"Don't let Katie get to you."

I chuckled as I threw my shirt over my head. This nigga really didn't know my life. I never let a bitch get to me; I got to her. "She's not getting to me."

"I like how you handle her." He watched me with an approving smile as I shimmied out of my shorts. "That's why I like you, ma."

"Like me?"

"You're different than the other girls."

"Look, no disrespect Slim, but you don't have to blow smoke up my ass. My daddy was a pimp. I know what this is." I lifted my hands and they landed on my thighs with a loud smack as I spoke to him. No way could I get away with talking to him like this in front of the other girls, but behind closed doors we had a mutual respect. I wasn't some meth or crackhead. To him, I was Brandie; a woman who lost everything when she lost her husband, then her job, went through all her savings, and wound up on the streets because she had no family. He knew that I was educated with street smarts. To him, he had talked me into this life and I wasn't doing it willingly.

He reached out, pulled me in, and made me straddle him. "You know what it is, huh?"

I smiled flirtatiously and nodded.

"Well, I ain't got enough smoke to blow up that phat ol' ass." He moaned lustfully as he gripped my ass. I could smell the liquor leaking from his pores. "Give me one sec. Let me take a piss."

I rolled over onto the bed as he stood. He started to take off his pants but stopped and reached in his pocket. The wad of cash that he pulled out was so big that my mouth watered. It was all of the money that the girls had earned that day. That's when it hit me. I couldn't steal from the girls, but I could definitely figure out a way to steal from Slim and get the hell out of Chicago.

CHAPTER 6

Chance

I looked at myself in the mirror a few feet in front of me. It was dark and smoky in the club, but I could see my reflection clear as day. I still didn't recognize myself.

I guess shorty didn't either.

"Wow. Look at you." I looked up from my drink. I already knew who the sweet, feminine voice belonged to. "Who knew you'd look ten times better with a haircut?"

I chuckled as Georgia leaned against the table. I was way back in the cut at Sunset. After weeks of being held up in the crib, I had to get out of there before I did something drastic; like kill myself... or kill Gia. It was official. I was stranded in Chicago, and there was no fussing, cursing or pleading I could do about it. Until Gia felt like she had enough paper to really stand on her own two feet in another city, she wasn't going anywhere.

"What made you cut your hair?"

I had to. Even though cutting my dreads off didn't make me look drastically different, I hoped that it, along with a fitted cap would help me go undetected on nights like this when I just had to get out.

I was trying real hard not to stare at baby girl as I answered, "Just wanted a new look." She was dressed in little to nothing, and the six–inch heels that she had on made her ass look like a thoroughbred.

Surprisingly, Georgia had kept her word and not said anything to Gia about our night in her hotel room. In the back of my mind, I wondered what made her be more loyal to me, a stranger, than her sister. I was waiting for her to flip out at any moment. Shit, a bitch like Simone had me looking at every chick sideways. I had been waiting for Georgia to turn state's evidence at any moment, but she was actually just cool as fuck. With her being closer to my age and the tension between me and Gia, I found conversation with Georgia during commercials as we watched reality shows replacing intimate time that I use to spend with Gia.

"It looks good," she said as she ran her hands over my waves.

"Thanks."

Just then, the DJ called Georgia to the stage. Her name was so unique that her stage name was her real name, but the DJ lied and said that she was actually "straight from the peach state with the ass to prove it."

As she walked away, I adjusted my hat so that it rode lower on my eyes. I knew that Gia was somewhere around, and I didn't want her to see the peek at Georgia's ass that I just had to steal.

"Gaaaawd damn," I groaned to myself. "Can't even believe I hit that shit."

"Over here talking to yourself, baby?"

I damn near dropped my drink. Gia laughed as I jumped out of my skin. "Damn, I didn't even see you."

"Didn't see you sitting over here either. I loved your hair. Can't believe you actually did it–"

"But I had to, right?"

Gia's eyes lowered with guilt. "It won't be for long, Chance."

"That's what your mouth say."

I was sure that in her heart, she planned on leaving soon. But every time she came to the crib with the racks she was use to making, every time she went shopping with Georgia or her girls that she had linked back up with, I knew we weren't going anywhere soon.

Ignoring my smart comment, Gia put her focus on the stage, where everyone else's focus was as well. Georgia swung from the pole like a tub of thick chocolate ice cream. I couldn't help but remember how I licked that shit up.

"Taught my sister well... Yeaaaa, Georgia!" She cheered on her sister with a smile.

I adjusted my hat, bringing it down even lower, and sneaking peeks every chance I got.

Simone

My little plan had actually worked. I had watched Slim as he opened the safe and repeated the combination over and over again in my head. As he returned to bed, and I robotically kneeled before him to suck his dick, I repeated the numbers over and over again. He was impressed with the way that I fucked him that night.

"Gawd damn, girl. This pussy good as fuck." He even chuckled as he looked down and watched his dick go in and out of me. "Damn, this is a good view. Look at that."

7, 31, 19, 4, 21, 9.

"Fuck, baby girl. What you tryin' to do to a nigga?"

All I wanted to do was make him cum so hard that he passed out in such a deep sleep that I could get into that safe without him knowing.

And that's what I did. I only took about forty dollars, though. Taking more would have been too suspicious and caused him to suspect a thief. Pinching that small of an amount would take forever for me to save enough to leave. But as long as it was eventually, I was willing to be patient. Yet, my stellar performance that night had Slim on my heels after that. Me being me, I put on extra sauce every time I was around him, to ensure that I was chosen at night to be with him. I threw my back into it every time I fucked him. I was nasty, freaky, loyal and anything else he wanted, all for a couple dollars to stash as soon as he closed his eyes.

The current night was no different.

"Again Slim?!" Katie was so pissed that she didn't even hide her anger from Slim.

He shot daggers at her. "The fuck you just say to me?!"

I lay across Slim's bed with my hands behind my head and a smile on my face. Katie was eyeballing Slim with tears in her eyes as she stood at the door, but her eyes kept falling on my taunting smirk. I even stuck my tongue out at her to fuck with her stupid ass.

"Daddy–"

"What the fuck did I say, Katie? Get the fuck–"

She didn't even know what she was doing when she allowed her tears and hurt to take over her better judgment. "Daddy, no! I love you!"

Slim moved like a fucking ninja. I didn't even see it coming. Katie damn sure didn't, until she was up against the wall, clawing at Slim's hands in order to free them so that she could breathe.

I was cracking up.

"Don't fuckin' talk back to me, bitch!" He was actually choking her with one hand and opening the door with the other. "Get the fuck out."

He threw her out; literally. As the door slammed shut, I could see her face hitting the concrete. "And what you laughin' at?"

Slim was staring at me with a smile as he walked towards me, unbuckling his pants.

95

"You," I giggled.

"I got something for you to giggle about."

"Bring it over here then."

I was on all fours with my mouth open as Slim made his last two steps towards the bed. As my mouth wrapped around his dick, he moaned. "Yep. That right there is why I like you."

7, 31, 19, 4, 21, 9.

Chapter 7

Omari

I was talking mad shit when I told Jasmine that she would have to be the one to call me. I couldn't imagine telling a woman like her that I had deleted her number. I held my breath for three days, waiting for her to call. My dick had been hard the entire time I waited, thinking about how soft those glossed lips were. I couldn't believe that I was actually waiting for her to call. But when I sat my manhood aside, I could believe it. It was something about shorty that relaxed me enough to even want to talk to her. When I was dancing with her, I felt like I had no worries. I felt alive again.

Even Capone had noticed the change in me that night at the club. As soon as we hopped in my car, he let me have it.

"Really, nigga?" he asked with a grin.

I tried to play dumb. "What?"

"Bruh!"

"What?!"

"Bruuuuh," he sang as his head fell back against the headrest. "You kissin' chicks outside the club? Really, bruh? ... No, really?"

I just laughed and tried real hard not to blush. I couldn't even say shit. He was right. My drunk ass just had to taste that mouth. It was perfect.

"Can't even blame you. I'd kiss her fine ass too. She thick like mayonnaise."

I had to laugh as I actually felt some jealously. Surprisingly, though he was my boy and meant no harm, I wanted no one lusting after that beauty but me. I'd had my reservations after meeting her the first time, but her cool swagger that evening had convinced me that I had to get some one–on–one time with her.

"Nah, for real. I haven't seen you like that in a long time."

"Seen me like what?"

"Happy."

Yea, I was. Even as I woke up the next morning, I had an extra pep in my step as I waited for her call. I just knew that she would ring my line. But Saturday went by, Sunday crept by, Monday rolled back... and nothing! I let another few days go by until it was yet again a Friday night. I was sitting in the trap house listening to the block boys turn up on the porch while I couldn't believe that I was obsessed with knowing why shorty hadn't contacted me. I started to feel like a real dumb ass for deleting her number. I had no way of contacting her since not even Capone was lucky enough to get her girl Tasha's number.

As I called Sprint, I had to pinch myself. *Am I really doing this?* I couldn't believe that I was going through so much to have yet another woman in my life that could possibly cause a hell of a lot more drama, but something was telling me that it was worth it.

The customer service operator at Sprint laughed at me when I asked if there was any way to retrieve deleted text messages. I was let down when she told me that there wasn't. Maybe I had no business talking to shorty. I was ready to give up until the operator reminded me that there were archives of my text messages in my Sprint account online.

Bet!

I still wasn't technically savvy. I could cut up some coke but I couldn't figure out Twitter for shit. So I had one of the block boys' thots come in the trap house and log on to my account on my laptop for me. Then I told her what I was looking for.

"There you go." Candy put the laptop on my lap, and I was able to see the text that I had sent Jasmine.

I felt so relieved to see that number that it was scary. The way that this girl had me feeling already was unreal. I mean, I wasn't in love or nothing, but a nigga hadn't been this into a chick since I was trying to get with Aeysha.

As soon as Candy went back outside and left me alone, I dialed Jasmine's number.

The smile that spread across my face was embarrassing when she answered.

"Hello?"

"This is not how relationships go. As my girl, when I leave something up to you, you're supposed to take care of that shit, ma."

She started cracking up. "What?"

"I told you that I would leave it up to you to contact me since you don't like when I contact you. It's been a week, and you haven't done it yet. I'm holding my breath over here, and I'm about to die."

"I'm sorry, Omari." Wow, my name even sounded good coming out of her mouth.

"Now you have to make it up to me."

"How am I supposed to do that?"

"Go out with me tonight."

I squeezed my eyes shut, waiting for her answer in fear.

When she said, "I'm busy tonight," I was so let down, but something told me to keep trying.

"Oh, I'm sorry. I didn't know you knew Barack and Michelle." She laughed again. "What?"

"Oh, wait. Is it Jay and Bey then? Because those are the only four people that you should be trying to kick it with tonight besides me."

I bit my lip, hoping that my humor was pulling at her heartstrings. "Just one date, ma," I said, persuading her silence. I could tell that she was contemplating and I wanted nothing more at that moment than to change her mind. "Give me one date, and if you don't want to, you never have to see me again."

Jasmine

"Do I look cute?"

Marcus looked up from Madden 15 for not even a whole second before he gave the TV back his undivided attention. "Yea. You look straight."

"Straight?" *Fucking teenagers.* I stomped over to the TV and stood right in front of it.

"Ma!"

"Pay attention, boy! This is important! I'm going on a date, and I want to make sure that I look good."

"A date?" I know that word was foreign as hell to Marcus. He was only use to two men being in my life; Kendrick and Ant. "Who is this, nigga?"

I waved my hand dismissively. "Boy, stop flexin'."

"Who is he?"

"You know what?!" I fussed as I stomped away. "Forget it, Marcus!"

Swear to God, I couldn't wait for that lil' nigga to go to college. I loved him to death, but having a soon-to-be-eighteen-year-old in my house was like living with a man that paid no bills, had everything to say, and always had his hand out for some money.

Once inside of my bedroom, I stood in front of the full-length mirror on my wall. Omari didn't say where we were going so I wore a black long sleeved fitted body con dress that fell a little bit past the knee. With a pair of burnt orange thigh–high stiletto boots and lots of gold accessories, I looked dressy enough for anything, yet casual if that's the direction that he was going. Pairing it with my Dark Knight leather jacket from Akira, I was prepared for anything. I was expecting Omari any minute, so I filled my purse with the necessities and sprayed myself one more time with my favorite Aqua Di Gioia perfume.

I was shocked to get his call earlier that day. I figured that he had written me off. For days, I battled with whether to give him a call. I didn't want the drama of talking to anybody, but I could not get him or his mouth off of my mind. My bullet got a good workout that week. Part of me wanted to call him, but then Ant would call and the argument that we would have would convince me not to call Omari. Then thinking of Kendrick married convinced me to totally stay away. Luckily, Omari made the first move. But I feared that he thought I was a slut and that all he wanted that night was to finish what that kiss had started.

I actually got nervous when I heard the doorbell ring. But when I saw Marcus' shadow going towards the door, I ran out of my room. "Marcus!" I whispered harshly. He looked at me like I was crazy. "Get back, boy."

"I wanna see who this nigga is."

"You are not too big for whoopings. *Get... back.*"

He was actually way too big for whoopings. He had taken after

102

his father. He was six feet and two hundred pounds. If I would have hit him, it would have felt like I was tickling him.

He walked away, shaking his head and telling me, "Be careful."

"I'll be back in a few. Love you."

"Love you too."

Perfection was on the other side of the door when I opened it. His skin was so dark that he almost disappeared amongst the backdrop of the night's sky. His piercing gray eyes were cat–like. His smell attacked me before I could even walk out of the house to meet him on the porch. I was happy to see him in a leather blazer, jeans, and a tee that looked more expensive than any suit. With Timbs and dreads that fell down his back in nearly architectural design, he was giving off the dope boy, street nigga swag that I loved. But I remembered the time we spent at Sawtooth that told me that he was way more than just that.

"Damn, I'm lucky," he said as he looked me up and down.

To hide my own nervousness, I started joking around. I put my hand on my hip and modeled for a few steps, even pivoting and giving him the duck lips.

"Awwww shit," he sang.

"You see that behind me?" I asked as I pointed behind myself. "That's a murder scene because I'm *killin'* 'em!"

We both bellowed out in giggles.

We smiled at each other like kids. When he took my hand, I didn't even feel the need to pull away. I fell into that small gesture of intimacy and allowed him to lead me off the porch. "C'mon girl. What am I going to do with you?"

I left that unanswered, giggled away the nerves and followed him.

I was highly impressed when he led me to what I assumed was his car. "Is this a BMW i8?" The only reason that I knew is because I was looking at them when I was trying to buy a new car when I got back to Chicago back in September. I settled for my little Jeep though, not wanting to bite off more than I could chew.

"Yea, it's one of my babies."

One of his babies. Hmmm. Touché, I thought as he opened the door and I climbed in.

"So," he sighed, after climbing in himself. "You know rap lyrics and cars. Are you a stripper?"

My mouth dropped. "No!"

"C'mon. You can tell me. I don't judge."

Since he finally let me in on the joke by laughing, I laughed too. "I am a teacher, for your information."

He was in the midst of starting the car, but, as soon as he heard that, his hand left the ignition and he sat back in shock. "You're a what?"

"I teach eighth grade math."

"Maaaan, I bet you be drivin' those lil' boys crazy."

I chuckled. "Something like that."

I couldn't really detect what his grin meant as he went ahead and started the car. It was a mixture of happiness, curiosity and disbelief; of what, I wasn't sure.

As we began to make our way, he turned down the radio, which I appreciated. That meant that he wanted to converse with me during the ride, and not ignore me by giving all of his attention to Boosie, Lil' Wayne or Drake. "So, besides the kids that you teach, do you have any of your own?"

I braced myself. I always got a fucked up response after telling people, "Yes, I have a seventeen–year–old."

His eyes darted towards me, but he quickly put his eyes back on the road. "You have a what?"

"You heard me," I reassured him through giggles.

Again, he looked at me in shock quickly before giving his eyes back to the road.

"I know, I know. I don't look old enough to have a seventeen–year–old. I'm not. I had my son when I was very young."

"Oh okay. That's pretty cool. Means you got all of that diaper changing and shit out of the way; unlike me."

Oh Lord. Newborn means new baby mama. "Unlike you? You have a little one?"

"Yea, he's seven months."

"Oh okay–"

"And no, me and his mother aren't together. We're super cool though, and she is a cool person. We get along great, so no baby mama drama over here."

"What about wife or girlfriend drama?"

"If that's your way of asking if I am in a relationship, the answer is no."

"And why is that? I can't imagine a man like you being single. You must have recently broken up with someone."

"Not broken up exactly." His tone changed so dramatically. The light in his eyes that was shining bright when he picked me up, suddenly went away.

"Not exactly?"

"She passed away."

The sadness in his eyes took over the once flirtatious and joyful atmosphere in the car. I could literally see the death in his eyes as I told him, "I'm sorry to hear that."

"Yea," he said as he cleared his throat. "Me too."

I wanted to know so much. I wanted to know what happened, how and when. He obviously still loved her very much and was still mourning her. Suddenly, things got awkwardly silent. I wanted to apologize for even bringing it up until he looked at me and smiled. "What about you? How many niggas I gotta fight off to get you out with me again?"

I was relieved that he was back, but I still wanted to pry. Something told me to just leave it alone, since he had so blatantly changed the subject.

The rest of our time together went by so fast that I didn't want it to end. The entire night I tried to ignore the reminder of the electricity that was between us when we drunkenly kissed that night at the club. As we ate dinner at Mike Ditka's, I tried so hard to resist those lips. He was so full of excitement as he talked about his son and his son's mother, even his friend, Capone. We both shared stories of our past; both good and bad. I purposely left out my heartbreak, trying not to appear like a bruised woman.

The time flew by, and not once did he inappropriately say or do anything. My thoughts were the only thing inappropriate at the table... that I could tell.

That is; until he pulled in front of my house at the end of the night. I would have loved to continue our night. I was actually sad that it was ending. But if I wanted to leave out of his car like a lady, I had to bounce.

I don't think Omari saw it that way though. As soon as I turned my head to say goodbye, he was on me like a leach... and I was leaking like a faucet. For a moment, I was right there with him; sucking lips, swapping spit, and allowing lust-filled growls to escape my throat.

"Omari," I breathed in a warning tone as I attempted to back up.

We were so close that we were literally breathing the same air. He looked into my eyes and saw my reluctance. "Damn, sorry, ma. I couldn't help it. I've been thinking about your mouth for a week."

I ignored the flips that my stomach was doing. My pussy was literally reaching out to him. It had been so long since I got fucked and gawd damn if Omari didn't look like the right lucky nigga to get some desperate pussy.

"I … I had a good time, Omari, but I'd like to take things… this… I mean, I don't really know what this is, but I don't want to have sex with you. We don't really know each other. So, if that's what you're on, then –"

"Whoa. Hold up. Jasmine, I just wanted to kiss you, baby. I wasn't trying to let you take my virginity."

I relaxed into his joke and laughed with relief. "Boy, whateva. Bye!"

"Wait."

He hopped out of the car and jogged around to my door. He opened it as I gathered my purse and leftovers. I planned to scarf them down as soon as I got in the house. The stress of eating pretty in front of a man that I was trying to impress was too exhausting to finish my food.

"Aye..." Omari looked deep into my eyes after helping me out of the car. "...We can take *this* as slow as you want."

I discreetly gasped.

Smiling, I told him, "Okay. Thank you."

I walked towards the house holding his hand with shaking legs. Omari had really impressed me. I was use to dates consisting of house parties and shots at lounges. I felt like I was in my own little hood romance that night, and it was so breathtaking.

Before I put my key in the door, Omari reached and held, not hugged, me. "Call me, ma."

"I will."

"No, listen…. *Call me.*"

The sincerity in his eyes was, like everything about him, scary. Humbly, I told him, "Okay, will do... and *see you soon.*"

Eboni

Terrance and Felicia were surprisingly still very much broken up. As the weeks went by, I was waiting for him to go back to her at any moment, but every time he came by to see the kids or pick them up, he reassured me that he was gone for good. He was even temporarily staying with his father until he could get his own place.

"But why? What happened?" I was just being nosy. I mean, at first I didn't give a fuck. Weeks later, I was very much curious.

Terrance was sitting at the table watching me cook the kids' dinner as they played and watched TV throughout the apartment. Jamari was surprisingly in Terrance's arms as he played with him. He was just doing that as overkill. That nigga wanted some more pussy; which I hadn't given him since that morning that I kicked him out. He was too much of a man to actually try to get it again, but he was trying to weigh me down by being super nice.

The sex was good, but, to me, that's all it was. After it was all said and done, after he moped out of my front door, I felt so stupid. I had taken so many steps forward. Fucking Terrance was like taking a thousand steps back. Yes, it boosted my ego to know that he still wanted me in some way. But who was to say that he was really done with Felicia? I wasn't trying to be in the middle of nobody else's relationship, even if I did have him first.

However, that small tease of having him there in the morning, like it is use to be, made me want it even more. It pained me to be reminded of what I use to have. It bothered me for days. Omari even saw it all over my face when I was at his house that day.

"I was just sick of her shit," he said with a frustrated sigh. "She's a bitch."

"Noooo," I dramatically said. "You don't say." I shot him a smirk over my shoulder, in which he met with a smirk of his own.

"How long do I have to suffer because of what I did?"

"Hmmm, let's see... We were at each other's throats for a little over a year, so you have to suffer for just as long."

"Eboni, I'm sorry."

"And I'm sorry, but your apology seems very conditional since it didn't come until over a year later." Just the thought of it made me stop stirring the taco meat that I was browning for the tacos that I was making. I turned my back to the stove and folded my arms. "You wouldn't even help me take care of the kids. You wouldn't even spend time with them."

"Eboni, she could do so much for what I was trying to do. I wanted to buy a house and start a business, and you couldn't help me with that. I know it wasn't your fault. I was basically the one that dealt you this hand. I kept getting you pregnant. I made you comfortable because I took care of everything. It's just... the grass looked so much greener on the other side, and she was so willing to help me get over ther–"

"So it was for the money, for her credit?"

He answered, "Yea," so blatantly honestly. "It's fucked up, but it's true. Yea, I was attracted to her, but I was much more attracted to a better life. I tried to have that with you, but you weren't down."

He was right. Terrance and I had so many conversations about me getting my life together, going to school, and fixing my credit. At the time, I allowed the amount of kids I had, talk me out of accomplishing any goals.

"Then, when I finally left out, she flipped on me. She could tell that our relationship was way different than yours and mine. She wanted to be close and be a family, but I didn't feel that with her. So she got jealous. She didn't want me around you and damn near did not want me around my kids. And, yea, for a while, I let her control me because of the business arrangements that we had. But that shit wasn't right. A few months ago, I said fuck her and started back coming around. I couldn't believe that she actually would argue with me about the time that I spent with my kids. That's when I realized that just as much as I was using her, she was using me. I wanted her stability, and she wanted to win me from you. That's what it was all about for her, so I bounced."

I had to put my attention on browning the meat again. I didn't want him to see the tears that were forming in my eyes as he continued to make this all sound logical. He was sorry, but it still hurt. Unfortunately for him, he could apologize and explain a million times, but it was going to take more than that to make the pain go away.

CHAPTER 8

Simone

Gawd damn it.

Katie looked all too happy to see me coming down the alley. The smile on her face was full of bullshit that I wasn't up for. I was trying to get the fuck out of the cold, after running around the corner for a gyro before getting in a nap. On a cold day like today, all I wanted to do was sleep and pray that Slim wasn't so thirsty that he made us work in the freezing temps. Shit, the man didn't think being on our period was an excuse to miss money, so I doubted that he thought the threat of dying from pneumonia was one too.

Anyway, as soon as Katie saw me, she went ham. "So you think you're just going to take my man from me?"

I had to chuckle. "He's everyone's man, bitch. Stop it."

She sucked her teeth because she knew that I was playing stupid. Slim might have fucked other women while she was sleeping in his bed, but over the past few weeks, the rotation was slowly starting to slow down, and I was becoming more consistent. The small amounts of cash that I was stealing were starting to increase, and soon I would be able to get away.

My nonchalant attitude pissed her off. I guess she was used to having her way. I just shrugged at the anger that poured from her eyes. Shit, I was on a mission. I had to get the fuck out of town, and if that meant taking her spot in that bed next to Slim, so *the fuck* be it. I had taken a bitch's man for way less meaningful purposes, so to take one to spare my life was a no brainer.

"Leave Slim alone." She was practically begging me.

"C'mon, Katie. You know how the game go."

She was so mad that she stomped her Puma's on the gravel. "You think he wants you? Bitch, I been his bottom for years. You bring your ass around here, thinking you the shit, but I know your story. You look down on me, but bitch, you ain't no better. Remember why you're here, bitch. Your man didn't want your whack ass? You wasn't good enough? He loved somebody else more–"

Her words were like honest shots that pierced my brain and triggered anger in me that I had learned to fear myself. Before I knew it, my hands were around her neck. She was so frail, and my anger was so powerful, that I had been able to lift her a few inches from the ground as I rushed towards the brick wall of the nearby building.

"Urgh!" She grunted as her head banged against the brick. But that was all that she was able to say as I squeezed my fingers around her neck so tight that the veins in my hands swelled in size.

115

I just wanted her to shut the fuck up because she was right. It wasn't the ex-husband that had left me broke; the story that I told everyone. It was Omari. It was DeMarco. It was Tre. It was any one of those spineless mothafuckas that had enough balls to fuck me, but not enough to choose me. They were the reason why I was in that fucking alley scared that some pimp was going to make me sell my pussy for change in negative ten-degree weather, and I had no choice but to do it. All because niggas didn't think enough of me to choose me.

Every time I thought about how right this crackhead bitch was, I squeezed until her face turned beet red, then purple. She clawed my hands like I had clawed at Jimmy's, and I watched the life begin to leave her body like I did Tammy's.

But just the thought of Tammy brought me back. I was able to feel the cold again. I felt my hands around her neck and let her go.

She fell to the ground, gasping for air, and I stood over her gasping as well, the fact that it was easy for me to snap taking my breath away.

"I'm not the one to fuck with, bitch," I spat. "You do *not* know my life."

I walked away, reminded again of how much blood was on my hands. I had done enough, so Katie lay there scared to death but very much alive. I knew how to take her life worse than physically, though. I didn't even want Slim or this life, but, since the bitch wanted to play, I figured I might as well entertain myself while I get myself out of this shit.

Jasmine

I did call Omari the day after our date. Surprisingly, we talked everyday afterward. It was cool talking to him. We just laughed and joked like friends. There was no "getting to know you" pressure. He didn't hound me with propositions to get in my panties, nor did he even pressure me for another date. I got the feeling that he was being just as cautious and careful as I was. But a few days later, after endless conversations between my classes and at night when I could spare an hour before bed, we were back on another date.

We eventually went out again... and again... and again.

Who would've thought?

Definitely not me.

But I wasn't going to complain. There was nothing to complain about really. I had a beautiful, Greek god like creature picking me up in a different one–hundred thousand dollar car just to kick it with me, feed me good food and drinks and make me laugh.

Like I said, no complaints.

This time, on a Thursday, we opted to keep it hood and get drinks at the Fifty Yard Line on 75th and Cottage. I was happy to because I didn't feel like attempting to be cute in some heels, while desperately trying not to bust my ass on ice, after fussing around with badass thirteen– and fourteen–year–olds all day. I was happy that I was able to throw on a velour jogger's set, some sneaker wedges, my hair in a ponytail and just go. Granted, I felt underdressed when he pulled up in a Porsche truck, but I felt a lot better when he got out to let me in appearing just as dressed down as me in cargo pants and a t–shirt.

Yet, Omari was the type of man that made anything look good. He was from the streets and in the streets, but he looked like he belonged on a billboard in Times Square in a Hermes ad or some shit.

"You are surprisingly down to earth."

He looked at me curiously as he leaned into me. We were sitting closely next to one another at the bar. I was practically in his lap with his hand on my thigh.

"What you mean?"

"I mean, you're nice looking, you're obviously well –off. Most guys like you wouldn't even waste time courting a girl, especially if she wasn't trying to give them any–"

"I told you, you couldn't take my virginity."

Laughing, I playfully hit his arm. I could feel the solid, strong muscles beneath his midnight skin. I quickly moved my hand away, since it wanted to act like it was melting against the touch. Omari noticed my lustful reactions and just smiled.

"No, for real." I ignored his gorgeous smile, curtained by full lips that he moistened often by licking them charmingly, and sipped from a Peach Long Island Iced Tea. "You know what I'm saying. You know how men are. They go from one to the next, especially if one ain't goin'. You... you aren't like that. You're humble."

"I have to be. I wasn't always in this lifestyle, and I came from the bottom. I never wanted to do what I do. It's what I had to do to take care of my girl."

"Your baby mama? Eboni?"

"No..." He hesitated. "My ex. The one that passed."

Once again, he became tight-lipped about her; just as he had been the few times she came up in our conversations. I didn't even know her name. His entire demeanor changed every time. Darkness came over him. Those bright eyes went black, like I was watching an eclipse. Therefore, I knew the subject was still way too touchy to talk about over drinks with a girl he barely knew.

I couldn't blame him. There were things in my past that I never wanted to visit again, that I wouldn't touch with a ten-foot pole. If he brought up Kendrick or Simone, I would probably jump up and run the hell up out of there. I kept them to myself as well, so I understood and let it go.

a month later...

CHAPTER 9

Detective Howard

"May I help you?"

"Hi, ma'am. Hate to disturb you on this Sunday morning. But is DeMarco Johnson living here?"

The elderly woman stared at me cautiously for a few seconds. She appeared to be a sweet old lady, and I was use to people treating me this way. No one wanted a detective at their door, especially in the hoods of Chicago. But it was now December. December in Chicago was no fucking joke, so if this little old lady didn't hurry up and let me in and out of these violent winds, I was going to knock her little ass down.

"What you want?" she asked. "What's this about?"

"Simone Campbell."

Her entire demeanor changed. She went from cautious to pissed. I even saw a bit of fear.

It had been a little over a month since Sam made my night with those dental records, but I hadn't gotten anywhere. There was still no trace of Simone Campbell anywhere. During my investigation, a few months ago, I saw that Simone was the victim in a rape case about twelve years ago. Knowing how deceitful and manipulative that Simone can be, I had to know more.

"It's pertaining to another case, ma'am." I figured I had to convince her if I wanted relief from the subzero temperatures. "A murder," I told her.

Still with eyes full of caution, she opened the wooden door further to let me into her single–family frame house on 76th and Luella, which smelled like strong, old perfume, cigarette smoke, and a dog. I hid behind the scarf that was once keeping me warm, to keep the stench from burning my nose.

"You can sat down," she spat. "I'll go get DeMarco."

I stared down on the couch trying to hold in a snicker. "Who in the hell still has plastic on the couch. Really, lady?" I muttered through gritted teeth.

I sat down anyway, listening to the sounds of heavy footsteps coming down a nearby hallway. I turned my head towards the sound of what I recognized as sneakers against a sticky tile floor. Coming towards me was the figure of a broken man. I had seen many pictures of him as I rummaged through his case files. Despite being much more handsome then, he had life in his eyes that was now gone. I could see remnants of the handsome man that looked back at me in the pictures. However, much of his pigmentation had lost its vibrancy. Years of alcohol abuse had changed him into a man that looked twenty years beyond his age. His 6'5" frame was slightly hunched over. His walk was slow and meaningless.

He had lived a hard life. After he was kicked out of UIC, he majored in petty crimes, robberies, and drug dealing; never anything major enough to give him the hard time that scared him into taking a plea that ruined his life.

"Detective." He addressed me with a simple nod as he sat on the loveseat near me.

We reached for one another and shook hands. As I told him, "Pleasure to meet you, DeMarco," I hated to lie to him. There was no pleasure in this meeting; only pain. It hurt my heart to see what Simone had turned this man into.

"As I'm sure your grandmother told you, I have some questions about Simone Campbell –"

DeMarco cut me off. "What about that bitch?"

His grandmother, who was standing close by, behind the loveseat, put a warning hand on his shoulder.

I held up my hand to stop her. "Ma'am, it's okay," I told her as I gave my attention back to DeMarco. "She's the suspect in a few murders."

Most people would have bulged their eyes in shock, but not DeMarco. The smirk he held on his lips that had darkened from years of weed smoke, told of the humorous irony that he found in all of this.

"I'm not surprised."

"Why not?"

He went on to tell me about how manipulative and conniving Simone had been when they met, how obsessed she was with being with him, despite him having a girlfriend that he planned to marry, how she threw herself at him every chance she could, until he gave in on a drunk night.

"I didn't even want to hit it again after that, but she kept sweating me." He shook his head and grimaced as he pulled a pack of squares out of his pocket. As he lit it, he continued. "I should have followed my first mind. Something told me not to fuck with that. But you know how niggas think with the wrong head." I chuckled, nodded, and he sighed. Years later, he was still punishing himself for choosing the wrong one. "Anyway, she came to a party that night at the frat house. I was upstairs chilling when she came into one of the bedrooms. She was throwing the pussy at me as always. She caught me at the right time, so I hit it. When she let my roommate, Cordel, hit it too, all I was thinking was, 'Wow. There is nothing that this bitch won't do to have me.'"

Chills ran down my spine at the irony in *that*. I was learning that there was noting that Simone Campbell wouldn't do to get what and who she wanted.

"How is Cordel?"

"I heard he was in Minnesota. He ended up doing a couple years for some drug shit. He fell off just as hard as I did. We haven't spoken since about a year after the hearing, though. I think he blames me for even dealing with Simone in the first place. I had a good woman and no real reason to even fuck with that bitch, Simone, despite just being a ain't shit nigga. We lost everything because of one nut; *everything*. Wasn't worth it at all." His head looked heavy on shoulders that weighed a ton themselves. "The school turned its back on us. We didn't have money for good lawyers. Public defenders encouraged us to take those deals... It was all bad, because of one piece of pussy."

I actually saw tears in his eyes as he stared off into space and I stared into his eyes. Watching him, I knew that, just as Simone wouldn't stop, I could not stop either. The longer it took to find her, my momentum had been depreciating. I was feeling defeated and felt as if Simone was slipping through the cracks yet again. But seeing DeMarco's face had done exactly what I thought it would do; give me the fire to keep going. Not only had Simone took lives and ruined them all for Omari, she had done the same to DeMarco. Aeysha wasn't a mistake. Dahlia wasn't an accident. She hadn't snapped. It was premeditated evilness and she had to pay. No longer should she be able to walk the same streets as normal human beings. And I was not going to stop until that bitch was in custody.

Eboni

After a while, having Terrance around was much more helpful than weird. I didn't have to rely on Omari so much, who was suddenly up in this girl, Jasmine's, entire ass. It was cute. It was good to see him feeling another chick after all that he had been through. I just hoped that she wasn't another delusional bitch. Omari had been through enough. *I* was ready to kill a bitch if she even thought about hurting that man.

They had only been talking for about a month, but he even wanted her to meet the kids and me. And I 'bout died when he told me that he had invited her over to his mom's house for Thanksgiving. Even though she didn't end up coming, the fact that he had even asked her to come was ... astonishing, to say the least. He was obviously really feeling her.

"What you doin'?"

When I looked up at Terrance, I had to laugh. He was out of breath from wrestling with Lil' T like some big ass kid.

Before I could answer, with his height, he was able to look over me as I sat on the couch. He laughed and shook his head. "What are you reading now?"

"*Main Bitch Dreams, Side Bitch Status.*"

"Is it good?"

"Yes, and you're interrupting me."

No matter how much Terrance was around now, I was still keeping distance between his dick and my pussy. I wasn't going and he knew it. That's why he just looked at me and shook his head. But rather than allowing me to finish my book as I hoped, he stood leaning against the wall just staring at me.

"What?"

He ignored my attitude and smiled. "You've changed."

The way that he looked at me made me feel funny. It was like he was... dare I say, admiring what he was looking at.

"What do you mean?" I asked, finally setting my Kindle next to me.

He shrugged, although he knew. "You're different. You're going to school ... and studying... you're focused... and reading books."

I only allowed myself to smile inwardly. The satisfaction that I got from his praise, he wasn't allowed to see. He needed to continue to think that I was doing, and would continue to do, my motherfucking thing without need of his consent or acknowledgement. I was intent on making him eat each and every degrading word that he had ever said to me. And so far, so good.

"Give me another chance."

I can't even lie, looking him in his eyes, seeing the sincerity in them, watching him as he looked at me in ways that he use to made me melt on the inside.

But it didn't melt away that hurt. It was good to have him there, it was great to have him at our kitchen table on Thanksgiving again, but it was what the fuck he was supposed to do as a father. It wasn't a treat and it wasn't a gift that I should be thanking him for. So I ignored the way that his words made me weak and want to run into those familiar, big arms.

"Give me a chance to fix it. I miss y'all. I miss... you. I miss being here."

I stood and excitement surfaced in his eyes. I adjusted my shorts as I grabbed my Kindle, and lust surfaced in his eyes. I walked towards him and he actually removed his hands from his pockets. He was getting ready to reach for me, assuming that his words had drawn me to him, but I stopped short before detouring towards my room.

I left him standing there. I had no words and I wasn't going to act like I did. I couldn't wrap my head around what he was saying or what was happening, so I didn't try.

No matter how bad I wanted it, I couldn't help but feel like it was too late. *Now* he saw potential in me. *Now* he wanted to be with me. It felt good to hear, but it was a day late and a dollar short.

Don't diss the caterpillar and then sweat it when it starts to turn into a beautiful butterfly.

CHAPTER 10

Omari

I never expected to like her. I know that "like" isn't a big deal, but for a man like me, I just never expected or even wanted it. I honestly didn't think that I deserved it. God had given me a very good woman and a beautiful child, that both loved me unconditionally. I threw all of that away with my greed. I didn't deserve a second chance, and I was ready to live with that.

I wasn't really sure that Jasmine was my second chance, but she was becoming damn good practice.

"You sure you wanna go in?" It really wasn't about her being sure, it was about me being sure. We were sitting outside of the trap in my ride. I had the most uncomfortable look on my face, when Jasmine was smiling coolly on the other side of her coat, that had some high ass collar that made her look like a sexy ass super hero.

"I'm cool. Are *you* cool?"

I really wasn't, but I waved my hand dismissively like I wasn't cringing on the inside. Jasmine knew what I did for a living. She knew I was a dope boy. Although I hadn't been willing to open up about Aeysha and Dahlia yet, I was up front about that. I didn't want to hide any parts of my life from her. I just felt that open being around her. One day, I would tell her about Aeysha, Dahlia and Simone, and I knew that she was unselfish enough to even help me through that, but I just didn't want to taint something that was turning out to be so dope with such sadness.

She brought light and life into what had been dark and dreary, and I just wanted to keep it that way for as long as possible.

That's why I didn't want to take her into that trap house. To me, in my eyes, she was perfect. Even with her drinking, obsessive cursing and son half her age, the way she looked at me, the way I looked at her, was pure, and I didn't want these dirty ass niggas looking at her with their nasty eyes. Yep, I was being possessive, because crazy enough, even without fucking her, even without really knowing if I was ready, I knew she was mine.

"Boy, c'mon." Before I could object, she opened the door and hopped out. I hurried out of the car and caught up with her on the sidewalk. I wrapped my arm around her waist to help her and her platform boots across the slick sidewalk covered in black ice.

Fred's eyes bucked when we entered the house. Even covered in a wool knee–length coat and gloves, Jasmine was a sight to behold, so I didn't blame the nigga.

"Hi." She smiled and waved at him like she had known him for years, one of the many things that made me so comfortable with being around her already. I felt that way the day that she finally went out with me; like I had known her for years. She was so fucking down to earth. There was no faking or no fronting between us, and I liked that shit. So, I basically called her every day since and got with her every time she could between teaching and being a mother.

"I'm in and out, Fred," I told him as we shook up. "Just came to get this shit real quick."

Before me and Jasmine caught the five 'o'clock show, I had to run some product over to one of my faithful customers. Usually I didn't make runs, but he had been waiting all day, and all of the other runners were busy or out of touch. I didn't need this hundred thousand getting away from me, so I opted to make the run real quick myself.

Jasmine followed me through the house, ignoring Fred's goo-goo eyes like a lady. The longer she was in there, the more I was laughing at myself for straight tripping. I had never felt so protective over a woman. Maybe it was what I had been through that had me wanting to guard every inch of her with my life.

I even had her stand right outside of the pantry as I ran in and grabbed a couple bricks out of the stash. I was in such a hurry that I was having a hard time locking the stash back up and cursing, making a lot of noise in the process.

"Omari, what are you doing?"

"Fucking up," I said with a laugh. "Here, hold these."

Once she reached and grabbed the bricks from me, I was able to secure everything back up with ease. "Ah ight. Let's roll."

As I went to take the bricks from her, she held one up slightly. "This weight is off."

"Huh?" I looked at her curiously as she handed me the brick.

"The weight is off."

"No, it's not."

"I'm telling you, it is. I know what I'm talking about. Go weigh it. Don't fuck up no money."

I had to pause, had to step back, look at her and just .... damn.

Phat ass, pretty face – none of that compared to *that*. That shit right there had me thinking of baby names like a straight up bitch.

She blushed in the midst of my eyesight. "What are you thinking about?"

"Just wondering how a girl like you ended up in a world like mine."

Jasmine

"Just wondering how a girl like you ended up in a world like mine."

Damn. He had my head spinning, literally. I casually leaned against the wall and smiled at him, when in reality I was trying not to pass out from the power of his sweet nothings and think of a smooth comeback.

I couldn't though. I mean, I didn't have a response for that. I was tongue-tied and he knew it, so he took my hand. "C'mon. Let's go before we're late."

That's what I liked about Omari. He was so catering to me. He was more than a gentlemen. He provided in every way a girl could ask for. Emotionally, I was fed. Spiritually, I felt a connection. He protected me, even when he wasn't near me. He didn't just give me what I wanted, he gave me what I needed.

I had my reservations at first. I was scared as fuck to even allow myself to be this close to another man. Even after we walked out the trap hand in hand, I was petrified, to say the least. But, after our first few dates, I couldn't help but allow endless conversation after endless conversation to draw me in. Now, a month later, this man had all of my free time outside of my son and work.

"Ooo, I love this song!" Without even asking, I turned the radio up as Omari and I fastened our seatbelts.

♪ *A definite silence*
You're almost exactly what I need
A definite maybe
Is sure to entice my curiosity
I can't help but think that this doesn't add up
I'm trying to separate the facts from all the fiction
We're living in a world of contradictions
And if baby you're the truth then I'm lying next to you ♪

"Yaaas!" I swooned as I snapped my fingers. "This is my shit!" My eyes closed as I swayed and basked in all the glory that was this song and Daley's voice. His words touched deep down into my soul. Though this song, "Alone Together," had recently released, it reminded me so much of the happiness that I use to have and what I wanted to gain again.

With my eyes closed tight and singing along to the lyrics, I almost forgot where I was. But my eyes popped open when I heard another voice singing along to the chorus with me, "*And you're the desert sand, I'll be your water. And you're the perfect plan I never thought of...*"

When my shocked eyes darted open and stared at Omari, he closed his mouth bashfully with a grin and pulled off.

"You can sing?!" I squealed, while ignoring the pulsating pinching sensation in my clitoris.

"I can do a little something."

"I didn't know that."

"I don't do it much. Not at all really."

"Why not?"

"I got teased enough for being a pretty boy back in the day. I already have gray eyes. I didn't need to be walking around singing like Prince, having niggas laugh at me for that too." He laughed at his own joke. "So I just never did and it became a habit."

"Well, you have a beautiful voice, and it's nothing to be ashamed of. You shouldn't be ashamed of anything about you, your past... nothing."

When he said nothing in return, I looked at him. Though those full heavy lips weren't saying anything, those beautiful gray eyes were saying so much. He traveled onto the expressway with a weird look on his face. Obviously, he didn't agree. Apparently, there was something that he was ashamed of that had him suddenly mute and deep in thought. Daley's voice was the only conversation in the car, but his words now helped me realize what I was feeling for Omari: "*I wanna know you. I wanna hold you. I wanna show you.*"

I didn't know much about Omari, nor did I even have a clue if this would lead to anything. But we had a connection that was definitely leading somewhere and, whatever those eyes were thinking about, whatever he was ashamed of, I was sure that I would find out eventually.

Gia

I rolled my eyes again as I folded towels in the living room. Every time Georgia and Chance laughed, I cringed. As always, they were in our bedroom playing video games. Over this past month or so, they had become like two peas in a pod. The age difference between Chance and me had never been obvious until Georgia came along. They were much closer in age. They got along so good, cracked jokes, and even knew some of the same people from back in the day when they were in grammar school.

I wasn't tripping. I didn't think they were fucking. I trusted Chance. Though I knew that he was pissed at me because we were still in Chicago, I knew that nigga loved me. He wouldn't disrespect me by fucking my sister.

It was that damn Georgia that was questionable.

Not that my sister had ever done me like that before; she just had been in so much shit as a kid that I didn't put shit past her motives or intentions.

That's why, when she came into the living room, heading towards the kitchen, I stopped her.

"Hey, Georgia, let me holla at you."

I caught her roll her eyes as she backtracked and came to sit by me on the couch. I was her big sister. We had been getting along well since she started dancing at Sunset, but of course, we weren't so cool that she wanted to hear my mouth.

"What's up?" she asked with a sigh.

I eyed her thick, long legs that fell from small varsity shorts that she always wore around the house. She was my sister, but I couldn't deny how thick she was; way thicker than me. When I looked in her face, her beauty made me cringe as she and Chance's laughter still rang in my head.

Cool out, girl, I thought to myself. *He wouldn't do that to you.*

"What's going on with you?" I asked her. "How much money have you been making at the club?"

Just as I had suspected, the manager at Sunset was too geeked to have my sister dancing there as well. It was like having a thicker, taller version of myself. The customers seemed to take a liking to her quickly, as she caught on even quicker to the pole tricks that I'd taught her.

"Enough," she told me.

"Enough for you to move?"

Georgia sucked her teeth and rolled her eyes. "Damn, you're kicking me out already?"

Even though she smiled innocently, I saw right through that shit. She was not about to take advantage of me like she did my mama. If she wanted to fuck up and lay up under ain't shit niggas, she could do that in her own damn house. Sure, she hadn't swerved onto that destructive path yet, but, knowing Georgia, it was only a matter of time before she was smoking weed, drinking, fucking recklessly and fighting again.

I wasn't having it. I had my own drama and my own dick to worry about.

"This is my mama's house too, ya know?"

"Girl, please," I said as I waved off her fake love for my mother. "When was the last time you were here before mama died? Besides, she had always said that she was giving me this house."

"This house, which you ain't supposed to be living in either? Aren't you supposed to be going back to Cali?"

I knew she'd mentioned Cali to fuck with me, but I didn't let her see me flinch.

She chuckled. "I know yo' ass ain't planning on going back. When are you going to tell Chance?"

"Why is that your business?"

"Because he obviously doesn't want to be here, and you keep lying to him."

"Again... why is *that* your business?"

"Sissy, I'm just looking out for you. The man is obviously miserable here. I know you 'bout that paper, but you got a good dude. You should kind of listen to him and do what's best for him too, ya know?"

"Chance, loves me," I said confidently.

"Yea, he does. But don't take advantage of it or him." When I glared at her, she quickly explained herself. "I'm just saying, you know I just came out of a fucked up relationship. I know how niggas can be. You could have a nigga that doesn't care, that would have left you here alone and went back to Cali without your ass... I'm just saying, don't take advantage of him."

Before I sounded like an insecure woman, I bit my tongue. I hadn't shared a lot with Georgia, so she had no idea what the fuck she was talking about. She thought she knew it all, and I just let her think it.

"Worry about your own man... Ooops, wait! You don't have one."

Georgia chuckled, smirked and stood to her feet. "Whatever, Gia."

"Yea, yea. Just make sure you save them tips for your *own place*."

I focused on the devious grin on her face as she said, "Whatever, Gia. Let me go get *Chance* a beer."

She had smiled and put emphasis on his name just to fuck with me ... and it was working.

Chance

I laughed when Georgia came back into the room and rolled her eyes.

She handed me the beer that she went to go get me with a pout that only made her look cuter. We were in a serious game of Madden. Madden just wasn't a video game to me. When I was younger, I always wanted to be in the NFL. I played touch football in the streets outside of Lexington when I could. But the older I got, and the rougher life got, I let those dreams go. For years, I could never afford video games. As a kid, all I wanted was a football and an Xbox.

Who would have thought that asking for so little would have been so much to ask?

So, Madden was like living out my fantasies in real life. I had never met a girl that actually played Madden before. Gia never wanted to play. I would spend hours in front of the TV and she wouldn't even watch. Georgia was actually good at it, so we spent hours in me and Gia's bedroom.

"What's wrong with you?"

She flopped down on the floor next to me as I sat on the bed. She always sat at my feet. For some reason, that shit turned me on; like she was submissive to me or something.

Ignore it, nigga, I thought to myself as I avoided the way her thighs fell out of those little–ass shorts.

I had been talking to myself a lot lately; talking myself off of the bridge and out of Georgia's pussy. She hadn't been flirting with me at all. It was like that night at the hotel never happened. But she was becoming the only friend that I had really. Besides Gia, I talked or hung out with no one, because I was basically hiding out in this house. Gia, and now Georgia, was all that I had. Georgia had kept me from losing everything that I had by keeping our secret. I appreciated that, so I kept telling myself not to ever fuck this up again by sticking my dick in her.

"My sister is bugging again."

"Yea? She been doing that a lot lately. But what she do to you?"

"Asking me when I'm moving out."

"I don't know why she's trying to kick you out when me and her need to be bouncing."

Georgia looked up, locked eyes with me and looked at me curiously. "Why do you want to go back to Cali so bad?"

I took a gulp of the Beck's to give me time to think of a good answer. Though she was her sister, Gia had never told Georgia, or anyone else, about the part I played in Aeysha's murder, or any of the things that happened in result of it. Georgia just thought that I was a dope boy that had fallen off and was desperately trying to get back on so that I could support my girl.

"I just don't like it here," I finally told her. "The weather sucks. There is more life in Cali... a lot more."

CHAPTER 11

Simone

Before heading in for the night, I detoured down a vacant block. Purposely, I stayed out longer than the other girls because I knew that I had to make this detour. The abandoned building was on the corner, so I should have been able to get in, out and to the hotel quickly and without looking suspicious.

Weeks after discreetly peeling off of Slim's stash, I had almost four hundred dollars. I could have easily kept the money that I made hoeing, but, in case there were eyes watching me, I didn't want to look suspicious. I had to be careful and meticulous if I wanted to get out of Chicago and stay out of Chicago, so nothing could be done fast or without caution and meticulous planning.

Once at the door of the abandoned building, I took my shoes off. I didn't want the sounds of my heels against the tile to echo outside of the broken windows.

On the second floor, in a hole in a wall covered by a picture, was where I kept the money that I stole. I couldn't keep it on me and risk one of the girls or Slim seeing it. He kept all of the money that we made and paid us by feeding, clothing and housing us.

"Arrrrghhh!!" It scared the shit out of me when I saw the shadowy figure out of the corner of my eyes. I must have scared it as well because it went running away, behind me and out of the front door.

"Urgh! Fucking hypes!" It was normal for crackheads and the homeless to live in abandoned buildings, especially in the winter time, so I thought nothing of it as the wind from the opened front door hit the back of my exposed legs.

But then it hit me. I rushed up the old stairs, tripping along the way.

"Shit, shit, shit! Please no!" I hoped aloud as I reached the hallway. I had always been so careful, making sure that no one saw me creeping in and out of here as the sun rose. It was impossible that that crackhead could have known to look behind that picture.

But he had. As I snatched the picture from the wall and dug my hand inside, I felt nothing but drywall and my freedom being snatched away.

"SHIT!"

I darted back down the stairs. If I had to run that motherfucker down and take my shit, I would. I hopped back into my shoes and ran down the stairs so fast that I slid down the last two steps.

But there was no use. The ground was covered in patches of black ice and two inches of snow had fallen over night. I was in six–inch boots. Running in them was a fail, to say the least. I could see the crackhead near the corner as I fell face first in the snow.

"Uh!"

Tears ran down my face. Who knew that crying would feel so good? I had been outside selling my ass since eight that night before. I had lost the feeling in my face hours ago. The tears felt so warm and inviting that I just allowed them to fall as I stood to my defeated feet.

"Fuck!"

Just as quickly as I had an out, I was back, stranded in this gawd damn city and no way out.

Jasmine

"I'm pulling up now."

"Cool. Let me open the garage. What you wanna get into tonight?"

I sighed, thinking about the day that I had. Three of my female students decided to jump another girl in my third-hour class. While trying to break up the fight, I got punched in my face. It took everything in me not to knock one of those little bitches out. The rest of the day was shot to shit; smart–mouthed kids, failing grades and a pregnant girl crying because she was scared to tell her mother.

Needless to say, I was whooped and didn't feel like being in some rowdy, loud club.

God, I'm getting old.

"I'm kind of tired. I had a crazy day–"

"What happened?"

"Some of my students got into a fight. I got hit... And some more shit–"

"I don't know why you choose to deal with these bad ass kids."

I chuckled. "I like teaching," I told Omari. "I wanted to stay home, have a drink and a hot bath, but I'd much rather hang out with you," I flirted. "Can we stay in? Do you mind?"

I bit my lip anxiously, waiting for an answer.

"Sure, babe." But I should have known that Omari would have given me exactly what I wanted. He was always catering to me. I blushed as I watched the garage door rise. It was crazy how he spoiled me with attention and affection so soon. It had taken me some time to get used to his attention and not fight it. I had been having such bad luck with men that I questioned his genuineness every chance I got. But within two months, he had convinced me that every dope boy, every hood nigga wasn't a cheating, selfish asshole. Some of them were loyal and loving, and I had been lucky enough to bump into one.

I climbed out of the car smiling for the first time that day. I was careful as the pointy heel of my boots touched the icy pavement of Omari's driveway. The last thing I needed to end my day was to bust my ass in front of Omari, but the sudden sound of booming rage made me jump out of my skin and damn near fall anyway.

"Jasmine!"

I clutched my chest as I braced myself against my Jeep. With eyes filled with fear, I looked towards the sound of his voice at the end of the driveway. There he was, stomping towards me, a running Range Rover blocking the driveway behind him.

"Ant?!" I was devastated. "What the fuck are you doing here?!"

"I need to talk to you."

I raced towards him, hoping to get rid of him before Omari came outside. "What are you doing here?!"

For the last month, Ant had slowed down on the stalking. He

149

called every now and then to curse me out for still not coming home, but he had finally gotten the point that I was gone and there was nothing that he could do about it... So I thought.

As soon as I was close enough to smell the weed coming off of his Moncler coat, he grabbed me by the arm.

"Ahh!"

"I been calling you and shit! Fuck! A nigga gotta come all the way to the Chi to bring your ass back home. Get in the c–"

"The fuck is goin' on?"

Instantly, my eyes filled with tears as I turned to Omari standing next to my Jeep in a t–shirt and jeans. Even in the most awkward moment, this man's presence pulled at my heartstrings. I felt like the most stupid girl in the world for bringing this drama to his house. All that we had ever told one another as we got to know each other was that we didn't want any drama. We had both gone through so much extraordinary bullshit that we didn't want to invite any more of that energy into our lives.

And here I was, bringing it to his front door.

"Who the fuck is this nigga?!" As he spoke, Ant squeezed my arm even tighter.

I winced, "Ow!"

That triggered Omari and he started to come closer. "Nigga, let her go."

"Ant, stop!!" I kept wrestling with him. I wanted to get to Omari so bad. I had to erase the doubt in his eyes that were looking at me with disappointment.

"You fuckin' this nigga?!" Ant barked.

"Let her go!"

The closer Omari came, the tighter Ant held on to me.

"OW! Ant, stop!" I couldn't believe it. I knew that Ant had to be doing some questionable things in his operation in North Carolina. But I had never known him to be this erratic. Even as he called me over and over again, after I left, I thought nothing of it. He had told me that I "bet' not be fuckin' somebody else," but I thought nothing of that as well. It was typical nigga shit. I didn't imagine he cared that much since he didn't care when I was lying in bed right next to him night after night.

As soon as Omari was in arm's reach, Ant pushed me to the side so hard that I slipped and fell on the icy driveway. "Urgh!"

Instinctively, Omari came to help me and that's when Ant rushed him. They were fighting like little ass kids and I could not believe it.

"Ant, stop! Get off of him!" I jumped to my feet and slid towards them, trying not to fall along the way. I pulled at Ant's coat to get him off of Omari, but soon Omari didn't need my help. He was taller than Ant and his size was filled with muscles, not fat filled with gyros, chicken, and weed like Ant's. He'd punched Ant so hard that his head flew back into the pavement. I cringed, "Omari, okay! That's enough!"

But he didn't hear me. It looked like Omari had blacked out.

The ass whooping that he was giving Ant had nothing to do with Ant. Omari was taking out some anger on Ant's face that I knew nothing about.

"Okay, Omari! That's enough!" This wasn't worth it. Ant wasn't worth it. "That's enough!"

Finally, he heard me. He stopped swinging and stood to his feet, glaring at Ant as he heaved in and out, catching his breath.

"C'mon, Omari." I pulled at his t-shirt and attempted to walk towards the house. At first he didn't follow me. He was still glaring at Ant, who was slowly standing to his feet.

Reluctantly, Omari slowly came with me.

Pop!

The gunshot came out of nowhere!

"Ahhh!" I yelled and screamed as I ran towards the garage.

Pop! Pop! Pop!

As I hit the floor in the garage, I caught a glimpse of Ant standing in the driveway, firing at us.

Pop! Pop! He let off two more shots before turning and running towards the running truck. I frantically looked around for Omari, not realizing that he was hovered over me.

"Omari!"

"You okay?"

When I heard his voice, I started crying hysterically. I felt like shit. "I'm so sorry."

I could hear Ant pulling off, his tires screeching along the way.

Omari stood to his feet without a word. He did help me off of the ground, but he stormed into the house without saying anything to me or inviting me in. I raced behind him, knowing that he was pissed. This was against everything that he wanted. He didn't want drama, and this was beyond drama. I had almost caused him his life.

My heart sunk deeper and deeper as I looked for him through his home. Omari and I were far from in love. We were taking a chance on each other. We had fun together, but I can't lie that it felt too good to be true. Ironically, I felt some relief as I roamed around his home. This entire time I had been anxious, wondering would it work and how heartbroken I would be if it didn't. Now that it was over, I was relieved that I could walk away without a heart that was aching and in pieces.

I just wanted to make sure that he was okay, then I would leave and he would never have to worry about seeing me again.

"Omari..." I called his name cautiously as I slowly approached him. He was in his bedroom, sitting on the edge of the bed with his head in his hands.

When he said, "I'm good," tears continued to flow even more. He was saying that he was okay, but his voice sounded like he was far from it.

I cried, "I'm sorry. I'm so sorry. I didn't know that he was even in town." He knew about Ant. I had told him everything about my ex. "I don't–"

I stopped when he raised his hand, still without looking at me. "It's all good."

He had never been so dismissive and that hurt. "Okay. I... I..." I sighed with frustration. "... I just wanted to make sure that you were okay. I'll talk to you later."

As I turned to walk out, he asked, "Where are you going?"

"Don't you want me to leave?"

Omari

"Why would I want you to leave?"

Seeing her cry almost made me forget about a nigga shooting at me.

Almost.

I planned on calling Capone first thing in the morning to take care of that nigga, but, for right now, I was going to wipe away those tears.

"Come here, Jasmine."

She walked towards me reluctantly. I knew what she was feeling. I had been adamant about not wanting any drama from any females. She was taking it slow because, I knew, that she didn't know what my angle was. Without her going into detail, I knew that her heart had been broken and she was guarding it with her life. But me, I was glad that she was taking it slow because, she was right, I wasn't sure where the hell this was going or if I even wanted it to go there. But I could never deny the soft spot in my heart for her that had been growing larger and larger every time we hung out.

I reached for her and sat her down on my lap.

"I'm so sorry." She apologized as I wiped her tears and more replaced the ones that dried against my hand. "I'm so–"

I kissed her; slow and steady. I could taste her tears as I sucked her bottom lip that was still trembling. I took off her coat and threw it on the sofa against the wall in my bedroom, all without breaking the kiss. I thought to myself why or how I could feel so strongly for a woman that I hadn't even felt on my dick. No matter how much dope I pushed or guns I toted, that feeling scared the fuck out of me. I had only felt that way with Aeysha and when I laid my eyes on Dahlia.

I stood us up and saw the weary look in Jasmine's eyes. Behind those lashes and mascara was fear as I began to remove each article of her clothing one by one. I had never even seen her naked, so the sight of her breasts and stomach made my dick hard as the bullets that flew by us just moments ago.

"Omari..." She called my name softly, but I ignored her. I knew what she was doing; she didn't want this, she didn't want to fuck. But all I wanted to do was take her tears away. Her sadness made me sad, and I was tired of feeling that way.

I kissed her again as I grabbed the waist of her jeggings and pulled them down over her ass. I laid kisses on her neck and trailed her cleavage and stomach as I kneeled down in order to pull her pants further down. Using my body weight, I forced her to sit on the bed. Her eyes looked questionably at nothing as she reluctantly lifted her leg to assist me in removing her boots and then her pants.

"I'll be back. Okay?" Sitting there in a bra and panties, Jasmine took my breath away. It was so hard for me to even look in her eyes. Her body was a road that I wanted to drive my tongue all over.

She only sighed and nodded, and I walked away.

JASMINE

I wasn't ready to fuck him. What we had was so different. We were actually getting to know each other. I actually felt a connection with him. It was different from these other niggas that wanted to fuck first and learn my last name later. That was what had happened so many times in my life. That was what went wrong with Ant. I fell for the dick while learning the man. He had also wifed me without even knowing me. After knowing me, obviously I wasn't enough to keep his focus. Hundreds of arguments and fights later, I was single again and heartbroken.

I didn't want that again. That cycle was getting old and tired. If I never had a love like Kendrick's again, I was okay with that, but I wasn't about to put my heart back out there with false hopes until I knew that it was right. Fucking Omari would surely prematurely put my heart out there. I knew it. I was already feeling him. He was everything that I had been missing in Ant. Beyond that, he was fine as fuck. I can only imagine how delusional the dick would make me. Once again, I would be in love with a nigga's dick so tough that I thought I loved him, and in a few years, it would be over.

I can't do this, I thought as I stood and looked at my clothes that were sprawled all over the floor.

When he walked back into the room, I was ready to tell him no.

I knew that my stinginess, along with my psycho ass ex, was going to put the nail in my coffin. He would be tired of me and tired of waiting.

But before I could say anything, he stood so close to me that his manly presence rendered me speechless. It was something about being in this man's shadow that made me weak. When he grabbed me by the back of the neck and took my mouth into his, my body went weak.

No. It's too soon. Not yet. I don't want to be hurt again.

The reluctance was in my head but never came out of my mouth. The only thing that managed to escape my mouth was evidence of the pleasure that his tongue in my mouth and his hand roughly in my head was making me feel. I breathed heavily and moaned into our kisses, while holding tightly onto his wrist as he cuffed my breasts.

When he ended our kiss, my common sense finally came back into the room. No matter how good he looked, I couldn't willingly follow him into another fuck–lationship that would end with me with a broken heart.

But he took my hand and said something before I could. "C'mon."

Curiously, I followed him out of the room and down the hall. I wondered where in the hell we were going until he walked me into his bathroom. The lights were off but flickers of light bounced off of the walls and illuminated the bubbles inside of the full tub.

159

"What's this?" I asked with a chuckle.

He had such a boyish bashful look on his face. He was just as shocked at his gesture as I was. "You had a bad day," he told me. "Just want to make you feel better. Get in. I'll be back."

I believe that he left out so quickly to avoid my response. I smiled from ear to ear as I removed my bra and panties. Then I used one of the rubber bands, which he kept handy on the sink for his dreads, to pull my hair up.

He was right, the water was so hot that it massaged away all the stresses of the day. I closed my eyes and forgot about those badass kids and Ant's crazy ass. I was in LaLa land until I heard him entering the bathroom. I opened my eyes to visions of him with glasses in his hands. He handed me a wine glass filled with what I learned to be the perfect mix of tequila and lime.

"Thank you," I said after a big gulp.

He spoke into his glass, "You're welcome," and also took a sip. Though he was staring off into space and trying damn hard to make me feel better, I could see that he was deep in thought and frustrated.

I was more than ready to apologize again for Ant, but he looked at me with a weak grin. "So... tell me about your day."

****

In most cases, the most intimate moments don't even involve sex. I was learning that with every day that I hung out with Omari.

We talked until the bath water got cold. All he wanted to talk about was me; how my day went, about the kids that I taught, about the relationships that I had with some of the students.

"You're so passionate. You do more than just teach," he told me.

"'Tell them, and they forget. Teach them, and they may remember. Involve them and they learn.'... That's the motto that I teach by."

He nodded, looked impressed, and continued to pull conversation from me until my skin started to wrinkle. When he stepped out to give me privacy to get dressed, I felt stupid for not fucking him yet. But I took the moment of privacy to make a phone call.

"Hello?"

"Tasha, what you doin'?"

"I was about to go to sleep. Why are you whispering?"

I turned on the water in the sink to drown out my voice. "I don't want Omari to hear me. Girl, Ant showed up at his house."

"WHAT?!"

"Yes, girl. He must have followed me from my house."

"What happened?"

"He got all rough with me, grabbing on me and shit. Then Omari came out the house–"

"Damn–"

"They started fighting–"

"Whaat?!"

"Omari was whooping his ass. Then when I finally got Omari off of him–"

"Why you do that? You should have let Omari whoop his a–"

"Listen! ... Girl, when I got Omari off of him and we started walking towards the house, this nigga started shooting at us!"

"WHAT?!" Tasha shouted. "Oh my God! Are you okay? Did anybody get hit?!"

"I'm fine. Nobody got hit, thank God."

With a sigh of relief, Tasha breathed, "That's crazy."

"I can't believe this shit. Do you think Tony told him where I stay?"

Tony was the dope boy that Tasha was fucking that introduced me to Ant. The question was rhetorical because it had to be him. I had just recently moved into that place. No one should have even known my address, but Tony had dropped Tasha off there a few times.

"It had to be him," Tasha told me. "I'm sorry, Jasmine."

"It not your fault or Tony's. I'm sure Tony didn't think Ant was going to go crazy like that. I think he just wanted to talk, but seeing Omari just pissed him clean off. I don't even think he was shooting at us. He was just trying to scare us."

"I'm sure. Omari would intimidate any man."

I smiled as she chuckled. Thoughts of Omari filled my mind and took me to a romantic place.

"Is Omari mad?"

"I'm sure he is, but he won't say anything about it. Ain't no street nigga gon' let another man come to his house and shoot at him. I doubt he's going to let him get away with that shit. But hopefully Ant takes his ass back to North Carolina before anything pops off. I just feel so bad. We both didn't want any drama, ya know? I came to Chicago to get away from this shit. This city is such bad luck for me."

"Yea, you're right," Tasha agreed. "You left this motherfucker to get away from Simone and–"

"No, I did not!" I laughed. "I was getting away from the memories."

That was actually the same thing, though. Simone and her antics had run me straight up out of this city. Just when I thought it was safe, I came back, and now I was still in a bunch of drama. But nothing was as bad as the bullshit that Simone Campbell could conjure up. Luckily, she was gone, and I had cut off all ties with anyone remotely close to her. Dead or not, I wanted nothing to do with her or anyone that had anything to do with her.

CHAPTER 12

Gia

"Ooo," Chance moaned. "Damn, baby. Well, Merry Christmas."

It was Christmas morning, and I was indeed waking Chance up with a gift. I was under the covers with his dick in my mouth. It was hot as hell under that down comforter, but the sweat was well worth it if it put a smile on Chance's face. Our one-year anniversary was coming up in January. This was our first Christmas together. Though we had been through so many horrible things, I wanted so badly for the good to outweigh the bad. I wanted it to so bad that I tried to suck his dick convincingly, to make him feel the same.

"*Shat*, girl! Gawd damn."

Hearing his moans on the other side of the blanket put a smile on my face, but I desperately wanted that smile to be on his. He had been miserable in my mother's house these past two months. He couldn't make a move because he didn't want to bump into anyone in Omari's camp. He would go outside briefly for this or that. But he was so uncomfortable that he could never fully enjoy himself. I was making all of the moves and hustling to take care of us. I didn't mind it, but he was a man, and he wanted to do the manly thing and take care of me.

I had managed to save some money, but it wasn't enough to put us in Cali. Saving that much money would take some time, time that Chance wasn't willing to give me. I feared that at any moment, he would run away, and I would never see him again.

"Arrrrgh! Fuck!" As he bussed into my mouth, I continued to suck his dick lovingly as his babies shot down my throat. He held my head and balled up into the fetal position, as he always did when I sucked his soul out of his body. "Fuck!"

I chuckled and came from up under the blanket. "Merry Christmas."

He was out of breath. His smile was weak as he said, "Merry Christmas to you too, baby." Then he grabbed the back of my head, pulled me towards him and kissed me quickly on the lips.

"You ready to open your present?"

The pleasure that I had given Chance quickly went away. "I told you don't get me nothing, baby. You're doing enough as it is."

"I know, but I couldn't help it."

I had to. I wanted it to feel like Christmas so bad. With my mother gone and Chance not being himself, the Christmas spirit had skipped this house.

Even though he didn't look happy, I reached over to the nightstand, opened the drawer, and retrieved the professionally wrapped gift box.

"Here ya go. Merry Christmas." He took it reluctantly. As he unwrapped it slowly, I told him. "It's nothing really. Just a little gift to show you how much I love you."

His eyes were full of questions as he pulled the frame out of the box. He looked at the professional photo inside and looked at me.

"It's a family tree," I explained. "I know that you don't have any family, and you've always wanted one. I want you to know that you have one now. You and me, we're more than boyfriend and girlfriend. We're family."

His smile was still weak and my heart went out to him. Despite how he felt, he leaned over and kissed me again. "Thank you, baby. This is nice."

But I was let down. The smile and happiness that I wanted wasn't there. The only thing that would have made Chance happy was spending Christmas in Cali, but I just couldn't give him that. The decision that I was making was for us, and I prayed that one day he would see that.

EBONI

"Thanks, Mommy! Thanks, Daddy!"

"Ooo! Oh my God! A Barbie doll house!"

"A cellphone?! Thank you, mommy!"

Terrance and I sat on the couch smiling at the kids as they tore up every gift box that was under the six-foot tree that Terrance and Lil' T had brought into the house last week. We had even decorated it as a family. The smile on my face was so big that it hurt. Last December, I had spent Christmas day crying as my kids opened mediocre gifts. It was all that I could afford. Terrance and I were at each other's throats. I had called him so many bitches and hoes that he refused to give me any money to help get the kids what they wanted. I watched my kids open gifts with visions of him doing the same with Felicia burning in my soul.

Now, not only did the kids have more than what was on their Christmas lists, but Terrance was there.

"You're happy," he told me as he sat back and put his arm around me.

I sighed and had to admit it. I felt it all over me. "Yea, I am."

"It wasn't a question. I know that you are."

I tried to roll my eyes at Terrance's cockiness, but I couldn't help but grin. "Whatever, Terrance."

"Don't you like this? Don't you like us all being together?"

"I always have. I wasn't the one who left." When Terrance rolled his eyes, I immediately apologized. "I'm sorry." I had promised that I would stop bringing that up if we were going to make this work... Yep, Terrance and I were officially back together. After two months of begging, he had worn me down. While Christmas shopping a few days ago, I gave in and told him that we could be a family again.

"Well, I'm glad you're happy, baby."

I blushed and relaxed. Finally, I was at ease and my life was on the right path.

Just as Lil' T lost his mind over Guitar Hero, the doorbell rang.

I gave Jamari to Terrance as I went towards the door. I figured it was Omari with gifts for Jamari. Omari talked so much shit about me getting back with Terrance when I told him. Omari thought I was crazy for giving Terrance another chance, but he said that he understood. I hoped that there wouldn't be any tension between the two. Though Terrance never expressed any ill feelings towards Omari, I knew that he felt some type of way about me having a baby by somebody else.

Once in the hallway, I hurried towards the front entrance. I opened the door expecting Omari, but what I saw was a pale faced, frazzled woman with desperation all over her face.

"Can you tell Terrance to come to the door?"

I didn't even bother to hide my smirk from Felicia. I leaned into the doorway and crossed my arms. "Bitch, you must be crazy if you even think that you can talk to my man."

"Your man?" she chuckled.

"Yes, my man. We're back together," I was happy to tell her. I was so glad that I was able to tell her face-to-face. The look on her face was priceless and a vision that I would keep in my mind forever. It was vindication for what she had done to me. "What did you think would happen? We're a family, and he's back where he belongs" I was being quite cocky, but the bitch deserved it. "*Bye, Felicia.*"

I closed the door as my kids' happy screams and shouts filled the hallway. Better than the sound of their voice was the look on Felicia's face that I caught as I peered through the peephole. She looked like she had just lost her best friend. I knew that expression all too well, because I had had the same look on my face when she took my man.

"Merry Christmas, bitch."

Jasmine

I wasn't expecting a gift from Omari. We had only been talking for two months and we weren't even in a relationship. I was just happy that he had invited me over. I wasn't surprised, though. Shockingly, he had invited me to his mom's house for Thanksgiving, but I declined then thinking that that was too much too soon. Now, I was more than happy and eager to spend Christmas night with him. I had spent all day with my mom, Marcus, grandparents, aunts, uncles and cousins, and happily got my ass out of there in time to meet Omari at his house after he had done the same at his mom's.

"Hey, you. Merry Christmas!"

Omari laughed as I jumped and wrapped my arms around him. "Merry Christmas, baby."

I was undeniably geeked that night. It had been so long since I spent an intimate Christmas with a guy that I liked this much. The last time was with Kendrick. As I walked into Omari's house, it hurt my heart to even think about Kendrick spending that day with his wife and kids. Holidays with Ant were filled with his kids and were little about me. He would throw me an expensive bag or piece of jewelry that morning and be gone most of the day playing Santa Claus.

So, obviously, when Omari led me through his house and into the living room, I was shocked when I saw the huge tree, lit and decorated with beautiful turquoise and gold ornaments.

"Omari, when did you do this?!" I was at his house the night before and the tree wasn't there.

"Today. This is for you and so are these." He pointed to the gifts under the tree.

"Wow," I breathed. "Really?! No fair! We agreed not to get each other anything."

Omari ignored me as he helped me out of my coat. Then he took my hand and sat us both down in front of the tree. I was taken away by this man's gestures. My heart melted when I tried hard to keep it as cold as ice. And with each gift that I opened, my heart melted more and more. He didn't jump the gun by giving me a bunch of expensive gifts that meant nothing. They were gifts with thought. I was always complaining about not having a necklace that I could wear with everything, so the white gold rope necklace in the first gift was perfect.

"Oh my gaaawd!!" I squealed. "It's so pretty. Thank you!"

He smiled, saying, "You're welcome, ma," and handed me more gifts to open.

The wine opener shaped like a heel was perfect for my alcoholism. The Louis Vuitton briefcase was exactly what I needed for work.

"These are so thoughtful, Omari."

His smile was breathtaking. He was happy watching me open the gifts, like I was his favorite girl opening Daddy's gifts on

Christmas morning.

He touched my heart when I opened the last box and pulled out a crystal apple, garnished with diamonds and engraved with the quote, "Tell them, and they forget. Teach them, and they may remember. Involve them and they learn."

"Oh my God." My voice was nearly at a whisper as I was tearing up at his thoughtfulness. "Omari, it's beautiful."

As I hugged him, I felt so grateful. After being unhappy and unsatisfied for so long, I was finally getting back to happy. I released him from my embrace hoping that he would be just as touched by my little gift that I secretly had for him.

"So, what you wanna do? Are you hungry?" he asked as I stared at the crystal apple with a smile.

"You didn't eat your mom's?"

"I had a little something, but I was waiting for you."

"Okay. Well, let me go to the bathroom first. Then we can go eat."

I hopped up and made my way to the nearest bathroom. As I locked the door behind myself, the butterflies started. I was nervous. I had a surprise for him as well and hoped that he liked it. As I prepared his gift inside of the bathroom, my heart began to race. I hoped that my gift wouldn't be too much or ruin what was turning out to be so perfect.

A few minutes later, I tiptoed out of the bathroom nervously. My eyes fell on Omari, who was on the couch going through his phone and not paying me any attention until he heard my entrance. When his eyes fell on me, his mouth dropped and so did his phone. I stood in the living room, in the middle of the floor, with my hands on my hips and a sneaky, lust–filled smile on my face.

"Merry Christmas," I crooned.

"Damn, baby. Wh… What's all this?"

"This…," I said as I turned slowly in a circle, "…is for you. This is your gift; me."

I was wearing nothing but a thong, pumps, and bows placed on my nipples and over the seat of my thong, where my wet, eager pussy, that I had gotten waxed just for him the day before, was waiting for him.

The way he just sat on that couch coolly and licking his lips made me even more excited and eager to give him this pussy. After two months, I felt like he deserved this pussy. He had done more for me emotionally than any man since Kendrick, and I wanted to thank him. So, I glided towards him. His eyes burned into mine. His glare was aggressive and strong. Gone was the gentleman that had been sweeping me off of my feet, and a beast was entering his soul.

Omari did well at hiding his street life from me. But I had a feeling that I was about to find out just how gangsta he was.

Omari

I was about to tear that pussy up. My dick had been hard for two months, waiting for the moment that she gave me her. I wasn't expecting that night to be the night, but when I laid my eyes on all those curves covered in milk chocolate, I thanked God, Buddha, and every other god that I knew of that it was about to happen. Seeing her naked, her perky titties staring at me, her mature curves hypnotizing me as she sashayed towards me, I didn't know which was better: seeing her with her clothes on or her clothes off.

When she straddled me, I took control. I had been kissing her for months, so it wasn't time for that. I carefully pulled the bows from her nipples and took them into my mouth. Never knew nipples to taste so fucking good. They seemingly melted in my mouth every time I sucked each one of them.

"Mmm. Shit." Her moans sounded like sweet melodies. Her fingers running through my dreads felt like a massage. I was dying to get in that pussy, so I stood up, careful not to drop her and sat her down on the couch. I knelt in front of her like I was serving her. She was about to serve me because I was about to eat that pussy like Christmas dinner. I threw her legs over my shoulders and didn't even take the time to remove her thong. I sucked her nipples again. I savored the taste of every inch of her between her breasts and bikini line. When I got down to what my mouth was watering for, I pushed her thong to the side and dove in.

"Ooo!"

Her moan was full of surprise at the way I took her clit into my mouth. I sucked it, my dick hardening more and more at the taste of her. It pressed against my jeans to the point that it was starting to hurt. My fingers played in her juices. She was so wet that it turned me on even more. I held her waist and forced her to grind her pussy against my face. "Damn, baby, you taste good."

"Shit, baby. Oh my gawd." She was taken aback by my raunchiness, and that was okay. I had been careful with her for months. I had been a gentleman. And now... she was about to get this dick.

I glanced up to see her eyes in the back of her head and her mouth stuck gaping open. I chuckled to myself, entered her center with two fingers, found that g–spot and started to rub it like I was giving it a deep tissue massage.

"Yessss," her moans almost sounded like cries. "Oh my gawd. Right there."

I finger fucked her while I sucked that wet pussy. As I sucked, I flicked it with my tongue and softly pulled it. I was so fucking ready that I growled into it, causing her to moan even more. "Shit, Omari. Come here, baby. Give me that dick."

I left her pussy, feeling her juices all over my face. I didn't even bother to wipe them off. Her taste was incredible. I wasn't ready for it to go away just yet. But she sat up and kissed me, cleaning her juices from my mouth. I damn near bussed a nut right then, but fought to keep it from happening. As we kissed, she removed my shirt and unbuckled my pants.

When I was before her, just as naked as she was, I pushed her back and kissed that pussy one more time. I was drawn to the taste of her.

I could feel her sit up and grind against my mouth. "Oh my gawd." Her breathing was so heavy and sporadic. "Fuck me, Omari. Please, baby. Give me that dick."

The way she begged for it drove me crazy. I pushed her back, regrettably pulled my mouth away from her pussy, and brought my dick to her opening. It rubbed against her wetness, teasing her.

"Omari, please," she breathed.

"You want this?" I asked as I kissed her mouth.

"You know I do."

"Beg for it then," I told her, never breaking our kiss. She had been making me wait, and now she had to... only for a few seconds. "Say 'please.'" I wanted her to feel the intense anticipation that I had been feeling since I laid eyes on her at the mall.

But when she breathed into mouth, "Please, baby," I lost it. I slid deep into her wetness and bit my lip in response to how tight and wet that pussy was. It wrapped around my dick like no one else had ever been in there, only verifying that it *belonged* to me. She gasped slightly at the pressure my dick inside of her stomach caused. I grabbed her by her legs, locking them in a tight death grip, and pulled her down on top my dick.

"Shit!" she breathed.

Now that I had her where I wanted her, in the perfect position, I let loose. I penetrated that pussy meaningfully, rhythmically and at a steady, deep penetrating pace. I wanted her to feel every millimeter of this dick. I wanted her to own it and regret every day she kept this motherfucker from me.

"Gawd damn! Shit, ba–" In one long, deep, slow stroke, I'd shut her up. She wanted to express how good the dick was but my dick had crawled up her stomach, wrapped around her tongue and left her speechless.

CHAPTER 13

Simone

"What are you doing out here?"

It was surprising to see Slim. He rarely showed up on the Ave. When he pulled up, he honked the horn, and Katie immediately started to run towards his car.

"Not you, bitch," he spat. Then he looked at me. "Bring your thick ass over here."

Katie was livid, but I had scared her straight. She knew better than to open her mouth to say one word to me. After that day in the alley, she hadn't popped off again. Now, she just looked at me like I was the devil himself.

I trotted towards Slim's car, teasing Katie with a taunting grin along the way. That bitch was lucky to be alive, and I was going to fuck with her every chance I got. Slowly, but surely, I had taken Katie's place, and she hated it. He had even taken me shopping a few times. I kept the tags on everything, until the day that I could sneak and return it all, whenever that might be.

When I got in the car, Slim had such a stern look on his face that it scared me. "What's wrong?"

"Somebody's stealing."

This was like deja vu. I had had the same conversation with Omari, and like when I had it with Omari, I lied and blamed someone else. "Well, with crackhead bitches on your team, you gotta expect to get robbed every now and then."

Slim looked at me, studying every word that I said. "You think its Katie?"

"She ain't the only crackhead," I chuckled.

"Yea, but don't none of the other girls know the code to my safe."

"Who else does?"

My heart beat frantically. He hadn't given me the code. He was so drunk that night that he didn't realize that I watched when he opened it.

"No one but Katie," he answered.

I shrugged my shoulders. "Well, there you go. How much has she been stealing?"

"I don't know. I just noticed that my shit been short lately here and there. That's recently though. Ain't no telling how long the bitch been stealing. I trusted her." He actually looked hurt. Katie had been his bottom bitch for years, and now she was untrustworthy. It was as if he had lost a friend, but he tried to hide it behind a mean mug as he stared at the girls walk back and forth in attempts to stay warm.

"She's disloyal, daddy." I rubbed his head as I talked in the sweetest tone to further convince him. "She keeps fucking with me too. She hates that I'm with you."

"And a jealous bitch can never be trusted."

"Exactly."

With a deep sigh, he said, "Ah ight. I'm out." Then he lightly smacked my exposed thigh. It was so cold though that I didn't even feel it. "Gon' get back out there. I'll see you later."

I hated to leave. That heat felt like the beaches of Punta Cana. I climbed out of the car and adjusted the mini skirt that I had on. I stuffed my hands in the fake short body fur that I was wearing and stood on the curb, waiting for him to pull off before I crossed the street. I watched him as he pulled off, hating that I even had to go back over there. Fucking these nasty motherfuckers was never a walk in a park, but it was definitely better when it wasn't ten degrees outside.

Just as Slim turned the corner, the loud blare of sirens scared the shit out of me. I was in the middle of the street when I turned and saw a police car speeding towards me.

I ran, and so did all of the other girls. I had heard of things like this happening. Someone had probably propositioned an undercover and now they were coming back to arrest us. I ran for my life. I couldn't get arrested. I didn't have any identification, but once they fingerprinted me, my real identity would be revealed.

I ran like a runaway slave, I swear. Suddenly, my heels felt like gym shoes. I didn't even look back for any of the girls. The fear that they had was miniscule compared to mine. I was facing something far worse than a misdemeanor.

I found refuge in the same abandoned building that I was using as my stash spot. I was breathing so heavy and loud that I feared I would be heard from the outside of the closed door. I sat against it, with my knees to my chest, attempting to catch my breath. The floor was spinning rudely as I sat on it. I hadn't seen any signs of the police since I was arrested on the plane to Mexico. Just the sight of them had put the fear of death in me. I was so scared that tears ran down my face and my teeth were chattering. Right then, I had the urge to pray for God to make me like a breeze so that I could finally go freely.

But I knew that I had done so much wrong, so much evil, that He didn't listen to me anymore.

****

"Brandie! We thought they arrested you." Peaches ran to the door to greet me as I entered Slim's room. "Where have you been?"

Now that it was all over, I had to laugh at myself. I had sat in that building for two hours, too scared to make a move. I sat there until the sun came up and my fingertips and toes were numb from the freezing temperatures.

"I ran. What you mean?" I hurriedly sat down next to the heater, warming my frozen body up against it.

Slim chuckled as he puffed a blunt in a chair in the corner. "I heard you ran like a track star, baby. It was only a misdemeanor. I would have gotten you out of there. It's not that deep."

I bit my tongue, fighting the urge to say more.

You don't know my life.

Omari

"So, we gon' go to North Carolina and kill this nigga or what?"

I grinned at Capone's bravery as he whizzed through the downtown traffic. We had just finished meeting with a customer who ensured that he could guarantee ten bricks a week. That was a definite two hundred thousand a week, which was great for business and would for damn sure impress our connect; solidifying our business relationship with him even further.

Business was booming. My family was good. Christmas had been good to us all. My personal life was even looking promising. The New Year approaching was starting to look a lot brighter.

"Nah. Let's drop it."

Capone quickly shot me a questionable glance and then put his eyes back on the road. "What? A nigga shot at you, in your own home, and you just gon' let it ride? Don't he got people here? We can't kidnap one of them motherfuckas or something?"

"You crazy, bruh," I laughed. Capone was a killa. I was the brain and he was the brawn. I wasn't no pussy, but I did my dirt on a need to basis. This nigga Capone didn't need no motivation to pop somebody that was getting in our way, fucking with our bread or threatening our family.

He looked at me again, but this time with a smile. "That pussy that good?"

"What you talkin' about?" I tried to play cool, but I couldn't help the grin that surfaced when he even mentioned her.

"Don't tell me you lettin' her make you soft on me."

"Man, we just made an extra two hundred thousand a week. I'm happy. I ain't in the mood to kill nobody. You shouldn't be either. Fuck that nigga."

Still he continued with the questionable glares between changing lanes.

"Nah, real talk, man," I told him. "It was just warning shots. He wasn't even aiming at us. We don't know what that nigga got goin' in the Carolinas. But we def got too much business in the Chi to be attracting unwanted attention from the cops 'cause we done started a war. Let it ride... But if that nigga resurface, you got my blessings."

Capone was cool with that, so he turned up Rick Ross and eased back in his seat.

I laughed to myself as I constantly checked my phone to see if Jasmine had hit me. We had been talking and texting off and on all day, but it was never enough for me. Usually, it was the woman that lost control once they got the dick, but after she gave me that sweet pussy, I felt myself losing control of every feeling in my body with each nut I bussed every time she gave me some. Initially, I was scared that having sex would mess up the friendship that Jasmine and I were slowly developing with each moment we spent together. But, contrary to what we were both scared of, we had only gotten deeper into each other every time we danced in the sheets; which was a lot. Since Christmas, we had made up for lost time in the bedroom, most definitely. I couldn't get enough of shorty. I found myself in amazement, wondering how I even had the ability to like another woman after all I had been through. It was indeed happening though, because I was head over heels.

I couldn't even blame Ant. I would kill over that pussy too.

GIA

♪ *I can never wife her*
Only one night her
Women full of lies
I just fuck 'em then pass 'em to my guys ♪

Wife Er was my anthem. I did my thang to that song every time it played in the club, so I was on the stage getting it! Singles, five dollar bills, and, I hoped, some tens and twenties were raining down on me as I hung upside down from the horizontal pole in the ceiling. After three months, word had spread through the city that Gia was back in the building at Sunset, and my tips were proving that my clients had missed me.

♪ *I live for today. Mothfuck tomorrow.*
We at the top, nigga. Where the fuck is y'all?
I'm so high I ain't coming back tomorrow. Rich crew shit, we finna go national.
Baby girl, I done heard it all. Fuck that shit, lemme see you take it off. ♪

I was hanging up there like a dark, sexy, curvaceous bat, shaking my head until my hair flew wildly like a rock star. Once the blood started to rush to my head, I used my stomach muscles to lift myself up, reached for the pole, and slid down into a hard split that made my heels bang against the stage.

The crowd went ballistic. There was so much money in the building, how it had been for the past two weeks over the holiday season. People were in the club from out of town and lots of people were off of work, so the club was packed and my pockets were fat.

This was what I was used to. Those motherfuckers in Cali weren't feeling me. They had their favorites, so my tips weren't anywhere near the couple grand that I was use to making in a weekend or on a poppin' week night at Sunset.

I hated that the song was ending. It was the last of my two songs, so I had to get off stage and leave that money.

"Thank you, Reese." I held the bouncers hand as he helped me down the steps.

"Man, Gia," he lustfully grunted. "It's good to see you back, baby."

I smiled as he handed me a plastic bag full of my tips. "It's good to be back."

It damn sure was. I was so happy to be back in my own stomping grounds, instead of fighting with bitches to make money in a new territory. But, as I caught a glimpse of Chance in his usual corner, with a stern look on his face, I knew that he was still far from being as happy as I was. Life wouldn't be completely perfect for either one of us until things were right for him.

I sighed and opted to go to the dressing room to pay house and get dressed. I had made enough money that night, and it was nearly two in the morning. I wanted to go home and spend some time with my man until a smile crept on his face, even if it was only temporary.

"Nah, let that bitch go! She want it; let her come get these hands!"

I flew into the dressing room when I heard my sister's voice. On the other side of the door was mad chaos. Three dancers were in front of Georgia blocking her from getting to the other side of the dressing room. Maliah, a dancer that I had known for years and was super cool with, was on the other side of the room being held back as well by some dancers. I noticed that her hair was a mess. It was all over her head and tracks were visibly loose.

"What happened?" I asked.

Maliah was pissed. She punched her fist into her own hand as she told me, "Gia, get your motherfuckin' sister before I whoop her ass–"

"Bitch, you ain't whoopin' shit!" Georgia snapped. "I tagged that ass already!"

"Georgia!" I shouted in a warning tone and made a beeline towards her. "What the fuck happened?!"

"This bitch was looking at me sideways, so I popped her ass," she laughed.

"Maybe she was looking at you sideways because you're drunk," one of the dancers in front of her told her.

I sighed, frustration taking over my whole being. This was the type of shit that my mother dealt with that I was not about to; drunk, fighting Georgia.

"Georgia, put your clothes on and let's go."

"Why?!"

Now that I was present, the dancers once blocking her had left and gone to the other side of the dressing room. I was so fucking embarrassed. In all my years at Sunset, I had never been in any drama. Sure, there were girl fights when working around so many women with so much competition, but the vibe with the dancers at Sunset was pretty cool. We hardly had drama. Management didn't tolerate it. We were about getting that money. And here my sister was acting a fucking fool.

I looked at her like she was crazy. "Because I'm leaving–"

"But I gotta get on stage."

I shrugged my shoulders as I went towards my locker. "You gotta leave if you don't wanna walk."

She sucked her teeth. "I'll have Chance take me home then."

I cocked my head to the side. "Excuse me?"

"I'll have Chance–"

"I heard you, but I was hoping that you weren't stupid enough to repeat it." I stopped entering the combination. I looked at her straight in the eye to let her know that this was not a game. "If I say

189

it's time to go, it's time to go. Ain't no asking my man shit. That's *my* man. Not yours. Let's be clear about that."

"Yea, *let's* be clear about it." The smirk on her face said a lot of subliminal shit that I was trying to decode. She was way too comfortable with my man. I wasn't even about to give her the benefit of seeing me sweat by asking her what the fuck that smirk meant, but my gut was saying something so loud that I couldn't ignore it.

CHAPTER 14

Chance

"You buggin' yo'."

"No, I'm not!" Gia fussed as she sat down on the bed. "That little bitch be comin' at me sideways about you."

We had just made it home from Sunset. Georgia got into it with some stripper in the back so we had to bounce early. I followed them in Gia's car as she drove her mother's, watching as necks twisted and hands flew in the air. I knew that they were getting into it heavy. I prayed that Georgia's drunk ass wouldn't say shit about what happened between us.

Apparently, she wasn't that drunk, because she hadn't.

"Maybe it's just some sibling rivalry shit. Maybe she is just fucking with you, because she's never comes at me."

Gia huffed and puffed as she took off her shoes and shirt. "She gotta go."

I chuckled as I sat down on the opposite side of the bed. Gia and I had only been together for a year, but I lived with women and their attitudes all my life. I was accustomed to the shit, so I just let it ride. I knew better than to think that I could argue Gia down about this.

"It's not funny, Chance."

"It is. You gon' kick the girl out on the holiday?"

Gia stared blankly as if she was just remembering that it was now New Year's Eve. "I'll wait 'til tomorrow."

Again, I laughed.

"It's not funny! That lil' bitch wants you."

"You're trippin'." Granit, Georgia and I had fucked.... and it was good.... real fucking good... but she had been nothing but respectful ever since. She hadn't said one word to me, hadn't touched me, hadn't even batted an eye.

"You don't know her like I do, Chance."

"But *you* know *me*, so you should know that, no matter what she wants, I would never do that to you." I had. I know this. But that was before I knew who Georgia was. I would never fuck with Gia's sister. That was disrespect on a whole nother level.

"I know you wouldn't. But it's not just about that. She's causing problems already. Fighting and shit at the club. I'm not losing my job, which I just got back, because she wants to be hot-headed. She can take her ass back to Idaho–"

"With the nigga that beat her?"

Gia turned around and eyed me questionably. "Why do you care?"

"Really?" I couldn't believe her. "You know what you're problem is? You're thinking way too much into this shit. Stop bugging. That girl is here trying to make a come up just like you are.

And you gon' kick her out–"

"You don't know her like I do! You don't even have a family! You don't have any siblings, so how would you know?"

Immediately, she looked like she wanted to take that back, but it was too late.

"I'm so sorry," she apologized as I glared at her.

"Don't be." I walked towards the dresser and snatched up the keys. "I'm out."

"Where are you going? It's four in the morning..."

I shot over my shoulder, "Don't worry about it," as I walked out of the bedroom and closed the door.

The fact that she didn't come out of that door to stop me made it ten times worse. Gia was bugging for real. She was turning into some selfish, insecure chick that I didn't know. I guess our honeymoon phase was over and we were really learning about each other. Funny thing is, I hadn't changed. I was the same nigga. Fucked up and all, I was the same nigga. But she was doing a dirty one–eighty that I wasn't feeling whatsoever.

I missed the girl that was so down for me that she would leave her entire life to be with me, the girl that would never argue with me.

I jumped in the car welcoming the New Year with open arms and praying that it came with new beginnings. I wasn't going anywhere. I just sat in the car, turned the music on and zoned out. I was in prison all of my life and now I was back in the same prison;

unable to live how I wanted, couldn't even come and go as I wanted. I had gotten a glimpse of the good life. For just a few months, I was happy, getting money, had family and friends. I closed my eyes as I listened to Drake and recalled those happy times, wishing like hell that it wouldn't have ever happened for me at all. You can't miss what you never had. Had I not ever experienced bliss for that short amount of time, I would have had nothing to compare it to. I would have had nothing to miss so bad that it hurt. Now, I knew how it felt to have a normal life, to have brothers, to have money and I wanted it back so bad. It hurt living every day struggling, wondering when and how I was going to make it.

Simone was lucky to be dead because this kind of life wasn't worth living.

Omari

On New Year's Eve, I invited my family over for a BBQ. Capone and I were BBQ'ing on the patio. Luckily, it was only about thirty degrees out and the patio was enclosed. With coats on, we were able to grill without freezing. My mama was in the kitchen cooking up all the sides while I waited for Eboni, the kids, and Jasmine to arrive.

I just wanted everyone that I loved and cared about to spend this last day of the year with me, enjoying one another and having a good time. The music was blaring throughout the house, and I even had some games for the kids. This year had been one long, crazy, heart–wrenching year. I was glad than a motherfucker that it was over. I was more than celebrating the New Year. I was celebrating the end of one of the worst years of my life. I'd spent the previous Christmas and New Year's Eve mourning Aeysha's death. When she passed last October, the rest of the year was a blur. I had spent the holidays in darkness, not wanting to talk to anyone, not even God. Then that new year began with Simone's craziness. It was one thing after another. The year was filled with investigations, allegations and more death. When Simone was killed this July, I thought it was all over, that I could finally relax. But even in death, she was haunting my life with the truth of what she had done.

Luckily, there was some light at the end of this year. Things were looking up, and I wanted to hold on to that as much as I could. A lot of good things were finally happening to a nigga, and life was starting to feel normal again.

"Omari!"

I turned around to see Lil' T running up to me. Eboni had followed him until she got to the doorway of the patio, not wanting to bring Jamari outside in the cold.

"What up, Lil' T?" We shook up like homeboys.

"Can I play your Xbox?"

"You know you don't have to ask me, man. Gon' head."

I told Capone that I'd be back as I followed Lil' T in the house. I could hear my mother talking to Tatianna and Tasia in the kitchen. She had grown close to Eboni and the kids as well. With my sister and Tre living three hours away, my mother hardly got the opportunity to spend as much time with their son as she could. Even though I was re-establishing my relationship with my sister, I still hadn't seen her much. I honestly think that, for whatever reason, Tre didn't want her around us much at all. He never really did fuck with me too tough after meeting him that day. So, the only grandchild that my mother got to spoil was Jamari. She was happy to adopt Eboni's kids as her own.

I had taken Jamari from Eboni and started playing with him just as the doorbell rang. I was only now expecting Jasmine, so I got off the couch to open the door for her. Things had been going so right between her and me. We got along great, and we got along even better in the bedroom. I just hoped that when she walked through that door, she wouldn't change on me. I hoped that she was ready for this, for my life, and all that I came with.

"He–heeeey!" The sight of Jamari in my arms surprised her. She had never seen him before. "Hi, little man. Wow, you look just like your daddy."

Though she was smiling at Jamari and holding his hand, I knew that she was thrown off. I could see it in her eyes. I hadn't told her that my family would be there because I didn't want her to have the opportunity to say no or back out of coming. She needed to meet them. It was time.

"C'mon in, baby."

She followed me while removing her coat slowly. I could tell that she was taking in all the sounds of people all over the house. She was doing a bad job of hiding that she was completely thrown off.

She looked curiously at the sight of my mother helping Tatianna and Tasia mix cornbread at the kitchen table. Her eyes got big as golf balls as she noticed Eboni and Lil' T in the living room.

"Mama, I want you to meet somebody." My mother looked up, met eyes with Jasmine and smiled.

"Mama, this is my woman, Jasmine. Jasmine, this is my mother."

Jasmine shot me a questionable glance, but quickly recovered and rushed over to shake my mother's hand. Instead, my mother hugged her, saying, "Girl, give me a hug. We give hugs around here. Nice to meet you, baby. I've heard so many *good* things about you."

"Jasmine, that's Tatianna and Tasia, Eboni's daughters. That's Lil' T over there and that's Eboni."

Eboni had come into the kitchen when she heard Jasmine come in. As I introduced them, Eboni approached her and hugged her. "Hey, girl. Nice to finally meet you."

"You too," came from Jasmine in a nervous pitch.

"C'mon, Jasmine," I said taking her hand. "Let's take your coat upstairs."

She looked all too happy to follow me.

Once inside of my bedroom, she let me have it. "Omari, why didn't you tell me that they were going to be here?!"

She was freaking out, but I had the biggest smile on my face. I felt so relaxed, so happy, so different than I had been, with all my family together. "Because I knew that if I told you they would be here, you would get out of coming."

Jasmine sighed and ran her fingers through her hair as she paced back and forth. "You should have told me. I would have dressed better! Your mother probably thinks I'm a skank!"

She was wearing high-waist jeans and a camisole with sneaker wedges. It was simple, but that ass looked juicy as fuck in those jeans. "Yea, you're ass does look... *huge.* Did it get bigger? I must be hitting that motherfucka right!"

"Omari, stop playing!"

As I laughed, Jamari laughed, and Jasmine's frustration warmed at the sight of his smile. "You can't be mad at a face like this," I told Jasmine.

Jasmine looked like she was falling in love the longer she looked at him. "He *is* adorable."

I pretended to feel some type of way. "I was talking about me."

"Whatever, nigga. Stop trying to make me laugh. I'm mad at you." She crossed her arms across her chest, and at that moment I wanted to lose my face in between those titties. Just looking at her confirmed me introducing her to my people. In nearly three months, she had become my people too, in more ways than the people downstairs. It was necessary for us to take this step. She was still fighting the connection that we had. She still had the reservations that she had when we met. I needed her to let those go because I had let go of mine. It was inevitable that we were going to be fucking with each other for some time. At the moment, I couldn't imagine not sticking my dick in her every chance I got, not talking to her on the phone for hours when she couldn't come over, not hanging out with her and watching her get tipsy. I didn't know what the outcome would be, but I was willing to do what I had to do to show her that she could let her guard down, because I had no plans to play with that pretty little heart of hers.

"Look... I just wanted you to meet my family. I want you to

know everything about me, and they are a very big part of me. My family is so important to me. I know that springing it on you like this was wrong. If it makes you uncomfortable, you can leave."

With every word, she seemed to warm up to the idea. She let out a sigh, saying, "No, I'm good. I'm staying."

That's why I liked her. She rocked with me and rolled with the punches.

I reached out for her hand and she held it with a flirtatious grin.

"I'm gon' fuck the shit out of you when they leave," I told her. "You know that right?"

She smiled. "Yaaaay!" And we giggled like two teenagers as we made our way downstairs.

Back in the kitchen, it was Jasmine's turn to shock me.

"Is there anything that I can do?" She joined my mother and the girls at the table, and my mother told her what preparations she needed help with.

I smiled at Jasmine's initiative as I watched them, admiring what I hoped to be what the rest of the year would look like.

****

"Your woman, huh?"

I looked up at Eboni and ignored the Chester Cheetah grin on her face. I was back on the patio helping Capone finish up the rest of the meat. Eboni had just stepped out there to bring a pan to transport some of the finished meat in.

"What you talkin' about?" I asked her.

"You introduced her as your woman."

Capone stopped flipping the wings and stared at me with the same smile.

"What? She *is* my woman."

"Since when?" Eboni asked.

I shrugged. "Since now."

"This nigga is pussy whipped," Capone huffed. "I can't believe it."

Eboni started cracking up.

"Really?" I asked her. "You can't talk, while you over there sitting on Terrance's dick."

"Ooooooo," Capone instigated.

"Whatever, motherfucka! I been knowing that nigga all my life though. Besides... that shit ain't all it's cracked up to be."

Suddenly, real sadness took over Eboni's eyes, so I asked, "What's wrong?"

"It's just not how it used to be. I can forgive, but I can't forget... The kids are happy though." Then she sighed and changed the subject back to me. "Are you happy? Is she sane? She not crazy, is she? Like you know who?"

I immediately shook my head. "Nah, she's good. So far, so good. I know it's kinda out of the blue. Trust me, I fought this shit for as long as I could, but I like shorty. She makes me... happy. I'm good."

Eboni smiled genuinely. "Good. Because I'll fuck her up if she does anything to hurt you. Make sure you tell her that."

I laughed. "I will."

"It's good to see you happy, though. I'm happy for you. You deserve it. Enjoy it... Please?"

I planned to... *soooon* as these motherfuckas left.

Jasmine

As soon as Capone left the kitchen and locked up behind himself, Omari was all over me.

"Damn, I've been waiting to do this all day." He kissed me so slow and steady, as if he was savoring every taste of my lips and tongue.

"Wait...," I spoke into his mouth, but he kept going like a horny, sexy beast. "Wait, Omari." I pulled back and ended our kiss prematurely. He looked at me, wondering what was up with the look on my face. I hopped up on the counter behind me and finally asked him, "Your woman?"

It had been on my mind all day. I acted like I didn't hear it. I acted like him introducing me as his girlfriend didn't rock my world while giving me an anxiety attack. But it had.

A grin broke out of my face as I caught him bashfully shy away from my questioning eyes.

"What was that about, Omari?"

He avoided me and looked at the clock. "It's almost midnight."

"Stop playing, Omari."

Again, he grinned at me. "We can't bring the New Year in arguing."

I folded my arms but I couldn't even get mad at him. It was so fucking hard to resist him. "Omari, I'm serious."

Finally, he gave me his undivided attention. Once bashful, he was now back to being masculine and overbearing. He came close to me, standing between my legs, causing a heat that was electric between us as always. The way he stared at me always rendering me speechless. "You don't want to be my, girl?"

I never expected to be here with Omari. We were both against feeling anything for anybody at all costs and now we were feeling every emotion for each other.

I still had reservations. I was so scared to be with a man like Omari. Now, I was mature and grown. Dating Omari was real, not child's play. My heart was worn out and tired. I had no more room in my heart for drama, lies and games. He had the ability to do way worse damage to my heart than Kendrick and Ant combined.

But who could say no to a man like Omari Sutton? How could I say no to him when he was rubbing my thighs intensely, bringing himself closer to my body, making our chests connect and speaking into my neck? "You don't want to be with me, baby?"

I wasn't use to this. I was use to men stringing me along while being complete assholes. I was used to being committed to them by default; because we had been fucking for so long. This was so different, and I was *so* scared. I was scared of his like for me and his eagerness to have me in his life. It was so foreign to me. But I guess my mama was right; when a man wants you in his life, it doesn't take him long to figure it out.

I smiled as Omari began to trace my neck with his warm tongue, forcing the answer out of me that he wanted. "Of course, I do."

CHAPTER 15

Gia

"Wow."

I couldn't believe it. When I woke up this morning with an empty space next to me where Chance should have been, I left the bedroom looking for him. I was totally expecting him to be in the living room, but what I wasn't expecting was for him to be sleep on the couch with Georgia.

They weren't on top of each other or anything; they were just sitting next to each other with their heads cocked towards the other, fast asleep.

Still in all, I was pissed at both of them. I had just checked this bitch the night before about my man and Chance was being the typical nigga; too gullible and stupid to see the shit.

I cleared my throat loud enough for them both to hear me, but the only person that opened their eyes was Georgia.

"What I tell you last night?"

She immediately rolled her eyes as she stretched. "We fell asleep playing the game. Chill."

"Ain't no chill, Georgia. I should not wake up looking for my nigga and find my man on the couch sleep with you–"

"Y'all had it out. He didn't want to sleep in there with you."

"And as my sister you should have made him take his as in there anyway."

Georgia sucked her teeth and stood up. My gut instinct grew enormously when I noticed the little ass shorts that she was wearing.

"Girl, it's not my job to tell your man what to do. Besides, didn't you just tell me 'ain't no asking your man shit'? Well, ain't no telling him shit either." She walked by me, ignoring my glares at her and those little ass shorts. "It's your job to make sure that your man wants to sleep with you and not somebody else."

"Bitch–"

"Aye, man! What the fuck?!"

I didn't even notice that Chance was woke, but I was glad that he was.

"Why the fuck are you in here sleep with her?"

Chance's eyes rolled in the back of his head. "Not this shit again. Damn, Gia."

While I was pissed at Georgia, I was sympathetic towards Chance. He looked truly tired of all the bullshit. He was fed the fuck up. He was a man on edge. He had so much going on. I couldn't blame him, but I didn't want any of the bullshit that he was fed up with to be me.

I sat beside him and placed my hand on his lap. That dick was so long and big that he greeted me with a warmer hello than Chance had. It was falling down his leg and was fighting to get out of his shorts. I wished to every fairy godmother that we were in our bedroom with his dick in me, instead of arguing like cats and dogs. The honeymoon stage of our relationship was over. That motherfucka had evaporated into thin air. It was at no fault of our own though. I don't think any relationship could have survived the things that Chance and I had gone through during the short time that we were together. The fact that we were still together told me that what we had was so special. I refused to let money and my badass sister get in the middle of it.

"I'm sorry, Chance. I'm *so* sorry. I didn't mean what I said last night."

At first, he didn't want to fold. He wanted to remain mad at me, but, just like the man that I knew loved me, he let his guard down and put his arm around me.

"I love you, Chance," I whispered as I lay my head on his shoulder. In return, he adjusted so that we could comfortably spoon.

"I love you too, baby."

He even sounded stressed when he said it. This stress on our relationship had little to do with what I said last night or Georgia; it was being in this city.

"I know that we have a lot going on. I know you don't want to be here, and that you hate being stuck. I just want to make this money for us. I just want to put you on, baby, so that you can be happy. You deserve to be happy."

I didn't hear him say a word. I just felt him kiss my forehead.

"We're going to be okay, Chance."

He still didn't respond, so I just prayed that he believed it and still believed in me.

Simone

Two days after New Year's, I found myself in a funk. Normally, I was so motivated by getting out of dodge that I rarely focused on my unfortunate circumstances. But, now, it was a new year, and I was realizing that, still, I was in the midst of the same shit.

Every time I sold my pussy for chicken change, I thought about just giving up and turning myself in. Every time I slept with Slim just to secure a better meal or the fulfillment of seeing regular life as he let me tag along as he drove around Chicago, I thought about just ending it and killing myself.

My pride wouldn't let me do it, though. So I was stuck. I literally felt stuck for the past two days. Currently, as I rode with Slim and Katie, I was in a cloud that was full of desperation. I wanted to be free so bad, I wanted my regular life back so bad, that I was damn near in tears as we rode the expressway.

I had no idea where we were going. Slim had only asked Katie and I to ride with him to take care of something. I found it weird that he had even asked Katie to come along; even weirder that he told her to sit up front. I figured that he was attempting to pacify her frustrations with being bumped down a level and shrugged it off. I didn't give a fuck either way. At this point, I was scared to hit his stash, since he now knew that somebody was stealing from him, so it didn't matter whether he found me his favorite or not. I hated what my life had turned into, but it was all that I had. I didn't want to be back in that homeless shelter, starving, and dirty, so I abandoned the plan of stealing from Slim and was trying hard to think of another way.

"So you wanna steal from me, bitch?!"

Slim's sudden rage brought me out of my trance. I looked up into the front seat to see him in Katie's face. He was damn near in the passenger seat with her as we sat in an alley off of a residential block. Rundown, abandoned buildings and filth surrounded us as we sat surrounded by two inches of snow.

"Wh... what are you talking about?" Sheer terror was in her voice. She was shaking already, but I couldn't tell whether it was fear, effects of the drugs, or a mix of the two.

He charged her and slapped the shit out of her. "Don't play with me!"

Oh fuck. Here we go. Now it all made sense why he asked Katie to come with us.

When he jumped out of the truck, I didn't know whether he was going to beat the shit out of her or kill her. Either way, I didn't feel any guilt. It was me or her, and her hype ass would have killed herself anyway with an overdose before I allowed myself to die in prison, so I figured it good riddance.

"Slim, no! Please!" She shouted as he drug her out of the truck by her hair. I peeked out of the backseat window to see him throwing her into the snow and ice.

"You stealing from me?! That's what you on?!" His voice was like thunder bouncing off the buildings around us.

"I didn't take–" Slim's fist in her mouth stopped all pleads that were trying to come from her lips. He hit it so hard, over and over again, until blood painted the snow.

"You fired, bitch!" he shouted as he finally stopped pummeling her.

As he walked away, she literally crawled towards him in the snow. "No, Slim! Please! Don't leave me out here!"

"You done! If I see your face again, bitch, you're dead!" He swung the door open so fast and hard that it damn near smacked her in the face.

"Please, Daddy!" Her voice was literally filled with trembles and shrieks. She was begging for her life, pleading for another chance, but Slim wasn't having it.

"Get in the front seat, Brandie," he ordered, and I quickly obliged. We were way out in Boomfuck, Illinois somewhere. He wasn't about to leave me out there because I didn't move quickly enough. I quickly climbed into the front seat as he started the truck. Over the sounds of the engine and the loud music blaring from the speakers, Katie's screams could be clearly heard.

"Don't leave me, Slim! PLEASE?!"

Blood flew from her mouth as we drove by. We made eye contact, and I recognized the fear in her eyes. I had seen it in the eyes of Tammy, that girl in the park, and Aeysha as she noticed Chance's gun pointed at her; it was the fear of death. It was the same fear that resonated in my heart, because I was running away from death myself; a life wasted in prison, if I didn't do what the fuck I had to do. Her fear was valid. Without Slim, she would be homeless, broke and left to feed her addiction on her own in the streets. She would die from starvation or some other unfortunate circumstance.

I hadn't physically killed her, but she was still going to die nonetheless.

Jasmine

You ever had a man pray for you, or even pray with you? Well, that's what Omari did the morning of New Year's Day. We'd spent the entire night bringing in the New Year on top of each other. It was quiet and low key, but exactly what we both wanted. Then, this morning, before I crawled out of the bed to shower, he stopped me.

"Wait a minute, bae. One second."

I looked at him, searching for a reason why he'd stopped me. He wasn't laughing and flirtatious, as he usually was. He was serious and his mind seemed like it was full of thoughts.

"What's wrong?" I asked as I nestled back next to him.

"Nothing. I just want to pray with you."

I was touched. My mother had raised me in church. I knew the power of prayer. I was fully aware of the fact that Omari was a brick slaying, street nigga, but the fact that he had even said the word "prayer" took my breath away.

I smiled and told him, "Sure." Then he held my hand and prayed for us. He asked God to bless our union, to help us make the right decisions regarding our relationship, and to make this a joyous year for us as we grew stronger. I was nearly in tears when he was done. I had never had a man care enough about me to consult God about "us," and, if Omari and I didn't stay together forever, I would always remember that moment.

It was sacred... and I made it all raunchy when I grabbed his face and kissed him. Omari was unreal. He wasn't perfect, by any means, but he was perfect for me at that moment and time in my life. He had come along when I had lost faith in men, when I had lost faith in the possibilities of me ever being a man's rib. Omari was restoring my faith in those possibilities, so I thanked him with kisses all over his body. I quietly asked God to forgive me. Omari had just said such thoughtful prayers and there I was, fornicating in the midst of them, but I just couldn't help myself.

I kissed him from his chiseled jaws and down to his body. *God,* that body. The moment we had just shared was so divine, but that body was sinful and was encouraging me to do all sorts of dirty, ungodly things.

"Sssss," he hissed as I wrapped my mouth around his dick. I couldn't believe how wet my own mouth was. I seemed to salivate in anticipation of pleasing him. Sucking his dick was just as satisfying to me as having his mouth on me. I was aroused just the same and felt my pussy dripping wet as it hovered in the air over his Egyptian sheets.

"Shit, baby." I felt him rhythmically rotating his hips. He was fucking my face, and I invited him. I allowed myself to gag and he loved it. "Fuck," he growled. "Gawd damn. Lay down, baby."

He slowly slid out of my throat and lay me down. He looked down at all of my chocolate curves with the same hungry gaze that I looked at his darkness with. He kissed my thighs at an agonizingly slow pace, using his face to open my thighs wider, revealing my already glistening, wet pussy. I shuddered and pulled at his locs the moment that big, pouty mouth met my pulsating clit. My toes curled as I forced myself to take the profound pressure that his sucking was causing between my legs.

Minutes later, I was sloppy wet as he left his meal and hovered above me. I wrapped my arms around his hard body and nestled my face into his chest, preparing for the moment that he thrust that fat dick in me. But he gently grabbed my face, and turned it towards the wall. My eyes were on my own weak reflection as this beast entered it in one swift thrust. I was forced to watch in the mirror on the wall as that dick exhausted me with so much power that his back muscles tightened with each thrust.

"Gawd… damn!" I was clawing at his back as my eyes squeezed shut in disbelief of how deep this man was inside of me. "Shit… this… dick… is *so* good! Fuck!"

"Unt uh. Open your eyes, baby," he breathed into my ear. I readily obeyed, opening my eyes and taking in the vision of his perfect ass gliding up and down as he swam inside of me. The curve of his back was impeccable. The coating of his dark, black skin was remarkable and shined like brass with his sweat. "Keep your eyes open, baby. I want you to watch. So that tomorrow when you're sore, you remember who did it to you."

That was two days ago, and I still remembered. How could I forget when we had had continuous sessions like that ever since

216

and every chance we got? As I stood in the shower, I shuddered at the memories of all the sex that we had been having for the past couple of days. I was off of work because of the holidays. Marcus was with his father for the same reasons. I had spent days under Omari; getting to know him, his mind and his past and vice versa.

I stood in his shower, with the hot water massaging body parts that he massacred, wondering what the hell I had gotten myself into. Though we had grown close over the past few months, I didn't really know this man. I had done exactly what I didn't want to do; set myself up to be possibly hurt again.

Just the thought of it ran chills down my spine as I dried off. After moisturizing my skin, I rubbed sweet smelling oils all over and in every crevice, just in case Omari wanted to be nasty and have another car session on our way home from our date that night. I sighed heavily as yet another thought of him made my heart grin happily.

I didn't want to do it and I didn't want to admit it, but I was definitely falling for Omari Sutton.

Shit.

Omari

"You gotta be kidding me."

Detective Howard couldn't have picked a worse time to be at my door.

"Thought I left this bitch in last year." I huffed and puffed as I opened my front door. I stepped out hesitantly and closed the door behind me, not wanting Jasmine to be able to hear anything that this chick had to say.

I still hadn't given her any details of Aeysha's death, and I had never mentioned Dahlia to her. I was still trying to preserve the cool swagger of our relationship. Jasmine was the one place that I could go where all these bad memories didn't exist. She didn't know, so it was as if, when I was with her, it never happened. I could be with her with a free heart. Having the conversation with her would only fuck that up.

"Detective Howard, you don't have a phone?"

She chuckled as she nodded. I even caught her look me up and down. I must say that my swagger was on point. Jasmine and I was on our way out. I had set aside the baggy jeans and Timbs and dressed in a casual pair of Ralph Lauren jeans, a fitted blazer, with a dressy tee underneath and Gucci loafers. Jasmine had a habit of tugging and pulling on my locs during sex, but I made her fix them earlier, so the fishtail that my locs had been professionally braided in for the holidays was back right.

"Yea, I got a phone," Detective Howard finally answered.

I folded my arms across my chest, preparing myself. "You don't use it to call people?"

"I do, Mr. Sutton, but I get to waste time on the clock by making special trips to come to see you." Then she smiled, but, once again, she looked reluctant to be there.

I didn't want to hear shit she had to say. I had been under a very special girl for days. I had been knee deep in some very good pussy for days. I was on cloud nine and I didn't want to come down. "We gon' have to talk later. I have company, and I don't want her knowing how fucked up my life use to be, if you understand what I'm saying."

She nodded like she more than understood but insisted, "It's important, Omari."

She walked further away from the front door so that she would be out of sight, and I followed. "I'll make it quick... I'm sorry to tell you this, but ...." She hesitated and bit the corner of her bottom lip anxiously. Then she spit it out. "... That body in the park wasn't Simone Campbell's..."

I was in the motherfuckin' Twilight Zone. I had to be. I *had* to be! This shit wasn't real life. This type of fucked up shit did *not* happen in real life. I was in a scary movie. I was convinced. Freddy Krueger was about to come out of the bushes and slice the shit out of me. I just knew it.

"What?!" I had to have heard her wrong. I *had* to.

"Dental records show that the body belonged to Briana Daniels; a twenty–two year old reported missing that day…"

I had to shake this shit off. I had to. I couldn't let Jasmine see my reaction. But it was hard. My mind was completely blown. The shit that Simone was capable of was beyond my comprehension. I couldn't make sense of any of this shit.

Detective Howard looked on at my perplexity with sympathy. With a deep sigh, she told me, "I'm sorry, Omari. I'm so sorry. I didn't want to tell you until I knew that she was in custody, but that is taking longer than I thought. There is absolutely no trace of that woman in this country. I am working day and night to find her. But I had to tell you, because I want you to be careful; you, and anyone close to you. I doubt that she will risk being caught by coming anywhere near you, but, just in case, be careful."

I just shrugged my shoulders barely because they felt like they weighed a ton. I had no words. I couldn't say anything. My tongue was tied tight with disbelief. She had nothing to say to make me feel any better either. She just squeezed my shoulder and walked away, towards the running squad car parked in front of the neighbor's house. I watched her as she made her way, wondering what can of worms her visit had just opened. I wasn't scared of Simone. In all her obsession and madness, she had never hurt me. But now I was prepared to protect everyone around me; including the vision on the stairs, staring at me with bright, happy eyes when I walked through the front door.

"Hey, babe. I've been calling you. Who was that?"

"That... that was just one of the neighbors, baby. Wanted to know if he could borrow my snow blower. You ready?"

She was. Her hair was bouncing in those curls that always took her twenty minutes to perfect. Her face was painted in utter perfection. My plans were to take her somewhere nice for dinner, since I'd had her in the house for days, eating her for dinner, so she dressed up for me in a winter white pencil dress that fit tight down to a little ways past her knees.

"I look okay?" She probably asked because, though I was admiring how she looked, I couldn't help but to fear what Simone could do to her just to get to me. I was smiling at the sight of her, but I was trying hard not to go back to a place where I was last year. I was sure that she saw the uncertainty in my eyes, thinking that it was meant for her, when it could never be. The only thing that I was certain about in my life at that moment *was* her.

"Yea, bae," barely came out of my mouth. I nervously cleared my throat. "You look beautiful."

Her carefully arched and penciled in eyebrows curled curiously. "You okay?"

"I'm fine." I had to be. Fuck Simone. She had ruined every other good thing in my life. I wasn't going to let her ruin this too. "I'm more than okay. Let's go."

222

Eboni

I forced myself to giggle in a giddy enough way that he believed me. "I'm sleepy, Terrance. Stop."

He moaned into my ear, "C'mon on, baby. My dick as hard as cement."

I rolled my eyes in the back of my head, hoping that he didn't see it in the darkness of my bedroom.

His dick was indeed hard. I could feel it against the other side of my panties as I lay with my back to him. It was pulsating against my ass, but I wasn't impressed.

"I'm tired," I said with a forced yawn. "I've been in school all day," I whined.

He sighed, but kissed my cheek. "Okay, baby. But I'mma get that ass in the morning... Good night."

Lucky me... Not. "Good night."

I could have cried. I couldn't believe that after missing Terrance for so long that I was feeling like this. Since the holidays, things just didn't feel right. I had allowed him to pressure me into taking him back with all of the nice things that he was doing for me. I had done it for my family, for the smiles on my kids' faces when they woke up to their father getting them ready for school, but I didn't have the same smile. Slowly, I was realizing that what I had been missing was *someone* being there, not him.

Don't get me wrong. He wasn't doing anything wrong. He was the same man that he was when we were together. But he was also the same man that had left me alone for a year just to love on my best friend. I obviously still wasn't able to forget. Every time I looked at him, I saw the pain that I had gone through last year, because he was the source of it. I saw the heartbreak, because he was the supplier. How could I get away from all of that, how could I grow and get better if the source of my issues was right there in my bed every night? Being with him had me feeling like a failure, like a weak, stupid bitch all over again, but had my kids on cloud nine, so I felt stuck.

I had spent so long feeling insufficient and angry because Felicia had done me so dirty and had won. Her disloyalty had won her a posh life, and I didn't think it was fair. But I was now realizing that if these hoes are winning, it's probably not a prize worth having.

I couldn't sleep, so I dimmed the screen on my phone so that I could read from my Kindle app without disturbing Terrance. An author, Chloe, had just released her debut book, *Dirty*, that I had been waiting for a few undisturbed hours to get into. Since sleep didn't seem like it was coming anytime soon, I got comfortable under the covers and scrolled to my Kindle app, just as a message from Omari arrived.

Detective Howard came to the crib today... Simone isn't dead. That wasn't her body. I can't talk right now, bc I'm with Jasmine. I still haven't told her. I'll hit you tomorrow...Be careful.

11:58 PM

I threw my hand over my mouth to muffle my gasp. I clutched my chest as I re-read the words over and over again, hoping that they would magically transform into another message. When it didn't, I closed the inbox in disbelief and sat the phone on the nightstand.

This was unreal. It boggled my mind how Simone had been able to dodge death over and over again. I wondered what lengths she had gone to get away this time. I thought about that girl burning alive in the woods and tears came to my eyes while eerie chills ran down my spine. Suddenly, I felt it necessary to cuddle up under Terrance. Even in his sleep, he open his arms, spooned with me and allowed me to lay under his protection.

Rather than reading, I started to pray, because, apparently, only God was going to be able to stop an evil like Simone Campbell.

CHAPTER 16

Simone

I was with a john that liked to ride around and get high off of coke before we fucked in his tinted back seat. I stared out of the windows of his Cadillac, watching the buildings on Michigan Avenue go by. They were the buildings that I use to shop in with Omari's money on so many occasions. I closed my eyes briefly, remembering those days, but quickly forced myself to open them and live in my reality.

It was after midnight, so the streets were mostly vacant. Only the light from the many stores on Michigan Avenue populated the streets, along with couples that had dared to come out into this weather on a date. I looked at them, holding hands, then looked over at my john, who was snorting cocaine from his fingernail.

Urgh, I thought as I stared back out of the window longingly.

"Brandie, what's up with you? You're different tonight." His voice annoyed me. I never liked white dick, and I definitely didn't like it now that I was forced to play with it.

I started to say something smart, but a woman's coat caught my attention. Not just her coat, but her. She looked fly as she walked toward us as we drove slowly down the street. It was a very stylish hooded black wool coat. The fur around the collar and the big cuffs was what were so eye–catching. I imagined myself wearing it on my way to work at Lexington House.

Yea, that's definitely something that I would have worn.

I salivated at her handbag. I damn near busted my head against the window when staring at her shoes... at that ass...

Hold the fuck up.

No matter how long it had been, I would know that ass anywhere. But laying eyes on her face as she came closer, I knew it was her.

"Jasmine," I sighed under my breath.

Seeing her was like seeing a blast from a past that I wanted back so desperately. My heart broke. The car was going southbound, and she was coming northbound on my side of the street. Her smile was so bright and real as she held hands with....

"Arrgh!"

The john that I was with hit the brakes! "What?! What's wrong?!" But we were in the middle of the street, so he had to keep driving. I pressed my face against the glass, staring at them as they walked hand in hand, watching their happiness and staring at their intertwined hands to the point that I was completely turned around in my seat attempting to keep a glimpse of them until I couldn't see them anymore. At that point, I slid down into the seat in complete despair. "Urgh!"

"What's wrong? You're scaring me, baby–"

"Don't call me baby!! Just shut up!"

He looked at me like I was a psychopath. I felt like one. What I felt in my spirit was so intense that I just wanted to reach into my chest and rip out my heart. This was beyond hate. It was beyond jealousy. It surpassed obsession.

There I was about to be forced to suck the dick of a coke head for fifty dollars and these motherfuckas was walking down Michigan Avenue looking like the high school year book's cutest couple!

"Oh my God," I winced as I clutched my chest. I couldn't believe it.

"You okay?" I heard him ask and it only irritated me further.

"Would you just shut up?! SHUT UP!"

"We're still gonna fuck, right?"

My eyes burned holes so deep that his skin burned red with fear as he approached the expressway. I buried my face in my hands to hide the stubborn tears that insisted to fall. I took deep breaths to keep my head from pounding. Memories of "them" swam in my mind. Tre, DeMarco, Omari, their inability to love me and put me first. That was why I was there, in an old caddy, with this white man expecting to put his dick in me.

It was them. It was all their fault, and I loathed each and every one of them and wished it was them that caught Chance's bullet, that I choked to death, that I hung from a fucking tree in that park.

The john's hands on my thigh brought me back. I looked up and realized that we were ducked off in his favorite spot to fuck me. I looked in his eyes and his lust repulsed me.

I immediately reached for the doorknob, but it was locked.

"Let me ou–"

"But–"

"LET ME OUT!!!" I screamed so loud that I caught the attention of people on the street that walked by. We were further west in Garfield Park. The Ave that I usually strolled was a few blocks away, but pimps had hoes on many corners in the area. A few of them were a few feet away, peering into the car curiously, but unable to see through the tint.

"Fine. I don't need this shit anyway. Get out."

I heard the doors unlock and charged out so fast that I nearly tripped over the curb. The air on the outside renewed the blood flow to my brain, but I was still delusional with despair and panic. All that I had done, the lengths that I had gone, to end up... *here;* still giving myself to men who would never choose me if given the choice.

Detective Howard

Once again, it was damn near three o'clock in the morning, and I was still at the fucking station. No matter how much work I did, no matter how many cases I solved, the only case that I could think about was Simone Campbell's.

I hated to have to tell Omari that she was still alive. The pain in his eyes was what I had feared having to witness first hand. But the longer it was taking me to find that bitch, I knew that I had to notify Omari so that he could protect himself and everyone around him.

"Marcia, what are you doing up here, girl?" I was happy to abandon my paperwork when I saw Marcia, a detective from Vice, walking into the squad room. Marcia and I not only worked for the same district, we were friends. We went through the academy together and climbed the ranks together. Yet, because of our hectic schedules, we hadn't gotten together to hang out in a while.

"Got something for you," she told me, and I was all ears. I was expecting her to give me some good tea on some station gossip, but she had something much better for me. "I just left the stroll."

Marcia was an undercover in Vice. One of her main undercover operations was posing as a prostitute to bust johns. Every now and then, I peeped her walking out of the station at midnight in booty shorts and a wig, her rather plump booty for a Mexican girl shaking along the way. The male detectives always loved that shit.

"Okay," I probed her. "What happened?"

"I saw your girl... Simone Campbell."

I was so happy that I jumped up and down, playfully smacking her in the arm over and over again. "You did not!"

"Swear," she smiled. "She jumped out of a car a few hours ago. Had to look twice. She had on a blonde wig, but it was definitely that bitch. I didn't follow her. Didn't want her to run, but I started asking around. She works for a pimp that goes by the street name Slim–"

I hollered with laughter. "Figures that she would be somewhere being a hoe."

"Yep. She's over on 47th and Cicero every night. Blonde wig, usually. Goes by the name Brandie."

"Thank you, Marcia!" I was beaming. You would have thought that I won lottery.

"Don't thank me. Stop standing me up for dinner."

"You got it! My treat!'

We hugged as she told me, "I'll see you later, girl. My feet are killing me and my husband will still want his dick sucked when I get home, no matter how sleepy I am."

"Do your thing, girl," I laughed. "Talk to you later. We'll have dinner next week, for sure. And thank you again."

As she waved goodbye and exited the squad room, I squealed again. "Yes!"

I was supposed to be going home to sleep next to my babies for as long as I could before they had to go to school the next morning. But tracking down Simone Campbell was a sacrifice that I was willing to make.

I was typing the street name Slim into the database as I dialed Michelle's number.

When she answered, sounding like she was in a deep sleep, I felt so bad for waking her. "Hello?"

"Hey, Michelle. Sorry for waking you, sweetie. Just letting you know that I'm going to be late coming home."

Jasmine

♪ A definite silence

You're almost exactly what I need

A definite maybe

Is sure to entice my curiosity

I can't help but think that this doesn't add up

I'm trying to separate the facts from all the fiction ♪

"We're living in a world of contradictions. And if, baby, you're the truth, then I'm lying next to you!" I was singing my heart out to my song in Omari's bathroom. My hairbrush was my microphone as I sang those words with all my heart. I meant them. Omari had been lying next to me for days and I was at that place I had feared the most when I met him; *in my feelings.*

He was downstairs taking care of some business while I showered before we went to breakfast. It was Sunday. I had to go back to work the next day. My vacation was over, so Omari and I were spending this last day of my consecutive days of freedom together, as we had done all the others.

"Damn, where is my lotion?"

I searched through my overnight bag and didn't see anything. Nothing was in the bathroom cabinets either. Omari had a nice house, but it was obvious that a man lived there. He had the bare minimal and I refused to oil my skin with that hard ass Vaseline, that looked like it had been in there since before he moved.

I wrapped myself in the bath towel and tip toed out of the bathroom. I started to yell downstairs, but the surround sound was so loud that I figured he wouldn't hear me. I knew that there was another master bath in one of the guestrooms, so I tipped toed out of the room in search of what I needed.

The door to the closet in the room was slightly ajar. When I saw toiletries inside, I went in expecting to find what I needed. But I halted when I noticed how many toiletries there were. Much of them were used and looked to be old. There were body sprays, curlers, flat irons; things that should have been out in the open if a woman lived there. Then I noticed the women's clothes that hung in the closet. They smelled of a woman, as if they had been worn. They had her smell. Curiously, I bent down and peered into the box on the floor. Pictures were inside. I lightly gasped as I realized that this must have been pictures of Omari's girlfriend that had passed. They say curiosity kills the cat. Well, it was definitely about to kill my heart. I should have walked away. I should have walked away right then. He hadn't shown me that closet for a reason, so I should have minded my business. But like a woman, I didn't. I dug further and further into the box until I found news articles that looked to have been printed off of the Internet. The words in the headlines broke my heart; "drive–by", "pregnant woman slain", "Aeysha Walker."

Again, I should have stopped right then, but I just couldn't help myself. I kept rummaging through the box. There were more pictures. These were more recent. They were of a little girl with eyes just like Omari and Jamari's.

"The fuck?" I wondered to myself as I kept staring and pulling out more pictures and more papers. This was Omari's shrine to Aeysha, and whoever this baby was. You could literally smell Aeysha in that closet. He wouldn't talk about her to me, but she was definitely in that house with him and us.

I was so taken aback that I decided to return the pictures to the box and leave. I felt like I was invading a space that I shouldn't have, that I was forbidden from, that was private and sacred to him. I stood and bent down to return what was in my hands to the box until a paper lying face up in the box flashed words back at me that made me literally scream: "Simone Campbell arrested and charged with the murder of Aeysha Walker."

"OH! Ugh!"

"Babe?!"

I didn't even realize that the music had gone off. I could hear Omari rushing up the stairs as I fought to regain the ability to breathe. I walked away from that closet like it was haunted and dashed out of the room. I ran down the hallway, right past Omari, and into his bedroom. I frantically looked for my clothes. I had to get out of there.

"Baby, what's wrong?!'

"WHY DIDN'T YOU TELL ME?!"

I had never yelled at him. I had never cried in front of him. There I was screaming at the top of my lungs like a maniac with tears in my eyes and he was confused.

"She was your girlfriend. She was *your* girlfriend," I cried as I put my panties on. "I can't believe this."

Omari grabbed my shoulders, making me stop. "Jasmine, hold on. What's wrong?"

I felt bad for the confusion in his face, but my confusion superseded his. "Aeysha! She was your girlfriend! The girl that my cousin killed... *Simone.*"

He backed away from me like I was the plague. That was fine because I wanted fifty feet from him too. Now I was free to get my shit and get the fuck up out of there.

"Why didn't you just tell me?" I fussed as I literally threw on my clothes. "We wouldn't have even had to waste each other's time if you would have been honest."

He finally spoke up. "Hold on. I *was* honest with you."

"No, you weren't! You said that you were being open with me! That you were being real with me! But you kept out a whole part of your life!"

Omari

I didn't know what to say. There was really no way to explain to her the depth of the pain that a person feels when they lose loved ones the way that I had. I couldn't find the words to explain to her why I chose to confine Aeysha and Dahlia in a closet in a room in my house and not into my everyday life by talking about them to strangers.

Yet and still I felt bad for the pain in her eyes. I reached for her. "Jasmine–"

She backed away from me just as I had backed away from her a few moments ago. Just as I didn't want to be near her because of Simone, it was like she didn't want anything to do with me because of the same reason.

"Where is the baby?"

She caught me off guard. I was stuck, wondering how she ended up in that room in the first place, and wondering how somebody so perfect could be related to somebody so fucking evil.

"Where is sh–"

"She's dead!" The words smacked Jasmine in the face. She stepped back, even further than she had before. "Simone killed her too."

She gasped and clutched her chest. "Ugh!" Her tears became uncontrollable.

I had made space between us like she was contagious when she said that she was Simone's cousin, but I couldn't understand why she was treating me the same way.

"I just didn't want to talk about it," I tried to explain while she put on her shoes.

"Well, you should have," she said as tears fell down her face. "You should have, Omari."

"Why?"

"You hid an entire family from me, Omari! A child! What else are you hiding?!"

That shit offended me. My chest swelled. "Nothing. What the fuck? Are you serious?"

She ignored me, continuing to collect the many things that she had in my bedroom from her holiday stay.

"I don't understand," I said, watching her barely able to hold her composure. "Why is this so hurtful to you?

She didn't answer me. She went into the bathroom and quickly came back out with her overnight bag. It was open and spilling its contents as she threw it over her shoulder. "Where is my coat?"

She was spastic. She was trying to catch her breath as tears kept falling from her eyes.

"Jasmine, I don't get it. I understand that I should have told you, but, damn, baby, I–"

"I don't want anything to do with Simone." It seemed to have come out in a confession. "That bitch ruined my life, and I don't

239

want shit to do with her. And I'm sure you don't either, even though she is dead."

"She's not dead." I hated to throw it on her like that but since she wanted to know everything, I was putting it all out there.

Her eyes filled with terror. "She what?!"

"She's not dead. That wasn't her body in the woods."

"Wh... What..." Her breath was leaving her body. She looked faint. I moved closer to embrace her, but I couldn't even do it.

I stopped inches away from her and stared at her tears, not believing who she was connected to.

"I have to go," she insisted.

"You don't look like you should be driving."

"Omari!" she said as she raised her hands. "It doesn't matter! I'm leaving."

"Why?" I didn't want her to go. I felt the repulsion towards her because she was related to Simone. I wanted nothing to do with her, but another part of me didn't want Jasmine to leave.

"Omari, can you honestly say that you want to be with someone that is related to Simone? Can you fuck and suck somebody who is related to the woman that killed your girlfriend? Your baby?" She urged me for the answer that she already knew. No matter how much I stared into her eyes with all the care in the world, she knew what my answer was, despite how much I liked her. "Can you?!"

I was defeated. No matter how much I hated to see her go, she was right. I wanted so far away from Simone that, when I once couldn't imagine never being able to touch Jasmine again, I now couldn't stomach ever touching her again. But I couldn't forget how she made me feel; how, though her cousin took my life, Jasmine was giving me back life, so I couldn't fix my mouth to say the answer that we both already knew.

Jasmine shook her head with disappointment at my silence. "That's what I thought."

Defeat wouldn't allow me to go after her. She stomped out of my bedroom, but the defeat was so heavy on my shoulders that I couldn't move. I just collapsed on my bed, staring blankly at the loss.

Simone had successfully taken everything from me. She'd won. She had made it so that if she couldn't have me, no one else would. And she had won again.

CHAPTER 17

Jasmine

"Mama, you okay?"

I didn't even remove my head from underneath my blanket or peel my head away from the pillow. I mumbled, "I'm fine, Marcus," barely opening my mouth.

He knew I was lying. Marcus sighed, saying, "Okay." I was hoping he'd walked away from my bedroom door, but I heard his voice again, still trying to get mommy to act normal. "Are you hungry?"

"No."

"Are you sure–"

"Marcus!" I stopped myself. I felt bad for yelling. I wasn't mad at him; I was mad at myself. "I'm... I'm not hungry, baby. I'm tired and... I have a headache. I don't feel good. Let me rest, baby."

I heard his footsteps going the opposite direction against the white marble towel in the hallway. Finally, it was safe to allow my crying moans to return without the threat of my son hearing them. I knew that he figured something was wrong. For a week, if I wasn't at work, I was in my bed, emotionally eating, crying when the mood hit me and sleeping.

I had been so careful, so cautious, with my heart. Yet, still, I let that fine Black motherfucka get me to a place that I swore I would never be again; heartbroken.

It had only been a little over a week since I ran out of Omari's house, but it was obvious that it was over. He could never date the cousin of the woman that tore his world apart, and I couldn't blame him. Besides, if he could hide a child from me, there were no limits to what else he was hiding. After leaving Ant, I vowed that I would only date men who lied *with* me in the sheets, not *to* me in my face. Omari had done a lot of lying and covering up the truth. I couldn't imagine why he would lie and what else he was lying about.

But, still, I was surprisingly miserable without him. I thought that I would be able to walk away from Omari with my heart fully intact. We had only been knowing each other for a matter of months. We were only in a relationship for a few days. Surely, I shouldn't have felt enough for that man to be as sick as I was without him, but I was.

It had only been a few months that I had known him, but it had been years since I felt that kind of connection with someone; twelve long years. I missed talking with him. I missed laughing with him. I missed laughing at the way he snored and sometimes mumbled in his sleep. Even as I lay in bed, I missed the way his arm would find me in the middle of the night and bring me under him as we slept.

"I knew that shit was too good to be true." I mumbled angrily to myself as I wiped my tears away and pouted like a ten–year–old girl, whose mother told her that she couldn't go outside and play with her friends.

I indeed felt like that ten–year–old girl that was on punishment and couldn't do anything about it. There was nothing that I could do about this. This wasn't the normal fuck up that men do. He hadn't cheated. There was no other woman. There was no suspicious text messages in his phone. It was deceit, death and misery. There was nothing that I could do to fix or change that. What was broken was something that I nor Omari could fix. I couldn't make Omari want to deal with me, nor could I make myself ready to be the black sheep in his life that constantly reminded him of the woman that took away his family. There was nothing that I could do about that; there was nothing that I could do about Simone Campbell.

Omari

"This shit is crazy." I watched Eboni try to wrap her head around the same irony that I had been trying to make sense of for the past week. "They're *cousins*?"

My head nodded so slowly. It was too heavy, too weighed down with all this bullshit, to move any quicker.

"Cousins?" Eboni repeated herself again for the fifth time since I told her while she rocked Jamari. It was nervously. He was already asleep.

Again, whiskey was my remedy. I wouldn't have thought that I would have cared this much that Jasmine was out of my life, but as each day went by, I felt like I was mourning yet another death of one of my favorite girls.

I was sick. I knew that I couldn't be with Jasmine because she and Simone had the same blood running through their veins, but, as the days inched by, I realized that I couldn't be without Jasmine, despite it all.

The pussy was good. It was great... incredible... *life changing.* But it wasn't about that. I missed her smile. I missed her jokes. I missed the way she would wild out to trap music and bagged dope with me, even though she spent years getting an education at some fancy HBCU. I missed *her.* And it made me crazy that my heart could even miss someone that I knew was related to that bitch.

"Has she called you?" Eboni saw how happy I was with Jasmine. Now, she looked at me like she was as disappointed as I was to see that, as quickly as that happiness came, it was snatched away by the same bitch that had been snatching every other light of happiness away from me.

I shook my head while taking more medicine, waiting for the moment that I was too drunk to feel any of this shit.

"Have you called her?"

I shook my head again, finishing off the entire cup.

Eboni stared into my eyes. Concern was all over her face. I knew what she was thinking. I knew what she was expecting. She thought I was gunning it towards the edge of that cliff that had me on my knees with a gun to my head. I was racing toward the complete opposite direction though. Even though I was using liquor to self-medicate my grief, I was still determined to keep it moving. I missed Jasmine, but it wasn't a total loss. I was still the same nigga that planned to stay away from any woman with drama attached to her pussy. Any woman in relation to Simone Campbell was exactly that. They were two different women in two different bodies, but there was no way that Jasmine and I could be together. Every time I would look at her, every time I would think of her, every time I imagined her, I would be reminded of the way I died emotionally and spiritually on October 30, 2013.

I couldn't live like that.

I couldn't live like that … but as I sat there, watching part of all that I had left, I had to be honest with myself. Since October 30, 2013, my life had been destructive, dark chaos. But even as I sat there, knowing who she was, who she was connected to, who she reminded me of, I couldn't deny how since Jasmine Mays walked into my life, my life had turned into beautiful chaos.

Eboni

"Has Detective Howard said anything about any leads on where Simone is?"

Shaking his head, as he reached down for his bottle of Crown Royal, he mumbled. "Nah."

That was disappointing to say the least. I wasn't a scary bitch, by any means. As a matter of fact, I was praying that I bumped into Simone before Detective Howard did. I was just hoping that that day came sooner than later. All of us would be able to sleep way better at night knowing that that bitch was behind bars or dead… *for real this time.*

"Well, I have to go to class." I stood up, with Jamari in my arms, and walked towards Omari. I lay Jamari in his arms, forcing him to put down the glass. "Can he spend the night?"

His head tilted as those silver eyes looked at me with a smirk. He knew what I was doing. I had done it before. He needed to know what he had to live for. He needed to know who mattered. He needed to remember his gains, even though his losses haunted him every day.

I put my hands on my hips and gave him the same smirk. "Can he or nah?"

Omari chuckled. "Yea, sure."

"Are you drunk?"

"Does it matter?"

"Nope. Sober up if you are, because he's staying regardless."

Omari just shrugged. I adjusted my purse on my shoulder and, before I walked out, scooped up the bottle of whiskey from by his feet. "I'll be taking this with me."

"I got people to bring me more, you know that, right?"

I walked out without even looking back. "You won't…. Oh, and he's teething. Have fun."

I walked out of the house, hating the fact that I actually had to double check that I locked the door behind myself and check my surroundings. I was living life like I was being stalked or something.

"This shit is crazy," I mumbled, checking my phone as I hopped in the car.

An even more eerie feeling came over me as I looked at the missed calls from Terrance. I was sure that he was only making sure that I was okay, but I didn't even want to call him back. Terrance was more and more comfortable being back home as time went by. He was adjusting quite easily back into his role as the man of the house. He had even started paying the bills and suggested that I quit my job at the salon.

I wasn't crazy though. I was still living on edge, waiting for him to leave me for Felicia again and trying to ignore the knot in my stomach that reminded me how much he didn't deserve me.

My kids deserved their father, though, and that was a sacrifice that I was willing to make.

Chance

"What's that?"

Georgia looked up from the table with a pin stuck between her lips. Even though we hadn't crossed the line since she moved in, I couldn't help but think about the moment that those pretty lips were wrapped around my dick. The memory alone made my dick began to grow rock hard in my True Religion jeans. I wore them motherfuckas faithfully. They were one of the few expensive purchases that I had made when I was serving for Omari. They were a reminder that a better life was possible one day.

"The classifieds."

I laughed as I sat down at the table in the kitchen with her. "You quittin' Sunset already? I know you not gon' let them chicks run you out of there."

"Run me out of three thousand dollars a week? Hell nah," she laughed.

Damn, three g's a week? I need to shake my dick somewhere for that amount of cash.

"I'm looking at the rental properties," Georgia told me. "It's time to move out."

I was kind of disappointed and didn't even try to hide it. Georgia had been great company to me while I was prisoner to these four walls.

"I gotta get out of here," Georgia sighed. "Living and working with Gia is like doing the same with my mother, and I hated that shit."

"So, you ran away from your mother, and now you are running away from your sister?"

"She hates our relationship, Chance. She's jealous. Me and you chill. We kick it. All you all do is argue. She hates it."

She wasn't lying. Granted, Georgia had popped off at Sunset. But Gia was judging the girl for who she was when she was a kid before she could even show and prove that she had matured or not. I didn't know this Gia, and I didn't like her.

If me and Gia weren't arguing about going back to Cali, she was trying to convince me that Georgia was a problem child that would fuck me the first chance she got. Even though she had apologized the other day, hadn't much changed. The tension was still there. It would always be until I was back in the sunshine state.

CHAPTER 18

Simone

Getting out of town was much easier than I thought. For months, I'd been wracking my brain trying to come up with a way to skip town. I had stolen from Slim and probably caused Katie her life. And then luck swooped down on me and like magic or a miracle, I was in Washington D.C.

It was right on time too. The night that I stormed into Slim's room, with visions of Jasmine and Omari holding hands in my mind, Slim told me that we were going to D.C.

"D.C.? Why?" I was acting like I was reluctant about going, while in my mind, I was already packing my cheap clothes and synthetic wigs.

"I got a friend in the game over that way. Its money to be made, so we about to go get it."

That was like music to my ears. I happily packed my bags and hopped in Slim's truck as the sun rose. With Francesca and Peaches in the backseat, and the other girls following us in a rental. We made the thirteen-hour drive to D.C. and had been there for two weeks.

Slim was right. There was way more money to be made in D.C. Because of the abundance of federal workers, labor workers, and executives, the stroll stayed in a heavy rotation on Vermont Avenue. We didn't even suffer from the cold as much. We were in and out of cars so fast that we barely felt the snow.

Slim was on a mission for a come up. He had us on a strict five hundred dollar a day minimum quota during the week and a grand on the weekend. That was bringing him in at least twenty–two thousand a week for all five of us. We were happy to put in the work because the more money Slim made, the better he took care of us. Our clothes were becoming higher end. We ate better and rested more comfortably in more lavish hotels.

I was so happy to be out of Chicago and the constant memories of what I was running from. D.C. was definitely starting to make life not seem so bad.

Now, all I had to figure out was how to stay there.

Jasmine

"Why don't you just call him, Jasmine?"

I looked at Tasha like she was crazy.

"Seriously," she shrugged as she flat ironed her hair in the mirror at my vanity. "You know you miss him."

I did miss Omari, no lie. They say you can't miss what you ain't never had. I was so mad that I had ever had Omari because I missed his presence, his taste and his smell. Each one of my senses was craving for that man.

"It's been two weeks, Tasha. He don't want to talk to me."

"Obviously, he does!" Tasha looked at me through the mirror of the vanity like I was the dumbest chick on the planet. "He called you, fool!"

"But it took him two weeks to do it!"

Two weeks. Two whole fucking weeks! I lay around and cried and got fat for two whole fucking weeks before that cat-eyed motherfucka picked up the phone to call me yesterday! I didn't answer either. Fuck him! And he didn't leave a message, so he was obviously thinking fuck me too.

"Of course it took him some time to call you. You went through his shit, first of all –"

"That was an accident. I was looking for lotion. I can't help it that I stumbled upon that girl's secret memorial!"

"When you go looking for something, be prepared to find it. You should have backed the hell up out of there when you saw that that was that girl's things anyway."

I lay back on my bed grimacing in her righteousness. "But I'm glad I found out. Can you imagine how heartbroken I would have been six months from now when he found out that I was Simone's cousin and he left me?"

"You're heartbroken now."

Again, I was grimacing as I rolled my eyes into the back of my head behind her back. I watched her as she flat-ironed her Brazilian body wave hair bone-straight. I wanted to smack her in that back of the head with those Chi irons.

"You wanna know why?" she asked me.

I sucked my teeth. "No, I–"

"*Because* you love him."

Now, I was sucking my teeth long, hard and slow. "Bitch, please. The nigga can fuck, but come on now. I do not love him."

"Yes, you do, friend. I have been knowing you since kindergarten. I know your life. You love him. Look at you. You ain't combed your hair in two weeks. You won't go outside. You keep calling off work. Have you even shaved? I bet your coochie looks like Chewbacca."

I stared into the ceiling wishing that she was wrong. Did I think that I loved Omari? No. But I missed him so much it was crazy. Life wasn't fair. This shit just was not fair! But I understood why Omari couldn't be with me.

"My cousin killed his girlfriend and his daughter. Girl, that nigga ain't fucking with me. Even if he wanted to, he couldn't. He probably just called to explain himself. I don't wanna hear the shit. Besides, the trust is gone now."

"There you again. You are tripping. Did you tell Omari everything about your past? Did you tell him about Kendrick? If you had been open about that, maybe you all would have been able to find out a lot sooner about you all's connection to Simone. You can't just blame him for keeping secrets. You fucked up too."

"Exactly! Which further proves that we shouldn't be together. This shit was cursed from the jump. I hate I ever met him."

As I lay back in bed, tears rolled out of the side of my eyes and down into my ears. I didn't even bother to wipe them away. I was so mad for even allowing myself to get close enough to a nigga that allowed him to cause me these tears. This wasn't me. I left my broken heart in North Carolina. I had allowed myself to sulk for two weeks, but fuck that. No more.

Anger grew like a wild weed in my heart. I was mad at myself and mad at Omari for breaking his promise to me. He was not only a liar but also a phony.

Tasha looked at me strangely as I jumped out of bed and started putting on my shoes. "Where you goin'?"

"Over to Omari's... You comin' with me?"

"Hell yea."

Omari

"I can't believe she still hasn't called me back." I was staring at my iPhone like if I stared at it long enough, thinking about her, she would call.

Capone sat in the den with me, watching highlights from the NFL playoffs. He was smoking a blunt. I was so stressed out that I wanted to hit it, but weed had never been my thing.

Capone shook his head, with a look of disbelief in his eyes as he stared at the seventy-inch flat screen on the wall. "I can't believe you actually want her to call you."

Knowing Jasmine's relationship to Simone, Capone didn't want me to have no parts of her. He was more than my business partner and friend. That nigga was like my personal top-flight security. Like Eboni, he was always trying to protect me. He wasn't going to let any harm come near me; male or female.

"I miss her, man. I can't front." I couldn't. I wanted to bad as hell. I really wanted to continue on with my life like I had never met Jasmine Mays. But the past two weeks proved that that wasn't physically or emotionally possible. Before I met Jasmine, I was fine with continuing on with life as a single man, avoiding all future Simone Campbell's. I didn't think that I would ever feel comfortable enough with another woman to get anywhere beyond fucking her.

With Jasmine, it was so different. That thick ass girl was like a breath of fresh air. She had renewed my faith in women. She showed me that I could have a relationship like me and Aeysha's again. Jasmine and I had a connection similar to me and Aeysha's. It felt like I had known Jasmine forever. The pussy was a bonus, and I missed the hell out of that too. If my mind didn't want any parts of Jasmine, my dick and heart sure did. Every morning, both woke up throbbing, in search for her.

Capone finally looked at me. When he looked into my eyes, it was like compassion came over him. He saw my genuine feelings for Jasmine and decided to be a friend, rather than my protector. "You don't care that she is related to Simone?"

I did at first. At first, I wanted her out of my house because I never wanted anything connected to Simone close to me ever again. But, as time went by so slowly without Jasmine that it seemed to stand still, that rejection slowly faded, and I didn't care anymore, as long as I had her. When I couldn't take it anymore, I called her, but she didn't answer.

I didn't want to sound like a chump, so I didn't tell Capone all of that. I simply said, "Nah. They might be related, but they are nothing alike."

Capone didn't say anything. It looked like he wanted to disagree. I knew that he didn't trust my judgment. Obviously, I wasn't the smartest man if I let a bitch like Simone into my life. But Jasmine's aura was different. I couldn't imagine her being anything like the pure evilness of her cousin. I was about to explain all of that to Capone, but I felt like he would just think that, like with Simone, I was being dumb. So I just sat in silence watching the highlights but not really giving a fuck about what team had beat whom. It amazed me how much of an impact Jasmine had on me. I knew her so well. That's why as I sat in the den and a familiar sound came from the windows, I knew it was her.

I jumped up.

"What's going on?" I could hear Capone ask as I ran out of the den.

I ran through the house with Capone on the heels of my Giuseppe sneakers. I knew the sound of that girl's engine. I knew that that was her car that had pulled into my driveway.

That was confirmed when I snatched the front door open and saw her Jeep backing out of the driveway. I almost tripped and fell over all of the things on the porch, but spotted them and jumped over them as I ran towards her moving Jeep.

But I had missed her by seconds. By the time I made it to the end of the driveway, I was only able to tap the side of the back passenger window before she threw it in drive and sped off. "Jasmine! Wait!... JASMINE!"

My voice ricocheted off of the houses surrounding us. White folks shoveling snow in their driveways looked at me like I was crazy. I could see Capone standing in the yard with his gun in his hand, but when he heard me say Jasmine's name, he put it back in his waistband.

I got my cell phone out of my pocket. I dialed her number, knowing that she wasn't going to answer. I was prepared to leave her a voicemail this time when she surprisingly did.

"What, Omari?!"

I knew that I had a problem on my hands when, even though it was full of venom, her voice sounded so sweet to me. I couldn't even be mad. At that point, I wanted her to turn around so bad. "Really?"

"Yes, really!"

"Jasmine, come back. Let me talk to you."

I closed my eyes, waiting for her reply and hoping that it was just as sweet as it used to be.

"No!" But it was the complete opposite. I could hear the tears in her eyes. "Now you wanna talk?! You haven't called in two weeks. *Two weeks*, Omari! Obviously, whatever you have to say isn't important if it took you this long. You should have been *saying* something when I met you! Then we wouldn't have wasted each other's time!"

Wasted each other's time? That hurt. My time with her had been far from wasted.

"It is important. I–"

Her tears and anger cut me off. "Well, at this point, it does–"

"Jasmine, plea–"

"NO!! It's over, obviously! What else is there to talk about?! Just let it be. Bye! It was *not* nice meeting you. Thanks for nothing!"

Then the phone fell silent. I regretfully looked at the screen and saw that the call had ended.

She was gone and I was standing on the sidewalk looking like a fool. I swallowed that fucked up feeling that came from nowhere in my throat. It was a lump full of some shit that I didn't expect.... I really missed that girl.

"What's all this shit?" Capone was curiously going through the bags on the porch when I walked up.

I didn't have to wonder. I recognized them. "Those are her Christmas gifts."

"Damn, she brought 'em back. She is mad for real."

I reached down and picked up the crystal apple that I had given her for the desk in her classroom. Again, I was ignoring the lump in my throat and trying hard to swallow it. But it was too big. It was growing with each vision of her driving away from me. "I guess so."

a month later...

264

CHAPTER 19

Detective Howard

I was sitting in an undercover car on 47th and Vermont, biting my lip nervously and watching every woman that walked by. For it to be after midnight, the block was surprisingly empty. As it had been for the past six weeks. I was told that any other time, this block was full of traffic. Now, it was a ghost town.

I was starting to think that Marcia was seeing things. But beyond my frustrations, I knew that she hadn't.

"They must have gotten scared and moved around," I told Marcia.

She was sitting next to me, nestled up with a large cup of Dunkin Donuts coffee. "Could be. Let's wait to see what KiKi says."

"Thought she was supposed to be out here by now. You said she said midnight."

"She's a prostitute, not a secretary. I doubt she's punctual, Keisha."

I found little humor in that shit, but chuckled anyway. I knew that Marcia was just trying to lighten the mood, but I didn't find shit humorous about Simone being able to constantly evade the law.

There were people sitting in jail for way less, for petty crimes. And yet this bitch had murdered four people, and was roaming wherever the fuck she felt like it.

It was time for this bitch to go down in a major way.

A knock on the driver's side door brought me out my trance. A frail dark skinned woman in a fake short body fur, sequin mini skirt and a long straight wig with a Chinese bang was standing on the other side of the door freezing her ass off.

"Open the fucking door, Marcia. It's cold out here."

The pink color of the wig reminded me of cotton candy and made her look like a really fucked up version of Nicki Minaj.

Marcia popped the locks of the car while checking her, "Bitch, don't talk to me like that. I will arrest your ass. Keep playin'."

KiKi hurriedly jumped in the backseat. She sighed as if the heat from the Charger was melting her skin deliciously like butter.

"Talk to me, KiKi. You find something out?"

"I hear Slim went to D.C. to meet up with his homie, Money. He's a big pimp in D.C. Makes a lot of money in that area."

"They comin' back?"

I cut KiKi off before she could even reply. "I'm not waiting until he comes back. I ain't got that type of time." KiKi thought that we were searching for Slim to arrest him for sex trafficking. She didn't mind since Slim and his girls were direct competition for her and her pimp. I didn't want anyone tipping off Simone that we were on her heels.

"They'll be back though. This is home. It's too much competition in D.C. He'll get his money, stack up and come back."

"In how long?" Marcia asked.

She answered, "A few months," like it was nothing.

I let out a deep sigh, told KiKi, "Thanks," and handed her a few dollars.

Marcia reluctantly watched me as I turned the engine. I didn't have a few months. In a few months, Simone would be in Egypt some damn where for all I knew. She was crazy, but she was smart. If I knew anything, I knew that Simone was trying her best to stay in D.C.

Eboni

"Right this way, ma'am."

This is so weird. That's all that ran through my mind as I followed the waitress to a booth in Cooper's Hawk. I had squeezed into a royal blue bandage dress. I hadn't worn heels in so long that my feet were burning at the bottom. Terrance was behind me. He'd dressed up well in jeans, a blazer and a bottom up.

It was Valentine's Day. The restaurant was full of couples.

I wonder how many of these bitches are just as unhappy as I am.

I sat at the booth trying hard to put an appreciative smile on my face. I wanted my smile to match the genuine happiness in Terrance's. I felt some type of way, but he was elated.

"You look so damn good." He watched me with a smile as I nervously played with the hair that he'd just bought me.

"Thank you," was all that I replied as I focused on the drink menu.

Yea, I definitely need a drink.

Being around Omari, as he moped around without Jasmine for this past month, reminded me of how hurt I was when Terrance left me. That reminder, coupled with what I was already feeling about being with Terrance, just made me feel that much more stupid for taking him back. He didn't love me like I needed him to. Omari had only known Jasmine for four months, and every day that he was spending without her had the nigga sick. But this motherfucka sitting across from me damn near did a marathon sprint out of the home that we shared with his three kids and into the arms of another bitch, whom I thought was my best friend.

His love for me wasn't the type of love that kept him by my side and out of the arms of the next bitch. I had matured since he left. My heart had healed since he left. Now, I would rather be alone than live with uncertainty every day, wondering when he would meet the next bitch that was better than me.

He was lucky that I cared more about my kids than my own happiness. For the moment, I was willing to be unselfish and uncomfortable for the sake of them. Beyond them being happy to have Daddy at home, with Simone being very much alive, I felt better having the security at home. I had Omari's only child, and I be damned if that bitch snuck her ass into my house to take one of mine.

Terrance started to go on and on about something that Lil' T had said that he thought was hilarious. I just laughed and nodded like I thought it was just as funny, when I was really wondering how in the hell I was going to get out of fucking him that night.

Omari

"I can't believe this shit." I was mumbling to myself as I parked in front of Jasmine's crib. I knew that if Capone knew what I was doing, he wouldn't believe it, because I for damn sure couldn't believe it myself. But I couldn't take this shit anymore.

It had been over a month since I'd seen her face or heard her voice. I had given up talking to her voicemail weeks ago. She wouldn't answer my calls, so I had given up calling her weeks ago. But it was Valentine's Day. It was cliché but I had missed her the most that day. I had anticipated spending this night with her since we met. The fact that I was at the trap house with niggas, thots, and buss-it-babies was fucking with me. So, like a chump, I went to the nearest florist, got her the biggest bouquet of flowers that I could find and headed to her crib on a hope, wish and a prayer.

"If it's a nigga in here, I'm killing her and him." I sounded like a desperate man and was so glad that nobody was around to hear this shit.

I took a deep breath as I stared at her Jeep and rang the doorbell. Like a bitch, my heart skipped a beat when I heard shuffling on the other side of the door. I positioned myself, trying to appear cool on the other side of the door, as I heard the latches unlocking.

She tried to look normal when she opened the door, but I could see the puffiness in her eyes. I could easily tell that the vibrancy in her spirit was gone. She wasn't the same woman. I would have liked to think that that was because we were apart, because without her I wasn't the same person either.

I knew that she missed me. She was letting that bitch come between us. She didn't want to be with me because of Simone. That wasn't fair. If I was willing to look past it, so should she. I was adamant to make her see that. I refused to lose another woman because of that bitch.

"Can I come in?" She eyed the bouquet of sixty red and pink tulips without saying a word. She leaned against the doorway with her hands folded tightly across her chest. She was only wearing a long Victoria's Secret sleep shirt. I wanted to wrap my hands around her and protect her from the cold air. Her hair was in a wild ponytail. She looked tired and weary, but still so fucking amazing. I wanted to rip that shirt from her voluptuous body, carry her into the nearest room and show her with my tongue and dick just how much I missed her.

"You know you can't come in, Omari." She was barely able to look at me. I was looking deep into her eyes, trying to steal some compassion from her soul. I knew that this was all a front. She was battling with herself. She wanted me; her fear of heartbreak just outweighed how much she wanted me.

"Why not, bae–"

"Omari, please," she warned as she raised her hand. Then her jaws clenched as she stared off into space. "What's up?"

"I want to talk.... about us. I miss you, Jasmine. I'm sorry for not telling you everything. I was wrong for not being honest. I had my reasons, but it was still wrong, nonetheless, and I'm sorry. I didn't hide or lie about anything else..." I was waiting for a reply. I would have taken anything; a smart remark, accepting my apology, anything. But I got nothing. She just avoided my eyes and stared emotionlessly at nothing. So, I told her, "Let me fix it." I wanted it so bad that I wanted to stomp my foot like a spoiled kid when she still gave me no response. She was being so stubborn and throwing this, us, away so easily that I was starting to think that she was using this as an excuse to run.

"Simone ruined your life," she finally responded. "She ruined mine too, but what she did to you was... evil. I can't imagine being around you every day, reminding you of that tragedy. I just... I can't do it, Omari. I'm sorry."

"I don't care about that. I'd rather deal with the reminder than deal –"

"That's just it! I don't want you to have to 'deal', Omari. You can find somebody else. It's not worth it. You can find anybody to kick it with and fuck at night, and she won't come with this much baggage."

I had to take a step back. That offended the fuck outta me. It hurt ... a lot. More than I expected it to. I was starting to think that maybe my desire to be with her was premature. Maybe she knew

272

better than I did that this, us, was nothing worth fighting for.

I cleared my throat in attempts to regain control of my feelings. I handed her the flowers and she barely took them. "Well, if that's all you think we were, then maybe you're right." Her eyes widened and, for once, her anger went away. It was replaced with a sympathetic glance that finally found my eyes. Her lips parted as if she was about to say something, but I cut her off. "I'll see you... Well, I guess I won't. Take care of yourself, sweetie." I bent down and kissed her cheek before she could know it or fight it. Then I turned and left.

Jasmine

I wanted to stop him. I watched him walk down the steps with his hands in the pockets of his Godspeed jacket. I knew that I was watching him for the last time. I wanted to run down the steps and stop him. I wanted to take him by the hand, sneak him by Marcus and into my bedroom, lock the door and fuck him senselessly. Then I wanted him to hold me with those strong arms while he kissed me on the top of the head during the night like he used to.

But I was right. He could find another woman easily. He was gorgeous. He had money. He was a gentleman and a protector with endless swag. Any woman would serve him, would submit to him and she wouldn't remind him daily of death. That's what I was to him, that's what I would make him think about every day; death.

I didn't give a fuck if it was Valentine's Day, Christmas Day or Resurrection Day; I didn't want to be death in a man's heart on any day, so as I watched him climb into his BMW, I sighed deeply, retreated into the house, and closed the door before he drove away.

CHAPTER 20

Jasmine

"So you just gon' let that bitch take another good man from you? That's what you gon' do?!"

I rolled my eyes into the back of my head as I stood in the full-length mirror in Tasha's bedroom.

Tasha continued to fuss without even letting me answer. "I'm just saying. Why continue to give that crazy bitch the upper hand? If you love him–"

I had to laugh. "I do not love him."

"Oh, yes, you do! The way you've been walking around with your lip poked out, you most definitely love that nigga. And it's okay if you do…" I watched her through the mirror as she sat on her bed, browsing Instagram. The smile on her face was slick and full of lust. "… I'd love that nigga too. Shat!"

"Whatever!" I fussed as I fought the chills that ran down my spine as I thought of how right she was.

"Jasmine, you're stupid as hell."

"No, I am not," I said, knowing she was right. I *was* being stupid. Simone had won at every wicked game that she played, and, now, I was letting her win again.

Tasha saw the contemplation in my eyes as I played with my curls in her mirror. "You know I'm right. And on a day like today, you should really be there for the man that you love. He needs you. He wouldn't have invited you if he didn't."

I sighed as I thought about it. "He invited me before I dissed him on my porch. He probably hates me now."

"That was two days ago. Love doesn't go away in two days–"

"Tasha–"

"And trust me, if that man went out of his way to go to your house, to invite you today, he does love you too."

Though Tasha was way off the mark with assuming that Omari and I loved each other, she was dead on with everything else. He had invited me, and, whether he had or not, I wanted to be there for him.

✳✳✳✳

I took a long deep breath and let it out slowly before unlocking the doors and climbing out of my Jeep. Nonetheless, I was still nervous. Omari had sent me a text, inviting me to a memorial service that he had planned for Dahlia, a week ago. He needed me to be there then. His exact words were, "I need you, ma." But that was before I was a complete bitch to him two days ago. I hoped that my sudden appearance wouldn't give even more grief that I assumed this day was bringing him anyway.

I nervously fixed my hair and made sure that my tunic was pulled down over my ass as I walked into the small church on 47th and Loomis. During one of our many conversations, Omari told me that Fellowship was his mother's church. He had also told me that, beyond losing her only grandchild at the time, not being able to mourn her death or even attend her burial had crushed her.

This was his way of making it up to her.

Of course, when I walked through the doors of the sanctuary, all eyes were on me, but they looked quickly and gave the podium back their attention. There was a man behind the podium singing *I Need You Now* by Smokie Norful and putting Smokie to shame. Only the first few rows were filled. I recognized Capone, one of his dips, Eboni, her kids and his mother. I even recognized a few of the dope boys from the trap houses over east and in the suburbs. I was too scared to even look for Omari, but I did catch Eboni's eyes. They were smiling and so was she.

I attempted to sit on a vacant row near the back, but she quickly looked at me like I was crazy and pointed aggressively towards Omari, who was on the front row.

"Fuck," I muttered under my breath. "Oops! God, forgive me. Sorry."

I didn't even know if I was supposed to be there, so I damn sure didn't want to sit in the front! But I inched my way towards the poster-sized picture of Dahlia surrounded by the most beautiful arrangements of flowers that I had ever seen.

When I reached the front row, Omari's mother looked up at me with the same smile that Eboni did, and immediately scooted over, making space for me to sit by Omari. A woman with Omari's eyes amazed me with how much she looked like him as she stared at me curiously. I knew that it was his sister, Erica. Next to her must have been her husband, Tre, who was holding their son. Tre had the most uncomfortable look on his face and never even turned his head to look at me.

My butt was squeezed so tight with nervousness as I inched over towards Omari and slid into the space that Omari's mother had provided me. I slid into the space, wondering what the best thing to do was.

Am I supposed to hug him? Say something? Urgh!

Luckily, "Smokie Reincarnated" started bellowing out the end of the song and caused the audience to clap, as well as Omari and myself.

♪ *I need you now, Lord,*
I need you now (ooooh)
I need you right now, right now, right now
I need you noooooooow!
Oh, not another second, not another minute, Lord,
Can't wait another day (oooh no, no)

Please, make a way ♪

Just as the clapping ceased, Omari reached and held my hand.

Omari

Seeing Jasmine had made this hour so much more bearable for me.

It had been months since Dahlia passed. I had come to grips with it, but sitting in this memorial service was heavy on the soul.

I was tired of funerals and death. I realized that, when I saw Jasmine, what I felt for her was something so real, because laying eyes on her gave me so much life and the energy to sit through the end of the service.

"Thank you so much, baby. Thank you for doing this for me." My mother's eyes were full of tears as she smiled up at me. The service was over. She stood in front of me, holding my hands while Jasmine stood next to me.

"You're welcome, mama. You were right. I should have done this in the first place." Now that the service was over, I felt like Dahlia had truly been laid to rest. She had been buried a long time ago, but her death felt like it was still lingering. Now that the truth was known about her death and we were able to celebrate her short life, it felt like the weight and burden of her death had been lifted from my shoulders.

My mother told me, "I'm going to ride with Erica and Tre to the restaurant," as she let go of my hands and walked away. Everyone else had pretty much said a few words to me before leaving the sanctuary. The only two people left was Jasmine and me as we stood next to one another with an awkward silence standing with us.

I leaned against the pew behind me and stared at her. She was still avoiding my eyes, like she had the last time that I saw her, but this time at least her anger was gone.

"Thank you for coming. I appreciate it."

She sighed, saying, "You're welcome. I'm glad I did."

This wasn't us. The distance, the sadness, the awkwardness; this wasn't us. I was tired of it being between us so I reached for her and pulled her towards me. I pulled her into my chest and wrapped my arms around her so tight, as if I was scared she would try to run away. But she didn't. She fell into my embrace, buried herself in my arms and held me just as tight.

"I'm sorry," I heard her say.

"I'm sorry too, ma." My eyes squeezed with sympathy as I heard her tears. "I'll never hide anything from you again, okay? Never. I promise."

I was waiting for her to fight it. I was waiting for her to say that she had come to support me but she still didn't want to be with me. I was waiting for it. I expected it, but feared it at the same time. Holding her was the best thing in the world next to being able to hold Dahlia or Aeysha again. I didn't want that taken away from me too.

When the simple word, "Okay," came from her lips accompanied with more tears and a deep breath, it surprised me how much better I felt knowing that she was back in my life.

I took her head into both of my hands and lifted her face until her eyes were looking right into mine. I used my thumbs to wipe her tears away as I told her, "I'll always try my best to do right by you. I promise... I love you."

Her eyes closed as she took in the words. Her grip around me became tighter as I softly grabbed her lips with my own and kissed her the way that I had been waiting to for a month and a half. She didn't say it back and that was okay. Her loving me too wasn't necessary at the moment. I loved her enough for the both of us.

Gia

After putting up with this lil' bitch, her attitude and disrespect, she was still fucking trying me! I walked in the house and found Georgia and Chance sleep on the couch again. The TV was on. A bottle of tequila was on the floor surrounded by cups.

They had spent the afternoon kicking it, while I ran errands.

The fuck?

"Georgia! Get the fuck up!" She and Chance stirred in their sleep. I didn't know whose ass to kick first; hers or his. This was some bullshit. I was on that pole every night, twerking for his life, to make money to put him on, and this bitch got all his time; playing video games and laying up with him like he was her man. I might have been a bit jealous, but there was a twinge of disrespect in the air that I did not like. "Get the fuck up! Both of you!"

"What the fuck is wrong with you?!" Georgia snapped as she jumped out of her sleep.

"You don't see nothing wrong with this shit?! You don't see nothing wrong with you constantly sleeping under my nigga?!"

When I caught eyes with Chance, he rolled his eyes. He stood and actually tried to walk past me. "Not again with this shit."

Before I could respond to him, Georgia's words hit me like a suckapunch.

"Maybe if weren't such a bitch, he would lay up with you!"

Even Chance's eyes bucked as he shot out a warning. "Georgia, chill!"

"No, fuck that! I'm sick of this shit. She ain't been nothing but a bitch since I got here. So what we hang out and have fun! Maybe if you chilled the fuck out, and did the same thing, maybe if you went back to Cali, like your man wants and needs, you wouldn't be so fucking insecure about our relationship!"

At first, Chance was about to stop her. He was holding her back, but with each word she said, his defense weakened more and more. He just stood there like she was right. I looked at him, waiting for him to take up for me. I was so pissed when he didn't, that I lunged at Georgia.

"Bitch, do–"

"Gia, chill!" When Chance stood in front of Georgia, protecting her, I lost it.

"Get out, Georgia! GET THE FUCK OUT!"

Georgia just looked at me and shook her head as she walked away. "Gladly. I don't need this shit from your crazy ass."

"You buggin', Gia!" Chance spat.

"No, I'm not!" I shrieked as I pushed him in his chest. "And why are you constantly taking up for this bitch?! How many times have you fucked her?!"

I should have known better than to ask, but they were too fucking close. He defended her like she was his fucking girl, not me.

"Are you fucking serious?"

285

"Yes!"

He shook his head. His eyes were full of disappointment. "You know what, Gia? I'm tired of this shit. I deal with enough bullshit. I don't need this shit too. You ain't gotta kick me out. I'm out."

I was too pissed at both of their audacity to stop him. He didn't have a dollar and this bitch wasn't even helping me pay the bills in this motherfucker. I knew that he would be back because he didn't have anywhere to fucking go. We both needed the space to calm down, so as he stormed by me with his shoes on and keys in hand, I let him bounce.

Chance

"Hello?"

I was fuming as I rode through the city. I had been gone for about an hour but my anger hadn't subsided. I was pissed, but I was angrier at myself than at Gia. This was all my fault. The tension between us, her insecurities; it was all my fault. If I hadn't killed a woman, it wouldn't matter where we lived. If I was man enough to make my own bread, I wouldn't be driving around in my girl's car with no money to get a bite to eat unless I called and got some money from her. If I had a family, or at least some damn friends, I wouldn't have been so into Georgia that my girl now thought we were fucking.

Calling Georgia probably wasn't the best thing to do at the moment, but, as always, I had no one else to call.

"Yo'. Where you at?" I asked her.

"Just finished getting something to eat. I'm about to go get me a drink and a room... Where are you going?"

Damn, all of that sounded good. "Nowhere. I'm just driving around."

"Are you going back home?"

"Eventually, but not right now. I ain't in the mood."

"Well, meet me at the Comfort Inn Suites in Lansing."

I hesitated. I didn't think that being in another hotel room with Georgia was smart, but with little gas, an empty stomach, and nowhere to go, I figured what the hell. "Bet."

Besides, Georgia hadn't come on to me since we fucked, so I assumed that we would be able to hang out in the room for a few hours without further fucking up my relationship. But a family size pizza and a pint of Tequila later, that wasn't the case.

The lights were off in the room. The effect of the Tequila had my eyes heavy as hell. I was fighting sleep as I sat up in the bed against the headboard. I was also fighting the urge to stick my dick in her. Georgia lay next to me with her head in my lap. Her ass was falling out of shorts that were so little that I felt like she had put them on only to entice a nigga.

My dick was hard as a brick. I knew that she saw it. It was even moving on its own inside of my jogging pants. My dick was so disloyal to me. I wanted to just be cool and ignore how sexy she was, how much opportunity we had to fuck since we weren't at the crib, but my dick was damn near reaching out of my pants and tapping her on the shoulder.

"Georgia, I'm about to go."

I had to go before I did something else to further fuck up my life.

She looked at me. I couldn't deny the yearning in her eyes, nor could she. I don't know if the yearning was for me to stay or fuck her. But I couldn't stay to find out.

She knew it too. She saw the lust in my eyes too, so she reluctantly watched me put my shoes and jacket on and followed me as I walked towards the door.

"Are you going to be okay here by yourself?"

Georgia smiled at my efforts. "I'll be fine, Chance. I'm a big girl."

"I'll call to check on you."

She smirked. "Don't let Gia find out."

I chuckled as I opened the door. "I won't."

Before leaving, I grabbed the back of her neck and kissed her on the forehead. Fuck it. If I couldn't fuck her, I at least wanted to taste her skin. "See you later."

I walked out biting the bottom of my lip and grunting as I grabbed my dick. I was in pain. My dick was aching to get back in that room. But no matter how good I knew the nut would feel, getting shit back right with my girl would feel much better.

I nodded at the receptionist as I walked by and got my cell phone from my pocket as I stepped outside. I was getting ready to call Gia to let her know that I was on my way home just as I heard my name called.

"Yo', Chance. Whad up?"

Instinctually, I turned around when I heard my name, but regretted it as soon I saw his face. "Ca–Capone... What's up?"

Fuck.

Simone

"Come on, shit!" I whispered hastily as I struggled with the zipper of my luggage. "Hurry up!"

It was time. After a month of getting familiar with D.C., it was time to bounce. I knew the city. I knew where I could run and hide and never bump into Slim. I also knew that he had over a hundred thousand dollars tucked away in a shoebox under the bed. I was gambling with my life by being willing to steal from Slim. I had learned during my stay in D.C. that Money was a feared man. He was not only a pimp, but also heavy in the dope game with many young soldiers ready to kill for him. Yet, I would rather run from them in D.C. than to continue running from the police in Chicago.

Finally, with my suitcases filled with the little that I owned and zipped, I was ready to run. Slim was somewhere kicking it with Money. The other girls were on the stroll. I'd faked the flu and a couple of throw up sessions. Slim would make us work on our periods, but he wasn't willing to risk money by me throwing up on the johns.

The coast was clear, and my palms begin to sweat with anticipation. I couldn't believe that after all of the plotting, scheming, and manipulated, fate had landed me in a new city. I imagined myself finally able to roam just a little bit more free, and it felt so fucking good, even in my imagination.

Just as dropped to my knees on the floor and got ready to snatch the shoe box from underneath the bed, the door of our room swung open so hard that it hit the wall with a loud thud and scared the shit out of me. "Argh!"

"Simone, we gotta go!"

I jumped to my feet. When Slim looked at me curiously, I faked nausea. I held my stomach and bent over. "I'm so happy you came back. I was about to go on the block to find one of the girls. I think I need to go to the hospital. I'm so nauseous that I can't stand up straight."

He looked at me up and down, his eyes lingered on my hands as they rested on my belly. "You think you're pregnant?"

I faked a stressed out sigh. "I don't know, Daddy."

"Well, fuck that. We gotta get you to the hospital back in the Chi. We gotta go... *now*. A couple pimps just got popped by the Feds. We outta here."

I quickly looked around the room for anything to use to take Slim down; a knife, his gun, anything. The fear of returning back to Chicago had me so spooked that I even considered using my bare hands to get the fuck away from him and out of this room.

"Come the fuck on! Why you just standin' there?!"

I jumped at the sound of his voice and avoided his questioning eyesight. I thought about if I would rather fight my way out of that room and lose, or go back to Chicago with the security of Slim still intact.

I sighed, saying, "Okay, Daddy."

And just like that– just as luck had showed her pretty face–
karma had reared her ugly head and I was on my way back to
Chicago.

CHAPTER 21

Omari

I finally felt better than I had in a long ass time. I sat in my den eating a bowl of Frosted Flakes, waiting for Capone and flipping channels while my baby lay upstairs knocked out. I had made up for lost time and knocked that pussy out indeed. But that was after we had a long talk. Finally, I told her everything. I gave her every detail of my relationship with Aeysha, even how much of a cheater I was. I told her about my bizarre relationship with Simone. I gave her every detail of the day that Aeysha was killed, when Dahlia was killed and all of the evidence that Detective Howard had against Simone.

She cried. Her family had their own version of what could have happened, but with Simone's parents dead and no family members really fucking with her, Jasmine didn't know the full story. Now that she did, she hated Simone even more.

Her own story of how Simone had ruined her life only validated how crazy that bitch was. Jasmine told me about the cruel joke that she now believe Simone played. She trusted her cousin when she told her that her boyfriend at the time had tried to come on to her because of his past of cheating on her ruthlessly. Simone used his past indiscretions to break her away from the one man that she ever had a connection to. When she shared with me what she knew about Simone lying on DeMarco Johnson, I was done. I couldn't believe that I had let such a crazy, psychopath into my life.

We didn't even have sex last night. The air in my bedroom was so eerie with memories of the detrimental path that Simone Campbell had left in both of our pasts. But as I woke up looking at Jasmine's beautiful brown face, I realized that it was a light at the end of this dark tunnel. Simone had taken away so much happiness, but her destructive hands in both of our lives had brought Jasmine and I closer than we were before. Our connection was that much stronger. Our loyalty to one another was that much deeper. We had an unspoken promise to give back the happiness in each other's lives that that bitch had taken away. So, I took it upon myself to tongue kiss that perfect pussy until she woke up and started to beg for the dick.

I stopped channel surfing when I got to the Channel Nine Morning News. I usually never watched the news, especially after news coverage of Aeysha's death took over every channel for days after her death. But the news cameras were on scene at the Comfort Inn Suites and that got my immediate attention.

"The body of Chance Rogers was found in the parking lot of Comfort Inn Suites located on 173rd off of Bernice Road in Lansing, Illinois at 12:15 this morning. The night clerk reports seeing the victim leave out and hearing two gunshots moments later. After calling 9-1-1, the desk clerk reportedly heard screams, but that was screams of pedestrians entering the hotel and seeing the body of Chance Rogers in the parking lot. No one reports seeing the shoo-"

Erin McElroy's voice was drowned out by the sound of my front door opening. It was Capone. I knew it. He was the only other person with a key to my crib.

"Yo', boss, you ready to roll?"

I sat my bowl of cereal on the table and sat back on the couch, the coverage of Chance's murder still playing in the background. I was trying to determine how I felt about it. It was wrong to wish death on anyone, but that was one of two people that I would not have regretted hearing about their death.

Capone entered the den, looked at the TV and didn't even flinch. "You ready?"

We were on our way to meet up with another buyer, but this shit had me shook. Again, I was trying to figure out if I was happy and if it was okay to be that happy about somebody being dead. I was also trying to figure out if my "security" had anything to do with it.

"You see this shit?" I asked as I motioned towards the TV.

"Nah, what's that?" he asked as he glanced at the TV and looked quickly away from Erin now giving a rundown of Chance's past as a murder suspect in Aeysha's death.

"You know anything about that?"

"Nah."

I chuckled. This nigga was always a bad liar. He couldn't do it to my face because he hardly ever had to. I looked at him, watching him, with both of my arms resting on the back of the couch, make a really bad attempt at keeping a straight face. "What, bruh? Damn, let's go."

"You mean to tell me that you don't know shit about this, when you told me that you was taking that broad to the telly last night?"

That blank face was slowly slipping away and giving this nigga up. "That's not the only telly in the Chi."

"It's the only telly that *you* go to."

Finally, the smile that had been threatening to surface did. "Would you c'mon? We gotta go."

He was lying and I knew it. That fucked up smirk on his face said it all. He didn't want me to have any details of it and that was fine by me. I had to chuckle at the irony in all of this though. "He could be like Simone. That bitch has nine lives, maybe he does too."

Capone shook his head, a cynical smirk spreading across his face. "Nah, I doubt it. He's dead for sure."

Eboni

"You need to talk to me?"

I looked up from my Kindle into eyes that were surprisingly scared to hear my answer. I had sent Terrance a text telling him that I needed to talk to him when he got off of work. He'd actually made it to my place an hour earlier than I expected.

I sighed, nodded and sat my Kindle down on the couch beside me. "Yea, I need to talk."

I patted the space on the couch beside me. I took a deep breath, not even believing what I was about to say. "I don't think we should be together anymore, Terrance."

He didn't even look surprised. I had a feeling that he knew this was coming. I had been acting funny since Dahlia's memorial service. After watching the passion that was between Omari and Jasmine, I just couldn't fake the funk anymore. Plus, Dahlia's memorial service had reminded me what I had been through. I had gone through too much to take three steps back.

"You don't want me, Terrance –"

"Yes, I do," he attempted to persuade me.

"If you did, if you wanted me like you are supposed to, you would have never left. You would have never left the way that you did. You did the unimaginable, and I'm embarrassed of myself that I am even fucking with you again." He flinched as if that hurt, but I had to keep it real. "You apologized and I appreciate that, but it doesn't erase what you did and how you did it. It's still in my heart. I think about it every day, and I can't live with it in my heart and you in my bed."

"So, we're going to do this to the kids again?"

"We are not doing anything. You did it when you left the first time–"

"I'm sorry–"

"You're not here because you want me, because if you were, you would have never left, or it wouldn't have taken you over a year to realize that this is where you wanted to be. You let her keep you away from your kids, from your family; if you loved me, us, if you were loyal, no piece of pussy would have been able to talk you into doing that... I know that you're sorry. I forgive you... but what happened was something a person should never forget." Since he looked like he wanted to keep arguing with me, I pled my case further. "I want somebody in this house that loves me so much that he would never leave, even if he fucks a random bitch outside, there is some loyalty in his cheating heart that won't allow another bitch to convince him to disrespect me and his kids. A man that will never fix his mouth to hurt me the way that you have. I deserve that. And even if I never get it, I would rather lie alone at night then next to you knowing how you can be convinced to feel about me with the right new pussy."

He shook his head as if I was the furthest thing from right. However, my women's intuition told me that, unlike my past, I was finally making the right decisions based on truth, not just fiction.

CHAPTER 22

Simone

Days later, we were back in Garfield Park. March was slowly approaching, so the cold weather was slowly crawling away. I felt relief as I walked back and forth on the Ave in a tight tube top dress and jacket.

"Damn, baby, that ass phat!" I smiled and waved, hoping that the Chrysler 300 on 24's was a john, but most men who could afford a car and rims like that, didn't have to pay for pussy.

The next vehicle that pulled up didn't have to pay for pussy either. He got it from me every time he asked for it or blinked twice.

"Brandie, come here."

I trotted towards Slim's truck as the rest of the girls smirked and giggled. They thought it was cute how Slim had slowly turned me into his bottom bitch. It was taking a toll on me though. Being a pimp's bottom bitch just wasn't about my pussy being at his every beck and call. My loyalty had to run deep. Every move he wanted to make, I was there, whether I wanted to be or not. I had to have his back with every decision he made, whether I agreed with it or not. It was stressful and a big responsibility to show such an amount of loyalty, to ensure that he believed that I was down for him no matter what. At that point, I actually had to give Katie some credit for doing it for so long.

"What's up?" I asked him as I sat and enjoyed the relaxation of my toes and the balls of my feet.

"Take a ride with me."

"I'm working," I reminded him.

He sucked his teeth. "This money ain't shit like what we were making in D.C. I ain't sweatin' it."

Slim was feeling himself. He had a pocket full of cash and was fucked up about the fact that he had to leave D.C. As he pulled away from the Ave, he even started to talk about plans of going back to D.C. when things died down and investing his money into something else like drugs or high-end escorting.

I liked the idea of D.C. much better and was getting ready to use every piece of willpower that I had to talk him into going back ASAP but lights and sirens caught my attention.

Slim pulled over without a second thought. Just as I had, he assumed that they weren't stopping him, but when the police merged into the lane behind him, I freaked.

"Fuck," Slim grumbled. "Stupid ass cops."

My heart began to beat out of my chest as he pulled over to the side of the road on Cicero Avenue.

I urged him, "Pull off, Slim."

He looked at me like I was crazy. "Why? It's probably just a traffic stop."

"What if it's not? We just left the Ave."

"They weren't behind us." Then he chuckled at the way that my eyes widened with fear. "Chill, ma. We left the Feds in D.C."

He didn't know that. He fucking didn't know that! I knew that this was something else. I felt it in my gut as I noticed that the car that pulled us over wasn't a squad car. It was unmarked.

Detectives don't make traffic stops, I thought as I took in my surroundings. I even kicked off my shoes. I was preparing to swing that door open and run. I couldn't get arrested. The moment that they would fingerprint me my life would be over.

My hand grabbed the door handle as soon as a flashlight shined into the dark car and blinded the both of us.

"Put your hands up and step out of the car!"

Shit, shit, shit! I was bugging out. I freaked when Slim put his hands up and stepped out of the car so willingly. I spazzed, jumped into the driver's seat and snatched his gun from his waistband as he got out.

Detective Howard

Slim got out of the car with no issue, just as we had planned hours ago when I pulled him over the first time.

"Look, Slim. I'm a homicide detective, not Vice," I explained to him once I pulled him out of his truck and put him in the back seat of my car. "I'm looking for Simone Campbell–"

"I don't know no Simone, yo'."

"She goes by the name Brandie." I watched his eyes widen in the rearview mirror. "She arranged to have a pregnant woman killed. She killed her friend, a baby, and most likely that girl that was burning in the Calumet City Forest Preserve a few months ago." His eyes widened even more as I continued, "I need your help to get her, and in exchange, I've talked Vice into turning a blind eye to your bullshit.... for a while."

He was down without a question. The plan was for him to go on the Ave and pick up Simone. I didn't think he really would, but as I watched him get her into his truck, my mouth started to salivate with the chance of finally getting this bitch.

And here we were. I had my eyes on Simone as he exited the truck. I couldn't wait to put handcuffs on this bitch.

The thought had just ran across my mind, *This was easier than I thought*, when I heard Slim say as he walked to the back of the truck, "She grabbed my gun."

Fuck!

I eyed Simone as she sat in the car nonchalantly. I eyed Marcia as she stood on the other side of the driver's side door with her gun drawn as well. I was inconspicuously placed a few feet behind the passenger side window. I didn't want her to hear or see me because she would recognize even my voice, but time was up.

As soon as I spat out the order, "Put your hands up, Simone! Put the fucking gun down!" I saw Marcia tense up. "Don't shoot!" I told her. Death was too easy for Simone. She didn't deserve to get away with all of the shit she'd done by dying. She needed to live miserably behind bars with women that shoved pointed objects up her ass because they hated her for killing a pregnant woman and a baby.

"Put your hands up, and get out of the fucking car, Simone!" The longer she took, that antsier I got. I knew that she was inside of that car trying to plot an escape route in that birdbrain of hers. Just as I was about to snatch the door open, it opened itself. Simone's hands appeared first and then her bare feet and legs.

Out came a woman that I hardly recognized. Gone was the woman with expensive weave and designer clothes. She looked poor. Beyond the synthetic wig and cheap clothes, she looked tired. When she stood in front of me and laid eyes on me, a smirk fell across her lips as she recognized me.

With my gun pointed at her, I inched towards her. It alarmed me as she inched away.

304

"It's over, Simone," I told her. "Put your hands behind your back."

Her arms moved, but not up in submission. Swiftly she reached into her cleavage. I wondered for what for only a few minutes before I saw the handle of the Smith and Wesson.

"Gun!" I heard Marcia shriek just as I reluctantly pulled the trigger.

Pow!

My heart broke as I watched Simone's forehead split open just before her body hit the ground.

Shit! I cursed inside of my head as I bit my lip with regret and ran towards her body with my gun still drawn. "Damn it," I grimaced as I realized what I had done, what I had to do, what she'd made me do. I fought the urge to cry. I fought to stay professional. But I couldn't. I was emotionally invested in this case. I felt for every one of her victims. My heart went out to Omari. I loved on my kids even more because of his pain that I witnessed. I had lost time with my kids to ensure that she paid for every life she took. Simone deserved to fucking suffer.

Out of my peripheral I saw Marcia coming towards the curb where Simone lay with blood and brain matter spilling from her wound. I stood over here, still aiming my gun as I kicked the Smith and Wesson a few feet away. But there was no more alarm.

Simone Campbell was dead.

Gia

I was waiting for the moment that I lost it; for that moment I took my own life, because living without him was like not living at all.

Ironically, as I lay on the floor in my bedroom, I could hear my sister's tears throughout the house. She was crying just as hard as I was. She was in just as much pain, and it sounded like her heart was just as broken.

What was even more ironic was that I had helped Chance run from this. I helped him run from any punishment for his involvement in Aeysha's death. I thought he was innocent because of his troubled past. But as I lay in the middle of the floor, gripping my chest, attempting to massage away the constant aching in my heart and praying for the pain to go away, I realized that this must have been how Omari felt when he watched Aeysha die. At that moment, for the first time in a year, I felt sorry for Omari more than I wanted to help Chance run from this. I felt bad for his loss, and, just as much as I was sure that Omari wanted to kill Chance – just as sure as I was that he had killed him or someone close to him had – I wanted to find Omari and do the same.

But I wouldn't. I would continue to live and keep Chance in my heart. I would be able to live because now Chance was at rest. There was no more missing the family that he never knew. He no longer had to feel inefficient. He no longer had to struggle in hiding and live his life looking over his shoulder. Ironically, as much as I missed him, I was happy for the freedom that he must now be feeling.

I just hated that he died without my last words being to him "I love you." He died because I lost faith, because I was insecure and allowed our circumstances to make him flee what should have been a sanctuary from what he knew as chaos. He ran away from me and into a bullet. I had pushed him away, and I would have to live with that forever.

Omari

Jasmine let out the giggle that always made my dick resemble steel.

"You like that?" I asked as her. My mouth was so close to her pussy that my lips brushed against her clit as I spoke.

Two of my fingers played with her g–spot and she moaned, "You know I do, baby."

I groaned. "Feed me, baby. Give me that pussy."

She lifted up and I used my tongue to open her folds and sucked on that clit just as she liked me to.

"Fuck," she moaned. "Yes, baby."

I locked my free arm around her waist, locking her down right where I needed it to be, and started my feast.

I loved this girl. She still hadn't returned the favor, she still hadn't said it back, but I still didn't need her too. She was still a little scared, but so was I. And I was prepared to fight and protect us from everything that tried to prove our fear right.

Shit, I thought as my phone started to ring again.

"Answer it, baby," Jasmine breathed.

"Unt uh," I managed to mumble with a mouth full.

"It might be important. They keep calling."

I kept eating but was interrupted when the ringing was right in my ear. Jasmine was handing me the phone. I reluctantly released her out of my mouth, leaned against her hip and answered without even looking at the Caller ID. I even continued to finger fuck her as I answered. Mesmerized at the sight of her juices as I went in and out. She covered her mouth with her hand to muffle her moans.

"Hello?"

"Omari..." It was Detective Howard so I took my fingers out of my baby, and I was drawn to how much of her dripped down my hand.

"I'm proud of you, Detective Howard. You finally learned how to use the phone."

She giggled. "Yes, I did."

"What's up?"

Suddenly, her voice changed to a triumphant tone. "I got her."

With my interest now peaked, I sat up in bed. "Got her?"

"You haven't seen the news?"

I hadn't. I looked at Jasmine and smiled. Instantly she smiled back at me, looking so beautiful with her hair all over her head and tired eyes from the long day we'd had in bed. "Nah. I've been a little... busy." Then I playfully pinched Jasmine's thigh.

Detective Howard let out a long satisfying sigh, "Well... Simone's dead... For real this time. She's in the morgue."

The feeling that came over me was better than any nut I'd bussed. It was even better than learning that Dahlia had survived the shooting. I was proud. No longer was my family's death lingering in the air above my head, taunting me because I hadn't made sure that somebody paid. I hadn't pulled the triggers but it finally felt like it was over. There was finally a period at the end of this tragic sentence. Aeysha and Dahlia could now rest in peace. They could finally use their wings and be free.

I closed my eyes. I fought the tears, fought looking like a bitch in front of my lady. But I relished in the feeling of there finally not being a bad thought when I remembered them. I could finally remember them without the black cloud of their killers roaming free, living and breathing, while they lay in the cold ground.

"Thank you," I told Detective Howard.

"I'm sorry it took so long… Take care of yourself, Omari."

"You too."

I hung up and met Jasmine's curious eyes. I tossed the phone to the side and fell into my baby's chest. She wrapped her arms around me asking, "What's wrong? Everything okay? Who was that?"

"Everything is okay." I sighed with relief because finally everything *was* okay. I had brought Simone into my life. I had had a hand in Aeysha and Dahlia's death, and I would pay for that by living with that fact for the rest of my life. That would be the sentence that I would serve for the rest of my life; living with the guilt. But moving on would be a bit easier now because their killers had paid the ultimate price. "They got her. Simone's dead."

"For real this time?" she asked with a chuckle.

"Yea, for real this time."

She let out a breath and I knew its meaning. Finally, her hurt had been vindicated as well. We could be in this relationship without the tension, without the hurt, without the constant fear and reminder.

I nestled closer into her warm embrace, even though physically I was as close as I could be. Jasmine wrapped her arms around me even tighter. We intertwined our legs with one another's. I felt her kiss my forehead and I promised, "I love you, baby."

"I love you too, Omari Sutton."

six months later...

CHAPTER 23

Jasmine

"Girl, look at them."

I followed Eboni's eyes and laughed. Omari and his mother were on the dance floor dancing to *It's Your World* by Jennifer Hudson. For a woman her age, Miss Dahlia could dance her ass off.

"It's her birthday for real," Eboni giggled.

We were sitting at a table in the banquet hall that Omari had rented for his mother's birthday party. He had paid for it to be decorated beautifully with crystal centerpieces and all white balloons and flowers. Everyone was dressed in all white as well. I was trying extremely hard not to drop food on my all white maxi dress as I tried not to embarrassingly smash the delicious plate of soul food in front of me.

"Look at my damn kids," Eboni huffed.

I laughed again as I spotted Lil' T, Tasia and Tatianna dancing around Omari and Miss Dahlia. Even Jamari, who was now walking, attempted to mimic the moves of his sisters and brother. They were having a ball.

"Leave them alone. They're having fun."

Eboni just shook her head with a chuckle as she stared at them.

Over the past six months, Eboni and I had gotten very close. She was nearing the end of her program at Malcolm X. She was now doing clinics at Mercy Hospital, which took up so much of her time, so Omari and I had the kids a lot. I was glad to help. She was a devoted mother. She worked so hard for her kids, which made me go harder for mine. She made me feel like if she could do it with four kids, I had no excuse. She'd come a long way, let Omari tell it. He was so proud of her being stronger than she'd ever been.

"Your son looks like a grown ass, man," she said as she looked at him while sipping from her drink, compliments of the open bar.

"Yea, he does. He better not be over there calling himself trying to holla at that girl." I smiled as I spotted Marcus a few feet away, talking to one of the little girls that came in with Omari and Capone's crew. He looked so mature and grown in his white fitted button up and slacks.

Everybody was at the birthday party, even my mother and Tasha, who had brought a beau thang along with her. Even though she had a date, it didn't stop Capone from trying to holla, as he always did when we all kicked it.

We had all become close. Family was very important to Omari. As our relationship flourished, he made sure that we all knew each other and were one big happy family. He loved on all of us immensely. He smothered us with love and protection. He went over and beyond to make up for what he could no longer show Aeysha and Dahlia.

"What's up, Jasmine." I looked up and greeted Tasha's beau thang's homeboy, Geno, with a smile. He'd come with the couple to the party as well. But he wasn't even looking at me. He was looking at Eboni like she was his next meal, while she was trying hard to ignore how he was lusting after her.

Through a laugh, I introduced them. "Eboni, this is Geno. Geno, this is my baby's mama, Eboni." I often called Eboni my "baby's mama" because her kids felt like my own at this point.

"How you doin', Eboni?" He stuck out his hand and with reluctance Eboni shook it.

"I'm good. How are you?"

"I'm great... *now*."

I giggled and Eboni tried to fight hers. However, she finally began to reluctantly take in his appearance. Any man looks good in an all–white suit, but Geno was a sight for any single, hard–working woman's lonely eyes. He was an even six feet, light–skinned and slender. His fade was accompanied with short curls of slick black hair that also lined his face and mouth, giving him a smooth, sexy look compared to his rough persona. Even in a suit, his tats snuck out of his collar. His bad boy status screamed out in his swag, walk and talk.

Geno noticed that Eboni's drink was on its last sip. Without asking, he took it from her hand. "Let me get you another one," he said and just walked away.

Eboni's mouth was left gaped open as I laughed.

"Girl, who in the hell is that?"

I shook my head at her instant rejection. That's how she was when it came to men. After she broke up with Terrance and he went back to Felicia, she was through with men for a while. Though she was comfortable that she had done the right thing by leaving Terrance, she said that she wanted a break from men to just focus on her studies and her children.

"That's Tasha's beau's homeboy."

"He has a lot of balls."

"He has a lot of money too. He gets money out west. You better pay attention." Then I winked just as we saw Geno approaching use with two drinks in his hand.

"Can I sit down so we can have these drinks together?" he asked Eboni as he took it upon himself to sit on the other side of Eboni. "I *need* to get to know *you*."

Immediately, Eboni's lips turned to the side. "You don't want to talk to me. I have four kids."

He laughed and waved his hand dismissively. "Girl, I got five…"

We both cracked up laughing as he grabbed her hand and kissed it. She couldn't hide the blush that appeared across her cheeks. I suddenly felt like the third wheel but me and Omari's song began to play and my heart melted. I looked up and his eyes were on me, asking me to join him on the dance floor. I stood happily to meet my man on the dance floor. I loved me some Omari. I loved me some him. After so much heartbreak and betrayal, I thanked

God for him. I was blessed to have him. Finally, I thought about my life with a smile. I glanced at Marcus watching me walk to my man and even he had a joyous look in his face. With two men in my life that loved and adored me, nothing could be better than this.

Omari

In her all white, Jasmine looked angelic. In my arms, she felt so precious, like a jewel. She was so quiet as we danced. I knew that she was deep into the song. She wasn't even thinking about her surroundings. She listened to every word when it played because, she said, it reminded her of us.

> ♪ *You're the desert sand, I'll be your water*
> *And you're the perfect plan I never thought of*
> *I don't wanna do this on my own*
> *And you shouldn't have to be alone*
> *I would rather be alone together*
> *Be alone together* ♪

I bent down and began to sing along to Daley in her ear. "*I always keep you safe in my arms. I will guarantee that I will never break your heart. I'll always put you first 'cause you deserve the world. I wanna know you. I wanna hold you baby. I wanna show you.*"

I could see the smile that spread across her face. As her head lay on my chest, we swayed back and forth with our arms around each other.

But I had to let her go. I released her and fell down to one knee. She looked at me curiously, wondering what I was doing. On cue, Capone appeared by my side, handing me the DJ's mic. I reached into my pocket for the ring that me, Marcus and Capone picked up after Eboni and me and Jasmine's mothers picked it out a few weeks ago. Photographers began to take pictures of every moment, just as they had discreetly since the moment that we started to dance.

Still, Jasmine's eyes were filled with wonder as I began to speak. "Jasmine, you *are* the perfect plan that I never thought of; that I never knew I needed or wanted. I want to love you forever, but forever isn't long enough. No matter where I am, no matter where you are, I will always call you home. I will always hold you down. I love you, my family loves you and I know that Aeysha and Dahlia are here, right now with us, smiling in approval... Jasmine Denise Mays, will you marry me?"

Over our song that now played a little lower, I could hear the tears and cheers surrounding us, but I didn't see them. All I saw was the pure joy and happiness in my baby's face as happy tears flowed from her eyes. She shrieked, while out of breath, "Yes!... Of course!"

The entire banquet hall erupted as I slid the platinum, eight-carat engagement ring on her precious finger. Before I could even stand, she was kneeling too, with her arms tightly around my neck as she kissed me like no one else was in the room.

"I love you so much," I managed to speak into her mouth, never breaking her kiss.

Just then, it was as if her body relaxed. She had let go of all the hurt, pain, and reluctance and handed it over to me to fix. "I love you too."

EPILOGUE

A year and a half later, Detective Howard was at the station taping up the last box on her now vacant desk.

She looked sadly at Marcia, who stood close by, holding some of the personal items that once sat on Keisha's desk.

"That's it," Keisha sighed. "I'm ready."

Detective Howard had took an early retirement. After over twenty years on the job, she was retiring home to her kids so that she could raise them and be the full-time mom that she always wanted to be. Well, it wouldn't be completely full-time. She had purchased a large facility that she turned into an after school and summer program for inner city youth from kindergarten to twelfth grade. Instead of fighting crime once they became criminals, she was now going to fight crime by preventing so many youth from becoming criminals. She hired athletes, teachers and coaches to mentor the youth, one including Demarco Johnson, who would form an inner city basketball team that would play in the Chicago Street Basketball Association.

"What are you going to do with all of this time on your hands?" Marcia asked Keisha as they slowly walked out of the squad room.

Keisha sighed deeply as she looked around for the last time. "Go home and shoot the shit out of some boogey men."

Oh, and speaking of criminals, Slim had taken his line of hoes, and relocated to D.C.

Meanwhile, Gia was at Sunset getting ready to go on stage.

"Thank you, Reese," she smiled as he assisted her on stage to the sounds of Big Sean and Nicki Minaj.

It took some time, but Gia was finally able to live with the fact that Chance was gone. Georgia had packed her bags and returned to Idaho shortly after Chance's death. She felt some guilt behind his death as well, and could no longer take living with the constant regret in Chicago. Gia, on the other hand, remembered her man every time she climbed that stage. That was where they met and shared so many good times. And because of that, for as long as she could, for as long as her youth and body allowed, she would forever be the baddest bitch in Sunset.

Hundreds of miles away, Jasmine, Omari, Capone, Tasha, Eboni, and Geno were departing a shuttle in front of Mantangi Private Island Resort in Fiji. Just hours before, Omari and Jasmine had exchanged vows on the beautiful beaches of Jamaica with family and close friends, then the crew escaped to enjoy the couple's honeymoon in Fiji. There was no way in the world that Capone would allow Omari go anywhere alone. There was also no way that Tasha was missing Fiji. Eboni and Geno had gone on a date a week after the engagement, and slowly became a couple that was attached by the hip. Jasmine and Omari didn't mind at all sharing this precious moment with the people closest to them.

"Damn. Can't believe a nigga is in Fiji! WHEW!"

The crew laughed at Capone as they took off into the resort. However, Omari, holding Jasmine's hand slowed his pace in order to linger in the moment. For once in his life, he felt whole and complete. He took a moment to look into the clear blue sky and smiled at his family up beyond the clouds, feeling blessed that they were there, with him, watching him, with the woman that he knew that they had sent him, be the man that he always wanted to be.

The End!

JESSICA'S CONTACT INFO:

Facebook: http://www.facebook.com/authorjwatkins
Facebook group: http://www.facebook.com/groups/femistryfans
Twitter: @authorjwatkins
Instagram: @authorjwatkins
Email: jessica@femistrypress.net

Made in the USA
Las Vegas, NV
02 July 2023

74173958R00193